THE BUTCHER BEYOND

Sally Spencer

Severn House Large Print
London & New York

This first large print edition published in Great Britain 2005 by
SEVERN HOUSE LARGE PRINT BOOKS LTD of
9-15 High Street, Sutton, Surrey, SM1 1DF.
First world regular print edition published 2004 by
Severn House Publishers, London and New York.
This first large print edition published in the USA 2006 by
SEVERN HOUSE PUBLISHERS INC., of
595 Madison Avenue, New York, NY 10022.

British Library Cataloguing in Publication Data

Spencer, Sally
    The butcher beyond - Large print ed.
  1.   Woodend, Charlie (Fictitious character) - Fiction
  2.   Police - England - Fiction
  3.   Murder - Investigation - Spain - Fiction
  4.   Detective and mystery stories
  5.   Large type books
  I.   Title
  823.9'14 [F]

ISBN-10: 0-7278-7474-8

Printed and bound in Great Britain by
MPG Books Ltd, Bodmin, Cornwall.

*For his generosity of spirit
in loaning me Inspector Paco Ruiz,
I dedicate this book to my alter ego,
James García Woods*

Prologue

There were four of them gathered together that night in the large and opulent drawing room which looked down on Cadogan Square. Three were sitting – though for one of them it was not a matter of choice. The fourth was standing with his back to the Adam fireplace, holding a month-old Spanish newspaper in his slightly trembling hands.

The man who had no choice but to sit was in a wheelchair. His clothes proclaimed that he was wealthy – and his clothes did not lie. Despite his left-wing leanings, the crippled man had a bank balance that several small countries might justifiably envy, and this house – for all its grandeur – was only one of the properties he called home.

The other two seated men looked far less affluent. True, the sharp faced one on the sofa was wearing a good jacket and a hand-made pair of shoes, but these were now so far from being new that they had almost given up the battle of trying to appear even respectable. His companion – facing him across the coffee table from an easy chair in which he did not look in the *least* at ease – was even more of a contrast. He was tall and thin, with a shock of grey hair, and wore his ragged grey suit as if it were *literally* no more than rags.

The stocky bald man by the fireplace screwed up the newspaper in a sudden bout of rage, and threw it on to the floor.

'You've all read the report, haven't you?' he demanded.

'Of course we've read it,' said the sharp-faced man. 'We wouldn't be here if we hadn't.'

'They're going to promote him to Provincial Governor!' the bald man said bitterly. 'That butcher – who should long ago have paid for his crimes by his own death – is to be made the governor of a whole province! It's an insult to us all.' He paused, as if to give more weight to his next words. 'But more especially,' he continued, 'it is an insult to the dead – to those who were willing to spill their own blood for something greater than themselves!'

A heavy solemnity fell across the room, as all the men in it put names and faces to those – many of them little more than boys – who had sacrificed their lives in that time, so long ago.

The silence was broken by a clattering

sound – the noise made by five small cubes as they bounced across the antique coffee table which stood between the sofa and the easy chair.

'Do you have to do that, Roberts?' the bald man asked angrily.

The dice thrower – the sharp-faced man whose clothes had seen better days – calmly examined the exposed faces of the poker dice on the table, then swept them up into his hand. 'It helps me to think,' he said.

Of course it did, the bald man thought. He should have remembered that. Most men had minds that worked on a single thread, like the winding tackle back in the pit. Their minds either went down – as did the lift when taking the miners to the coal face – or went up – like the lift bringing the scarred and blackened men back to the surface. Roberts had never been like that. His mind could go up and down simultaneously – and sometimes even to the side – without one operation ever getting in the way of the others.

'So you're thinking, are you?' the bald man asked.

'Yes.'

'And could we know *what* you're thinking?'

'I'm thinking that I share your outrage – but not your surprise. The world isn't fair, Pete. I've always known it, I suppose, but that bullet in the leg really brought it home

9

to me. I'd never quite realized, before that point, just how educational a hot piece of metal can be.'

'You survived,' the bald man said, sounding more callous than he'd intended to.

'I survived,' Roberts agreed. 'But I still bear the scars. Here – ' he pointed to his leg – 'and here – ' pointing to his brain.

The meeting was somehow slipping off the rails, the bald man thought. They were there to map out the future, not relive the past.

He cleared his throat. 'We must decide whether or not we go back – whether or not we are prepared to face our demons,' he said.

The man in the wheelchair narrowed his eyes thoughtfully. 'If you did go back, how many of the others could you rely on to support you?'

The bald man looked suddenly uncomfortable. 'How many? Do you mean, from this side of the Channel?'

'Yes.'

'Then the answer is none.'

'None?'

'Like you, Henderson, my old friend, their hearts are in it, but their bodies are no longer up to the task. They couldn't even make it to this meeting, though they sorely wanted to come. What chance is there, then, that they could make the journey back to old battle-grounds?'

'And what about the foreigners?'

'I haven't asked them. There seemed no point until we had reached a decision ourselves.'

Henderson nodded sagely. 'You say our absent British comrades' hearts are in it, Pete, but is *yours*?' he asked. 'Because without you, you know, there can be no operation.'

The bald man's discomfort increased. 'I am just one member of the group,' he protested. 'My personal decision should carry no more weight than anyone else's does.'

'You were *never* just one of the group,' Henderson contradicted him. 'You were our leader.'

'We *had* no leaders,' the bald man said defensively.

'We had no *acknowledged* leaders,' Henderson agreed, 'yet you were the man we'd have followed all the way to hell and back, if you'd asked us to. And since hell is precisely the destination we're discussing, I'll ask you again – is your heart in it?'

'I'd be lying if I said I *wanted* to go,' the bald man admitted. 'I have a wife who I love dearly. I have a responsible job in which I feel I'm doing some good, in which I feel I'm fighting for some of the things we fought for back then.'

'But...?' Henderson asked.

The bald man waved his podgy hands

11

helplessly in the air. 'No sane man would happily risk all that to go back to a country in which he is still regarded as a criminal, in order to carry out an act which will certainly be classified by those in power as a crime.'

'But...?' Henderson asked for a second time.

'But there's no choice, is there?' the bald man said, almost angrily.

'You're wrong about that,' Henderson told him. 'You don't have to do the job yourselves. I could hire a man to do it for you.'

'Are you talking about a professional assassin?'

Henderson smiled. 'Perhaps it would be more constructive to look on him as a professional vermin controller,' he suggested.

'And do you know where we would find such a man?'

'Of course not. But I could certainly find out – and by tomorrow night, at the latest.' Henderson smiled again, self-deprecatingly this time. 'When you're as rich as I am, Pete, everything and anything is possible. So now you *do* have another option. The question is, are you willing to take it?'

The bald man hesitated. 'It's not up to me alone,' he said. 'We should put it to the vote, as we always used to.'

Henderson nodded. 'Very well,' he agreed. 'But since I am unable to assist you, should you decide to go yourselves, I do not feel that I have any right to a voice in taking the decision, either.'

'I understand,' the bald man said. He turned to Roberts. 'Which way do you vote?'

The gambler rolled his poker dice again. Two jacks, a queen, a king and an ace.

'Let's first be clear on exactly what we're voting for,' he said. 'When we first walked into this room – and a very tasteful room it is, by the way, Henderson – the question we had to answer was whether we should put our pasts behind us or whether we should deal with unfinished business. But that's no longer the question at all, is it? Now the only issue is if we do the job ourselves or hire a professional killer. Am I right, Pete?'

'Yes,' the bald man said.

Roberts shook his head admiringly. 'Neat footwork. Very neat. You were always good at twisting the situation around – at talking us into things we would have considered unthinkable a few minutes earlier.'

'Back then, I did what I had to do,' the bald man said. 'If I persuaded you to put your lives at risk, it was because I thought that was what was necessary to achieve our objectives. But times have changed – and so have circumstances.'

'Have they really?' Roberts asked.

The bald man smiled. 'Yes, and you do not have to look at the outside world to realize that – you have only to observe the four of us gathered here. So no pressure – not any more. If you wish to put the past behind you, I'll respect that. If you wish to leave before any vote is taken, that is no more than your right and I wouldn't blame you at all.'

Roberts rolled the dice. Two kings, three aces.

'A full house,' he said. 'Alone, each of the faces adds up to nothing. Together, they are a winning combination. But, of course, there are other throws which can still beat them.'

'Is that a "yes" or a "no"?' the bald man asked.

'When have you ever known me to let anybody cut me out of the action?' Roberts questioned. 'I vote we go back ourselves. It will certainly be cheaper – and probably much more interesting.'

The man in the tattered grey suit had said nothing during the course of the whole meeting. Yet he had been silent only in the way a volcano on the point of eruption might have been called silent – and while his mouth had been shut, the room had been full of his mental rumblings.

Now, when he spoke, it was as if fire and brimstone were gushing forth from him.

'We are the strong right arm of the Lord – His instrument of justice,' he said. 'We will smite the unrighteous and the unclean as He commands us. Yea, even unto death.'

'Even more enigmatic than my answer,'

14

Roberts said, greatly amused. 'But that's a "yes" too, wouldn't you say, Pete?'

The bald man nodded, but there was a troubled expression on his face.

He was worried about the man in the grey suit, and realized now that he had *always* been worried. In the old days they had all been branded as extremists and fanatics, and had taken it as a badge of honour. But even then he had seemed *more* extreme – *more* fanatical – than the rest of them. He was a loose cannon. He was teetering on the edge of insanity. But if the mission was ever to succeed, he was an essential part of the team.

'How do you vote, Pete?' Henderson asked.

The bald man shrugged. 'Does that really matter now? Two out of three is a majority, isn't it?'

'I think we'd like to hear, anyway.'

The bald man sighed. 'I was listening to the wheels of the train as I was travelling down here. They seemed to be saying, "You-don't-have-to-go, you-don't-have-to-go." By the time I got off at Euston, I was almost convinced they were right. And when I was standing on your doorstep and ringing the bell, my mind was already searching for an excuse – a way to back out. Then you, Henderson, came up with that excuse. We didn't have to go ourselves, you said. We could hire an assassin. It would be safer for us, I thought, and a professional killer would have a much greater chance of success than a group of middle-aged men who the years had made soft. It seemed like the perfect solution!'

'Perhaps it was,' Henderson suggested. 'Perhaps it still is.'

The bald man shook his head violently. 'No! A thousand times no! I felt no relief when I heard your idea. I experienced *despair*. And it was at that moment I realized that whatever the others decided to do, I had to go back. Even if I fail! Even if I'm killed myself! There is simply no other option for me.'

Roberts rolled the dice again. A pair of nines! It simply wasn't possible to score any lower.

'Apparently, there is no other option for *any of us*,' he said.

One

The immigration officer wore a green uniform, dark glasses – and a scowl. He examined Woodend's passport carefully – holding it as if it were an unexploded bomb – then looked up and said questioningly, *'Policía?'*

'I'm awfully sorry, but I'm afraid I don't speak any Spanish,' Woodend said apologetically.

'Oh, for heaven's sake, Charlie, it's obvious that he wants to know if you're a policeman,' Joan said exasperatedly.

Woodend nodded. Of course that was what he'd meant. 'Yes, I'm a bobb— a policeman,' he said.

The immigration officer did not seem to welcome the news. 'A sheaf inspector?' he asked, peering even closer at the document.

'That's right.'

'You are here for to work? To investigate?'

'Good God, no!' Woodend said.

Joan dug him in the ribs. 'You shouldn't blaspheme, Charlie,' she hissed. 'They're

17

very religious, are the Spanish.'

'We're here on holiday,' Woodend said, forming the words slowly and carefully, letting each one rest on his lips for a second. 'The doctor said my wife needed a rest.'

Joan sighed theatrically. 'They know nothin' at all, do they?'

'Who doesn't?' Woodend wondered.

'Them doctors. They might have all those certificates up on their walls, but they haven't an ounce of common sense between them.'

'Is that right?'

'Course it's right. If the doctor thought I needed a rest, he should have told me to leave you at home.'

Woodend grinned.

The man behind the desk did not. 'You would have allow your wife to travel alone?' he asked incredulously.

Culture clash, Woodend thought. That's what they called it.

'It's a joke,' he explained to the immigration officer.

'A joke? What is funny?'

'She's pretendin' to think that it'll be no rest for her with me here – because I'll be expectin' her to wait on me hand an' foot.'

'But of course you will expect it,' the official said. 'It is no more than a wife's duty.'

'No, you see...' Woodend began.

And then he gave up, because it was plain

he was never going to get through to this feller.

The conversation was obviously starting to bore the official. He picked up a large rubber stamp and slammed it down with some force on an open page in Woodend's new passport.

'You may go,' he said. Then – as if suddenly recalling a half-forgotten directive from the immigration officer's handbook – he gave the two visitors an insincere half-smile and said, 'Have a pleasant stay in my country.'

'Aye, I'll certainly try to,' Woodend replied.

Woodend stood at the airport exit, taking his first look at Spain. Last time he'd set foot on foreign soil it had been on a beach in Normandy, under the hail of enemy bullets. This time, he thought, his welcome had been a little friendlier – but not *that* much friendlier.

'It's a bit barren, isn't it?' Joan said.

It was indeed, Woodend agreed.

Lancashire was green – it rained too bloody much for it to be anything else – but the Spanish coast had an arid look which reminded him of another wartime memory, his time in North Africa.

'Still, I expect the hotel will be nice,' Joan said, with the optimism of a woman who had never travelled abroad before – and could not therefore imagine that there was any place in the entire world which did not have its share of British fish and chip shops.

'You will come now, please!' called the young man in the blue blazer who had met them a few minutes earlier and informed them that he was Jesus María, their courier.

Woodend picked up the suitcases – what the hell had Joan put in them to make them so heavy? – and carried them over to the bus. The vehicle had hard wooden seats, he noted, but at least it looked more road-worthy than most of the battered cars parked around it.

He found himself, instinctively, running his eyes over the other passengers who were waiting to get on the bus. The greater part of the group was made up of families – mum, dad and two or three kids. But there were also several young couples, probably on their honeymoons, and one other pair who – like the Woodends – were no longer *quite* so young.

Judging by their dress, Woodend decided that the majority of the men were either low-ranking office workers or skilled craftsmen. From their looks of uncertainty, he deduced that this was their first holiday abroad, and they were not yet quite sure whether they were going to enjoy it. They were, in other words, just the kind of people he would have expected to be travelling with.

It was not until most of the party had climbed on to the bus that Woodend even noticed the man who *didn't* fit in. He was in his late fifties, the Chief Inspector guessed, and had a bald head which – since it seemed to be covered with sweat – was reflecting more light than the average mirror. He was sporting a moustache thick enough to be called fully mature, yet he kept fingering it as if surprised to find it there under his nose. He didn't look comfortable in his suit, either. He twitched and stretched his arms, as though he were used to a much better fit. And despite the fact that he had taken his tie off – as most of the other holidaymakers had – he didn't seem at all at ease about it.

But it was his general demeanour which made him really stand out. He was not looking as if he didn't know what to expect next, but rather as if he *did* – and was greatly troubled by the knowledge.

'Stop it, Charlie!' Joan said sharply.

'Stop what?'

'Stop bein' a bobby, for goodness sake! You're on holiday. An' you're goin' to enjoy it if it kills you.'

As the bus bumped along the coast road, Woodend looked out of the window at the blue sea, and felt almost like a kid again, on the way to his annual holiday in Blackpool.

Except, of course, that it was not really the same at all, he thought somewhat ruefully.

He was forty years older, for a start –

21

though there'd been times recently when he'd felt as if at least a hundred years had passed since he'd last worn short trousers and knee socks. And this was not the Fylde Coastline – not by any stretch of the imagination.

On the Fylde, the only donkeys you saw were carrying screaming children along the beach. Here, on the open roads of Alicante, the animals seemed to be being used as everything from goods vans to taxis.

There were other differences, too. The villages they passed through had several small shady bars instead of one big public house. The shops were little more than holes in the walls, and while shopping in them might turn out to be a slow business, they held out the promise of unexpected trea-sures which would never be discovered in the shops back home. And then there were the people themselves. They were darker than their Lancashire counterparts, less en-cumbered by layers of clothes, and seemed to be going about their business in a far more leisurely manner.

'It's a rum sort of place this, isn't it?' said a voice from a few seats behind him.

Aye, it was, Woodend agreed silently. Very rum. Like nothing he had ever seen before. Yes, the more he thought about it, the more he was convinced he was really going to enjoy his time in the town of Benicelda!

'Your mind's still back in Whitebridge, isn't it?' Joan said, in an accusing voice.

'No,' Woodend promised.

'You're sure about that, are you?' Joan persisted.

'Yes! Honestly!'

And he meant it. Here was a whole new world, full of exciting new experiences, and he meant to savour them all.

Then he thought of the bald-headed man again, and realized that while the mind of the Holiday-Woodend might be in Spain, he had brought the mind of Policeman-Woodend along with him for company.

Two

The road entered Benicelda at the edge of its sweeping bay, so that most of the town's treasures were spread out in front of the coach party from the very start.

At first sight it was a difficult place to categorize, Woodend thought, as he looked through the bus window. It would be easier to describe what it had been – and what it was about to become – than to talk about what it actually *was*.

What it had *been* was a fishing village. There was ample evidence of that in the whitewashed shacks the bus was trundling past. They were spread out, these shacks, and they put Woodend in mind of a row of decaying teeth, separated by wide gaps. The reason for the spacing was obvious. Each house needed somewhere to beach its sturdy wooden fishing boat, and – more importantly – somewhere to spread out its large trawling net, so that it could be mended between expeditions. A number of men were at work on their nets at that moment – small, broad men with strong arms and weather-beaten skins. And while they were busy painstakingly repairing the mesh, their women – all dressed from head to foot in black – were either washing clothes in large wooden tubs or grilling fish over charcoal.

As he heard the cameras of his fellow passengers clicking all around him, Woodend found himself wondering how long the way of life they were photographing had been playing itself out undisturbed – and how long it would be allowed to remain now that the tourists had started to pour in.

They were approaching the other part of the town – the town as it was about to *become*. And *what* it was about to become, Woodend thought, was a kind of small-scale Blackpool, with the added advantage of guaranteed sun. The bus passed a number of four- and five-storey hotels – with names like *Gran Sol* and *Vista del Mar* – which looked so new that it was possible to believe the paint had scarcely had time to dry. And clustered in their shadow were smaller buildings which owed their very existence to the hotels – bars and restaurants, offering enticing *menús del día*; chemists' with prominent displays of sun cream; accessory shops which sold mats, buckets and spades, everything the visitor needed to take with him for his days spent turning crispy brown on the beach.

Progress! Woodend thought – and was not sure whether or not he was being sarcastic.

As the holidaymakers trooped off the bus – mothers telling their children to be careful, kids not taking a blind bit of notice – Woodend caught himself watching the bald man again. He was still wary, the Chief Inspector thought, but now he too seemed to have been caught up in the holiday spirit.

Except that that was not quite right either. He was looking round – taking in the sights – but not, Woodend suspected, with the eyes of one who had never seen them before.

And even that wasn't *quite* right. He was looking at them as if to note the changes which had occurred since the last time he had been there – whenever that was.

'The bags, Charlie,' Joan said.

'What?'

'The driver's taken our bags out of the boot. They're sittin' there on the pavement – ready for you to carry them into the hotel. Or are you waitin' for me to do it?'

'Of course not,' Woodend said hastily.

No Northern man worth his salt would ever allow his wife to hump the cases while he was around to take on the job himself. Yet even though he didn't expect Joan to do it, there'd been a time when she *could have* – easily – Woodend thought, as he bent down to pick up the suitcases which his wife had obviously packed with large rocks.

Joan had always been what he'd considered a *real* woman, but like most Northern women of her generation – brought up to pound the washing in the boiler, and then wring it through a heavy mangle – she'd never have been taken for a delicate flower. Yet all that had changed over the last couple of years. She'd started getting tired. She'd asked him to do things around the house which she would once have done herself without a second's thought.

'I'm not saying there *is* anything seriously wrong with her,' the doctor had told him, in a private chat after the consultation, 'but I'd certainly like her to have a complete rest before we do any more tests.'

I'm not saying there *is* anything wrong with her, Woodend repeated silently. But that was a long, long way from saying that there *wasn't*.

The foyer of the hotel was as bright and modern as any English tourist worried about travelling in foreign parts could possibly have wished for. Yet with the decorative tiles on the walls and the fans overhead, it could never have been accused of being like a new hotel back home.

Woodend sat Joan down, then joined the queue to register. The bald man was a couple of places in front of him, he noticed – which was just the position in the queue he would have chosen for himself if he'd been trying to remain relatively inconspicuous.

Stop bein' a bloody bobby, Charlie! he rebuked himself silently.

He looked around. Prominently displayed behind the reception desk was the photograph of another bald man, though this one was wearing a military uniform, rather than a blue suit. The face of the man in the picture showed none of the uncertainty of the man in the queue. Quite the opposite, in fact. His jaw was set in arrogant contempt, and his small, piggy eyes were looking straight ahead and seemed to express both disapproval and distrust of what they were seeing.

'Who's that, Dad?' asked one of the children in the queue. 'Is he the king or summat?'

'Nay, lad, that's General Franco,' his father told him.

It was indeed, Woodend agreed. Generalissimo Francisco Franco. The *Caudillo* – by the grace of God, the absolute ruler of Spain.

The bald man had reached the front of the queue, and Woodend strained his ears in an attempt to hear what words passed between him and the young male receptionist.

'This is your first visit to our country, Señor Holloway?' the receptionist asked.

'That's right.'

What was the accent? Woodend asked himself.

Northern, certainly. And semi-posh, although undoubtedly *acquired* semi-posh. The man came from a modest background much like his own, the Chief Inspector guessed, but had now risen above his origins and was either a civil servant or a successful business executive.

So what the bloody hell is he doin' on holiday with a bunch of plebs like us? Woodend wondered silently.

'The reason I ask if it is your first visit is because you have already had a phone call,' the receptionist told Holloway.

'A phone call?'

'Yes, a gentleman – a foreigner, but I do not think English – called up and asked if Mr Holloway had already arrive.'

'Must have been another Holloway.'

'*Another* Holloway?'

'It's a common enough name in England.'

Someone in the corner of the room coughed. Woodend turned his head. Sitting on one of the cane chairs, close to Joan, was a man dressed in an olive-green uniform and a three-cornered hat. He was also wearing full-length black boots, despite the heat, and had a pistol strapped to his waist.

A policeman of some sort, Woodend told himself – but not the kind of jolly local bobby who helps old ladies across the street, and let's kids off with a clip round the ear when he catches them stealing apples.

'The gentleman who called described you most clearly to me,' the receptionist insisted to Holloway. 'I recognize you from that description.'

The bald man shrugged, though the shrug did not, perhaps, appear quite as casual as he would have liked it to.

'Still doesn't ring any bells with me,' he said.

'*Qué?*'

'I still don't know what you're talking about.'

The policeman in the corner was watching the scene intently. It was obvious from the expression on his face that he did not speak enough English to understand the exchange properly, but it was equally clear that he knew that something was not quite right.

'It has to be a mistake,' Holloway said. 'If the man rings again, please tell him he's got the wrong person.'

'As you wish,' the clerk said. He reached up to the pigeon holes and took down a heavy metal key. 'Your room is number twenty-six, Señor Holloway. It has a balcony with a splendid view of the sea.'

'That will do fine,' Holloway said, in a tone which made it perfectly clear that he couldn't have cared less if it had given him a splendid view of the ventilation shaft.

The bald man picked up his suitcase. It was obviously new, but was made of cardboard rather than leather. It was as much a part of his disguise as the suit and the newly grown moustache, Woodend thought. But why should he bother with a disguise at all?

The queue shuffled a step forward, and Woodend with it. When it came to his turn to be processed, he would not have been totally surprised if the receptionist had told him that some mysterious man had called up and asked to talk to him, too, but all the clerk actually said was that his room was number 27 and it had a splendid view of the sea.

Three

The hotel that Joan had selected, after first carefully studying all the glossy brochures, was not one of the newer ones built near to the beach – although, travelling vertically, it was undoubtedly even closer to the sea than they were. It had been constructed at the top of the town's only hill – a steep-sided rock which the bus had coughed and complained about as it had struggled to reach the summit – and standing on his balcony, Woodend could look down at an almost sheer drop of perhaps two hundred feet to the water below.

The balcony afforded Woodend an excellent view. To his left he could see the fishing shacks they had passed earlier – square white blocks alongside which tiny figures were still working on their nets as the sun began to set. To his right were the fronts of some of the other buildings which shared the hill – buildings which, like the hotel itself, seemed to be teetering dangerously close to the crenellated cliff edge.

There was a church, amber-brown in colour – 'You can't go paintin' a church *amber-brown*,' they would have said in White-bridge – and though it had a bell tower like the churches back home, that tower contained only one single, lonely bell. There was an official-looking building with plateresque decoration on its façade, which was probably the town hall, and would be considered effete by the local councillors in Lancashire, who were used to conducting their business in solid and stolid Victorian edifices. And there was a square which contained no statues or municipal gardens, but was filled instead with bars at which people seemed to be actually *enjoying* themselves.

Woodend closed his eyes and tried to picture the scene as it would have been several hundred years earlier. This hill must have been where the local people fled to when pirates appeared on the sea, he thought. He saw them driving their goats up the steep paths, while desperately holding on to the rough sacks containing the few valu-ables they owned. He imagined them – simple fishermen, olive growers and shep-herds – armed with whatever crude weapons they could muster, and ready to fight to the death against these invaders who were intent on raping their women and selling their children into slavery.

Now those days seemed so long gone – and

if this were England, they would have been –
but Woodend reminded himself that less
than thirty years earlier thousands upon
thousands upon thousands of innocent
Spanish civilians had been massacred simply
for holding views that were not popular on
their particular side of the battle lines.

He went back into the room. Joan was
lying on the bed. She looked very pale, and
though she was making an effort to control
it, he was almost certain that she was short
of breath.

'Is there anythin' that I can for you, lass?'
he asked worriedly.

His wife shook her head. 'I'm just a bit
tired from the journey,' she told him. 'I'll be
right as rain after a good night's sleep.'

Woodend nodded, and started to take off
his jacket. 'Well, I suppose it won't do either
of us any harm to have an early night for
once,' he said.

Joan laughed weakly. 'What rubbish you do
talk sometimes, Charlie Woodend,' she said.
'You've never gone to bed before the pubs
closed for as long as I've known you.'

He grinned, self-consciously. 'That's not
strictly accurate, you know, love,' he said.

'It's accurate *enough*,' Joan countered.

'It's mainly been work which has kept me
out so late,' Woodend protested, feeling in-
creasingly uncomfortable. 'We're on holiday
now.'

'Exactly,' Joan agreed, 'we're on *holiday*. So why shouldn't you have a few pints before you turn in?'

He shrugged. 'I don't like leavin' you alone.'

'I'll be all right.'

'Anyway, there's not much point in goin' out, is there? I'll never be able to find any Lion Best Bitter in a place like this.'

'You'll find somethin' else that'll suit you just as well. So stop fussin', get off out an' start enjoyin' yourself.'

He didn't want to go – he *really* didn't want to go – but he could tell that Joan would continue to argue with him until he *did* go – and that she was already finding it a strain to do so.

He straightened his jacket again. 'I won't be long.'

'Be as long as you like, you daft 'apporth. I'll probably be asleep when you get back, anyway.'

He walked to the door, opened it, looked back once, and was gone. Joan breathed a sigh of relief. The pain in her chest had been bothering her for some time, and now that Charlie had left she could let it show.

The streets in the old town were narrow, twisting, and designed for hoofed traffic rather than the motorized variety. Even in the early evening, many of the small shops were still open, and the bars – most of which had managed to squeeze at least a few tables on to the crowded street – were doing a thriving business.

Woodend came to the shady square in front of the old church. He had several bars to choose from, he thought. In fact, he was almost *spoiled* for choice, but since there was no point in wasting valuable drinking time by weighing up their respective merits, he selected one at random, sat down, and signalled a waiter.

'Beer?' he asked hopefully.

The waiter looked perplexed. 'Bee-yar?' he repeated.

Woodend mimed a pint pot. 'Beer.'

'*Vino?*' the waiter asked.

'Could be,' Woodend admitted. 'Given that I don't speak a word of Spanish, it could very *well* be.'

'*Blanco o tinto?*'

'*El señor quiere una cerveza,*' said a voice to Woodend's left. '*Una cerveza grande.*'

'*Ah, cerveza!*' the waiter said, and disappeared into the bar.

Woodend looked up at his rescuer. The man was in his early sixties, he estimated. He was not particularly tall, but he had a good, well-muscled body for his age. He also possessed a pair of quick, intelligent, dark eyes, a firm jaw, and a mouth which betrayed a sense of humour.

'You speak English?' he asked.

'Enough,' the Spaniard replied, in an accent which seemed to have a slightly American edge to it.

'Would you care to join me?' Woodend suggested.

The other man shrugged. 'Why not? It is always pleasant to speak with visitors to our beautiful town. And it is a long time since I have been able to share a drink with a policeman.' He sat down awkwardly, as if there were stiffness in his left leg, then held his hand out across the table. 'Paco Ruiz.'

'Charlie Woodend,' the Chief Inspector told him, taking the hand and shaking it firmly. 'How did you know I was a policeman?'

Ruiz smiled. 'A guess,' he admitted, 'but an informed one. I was watching you as you made your way to this table. You were looking around. Taking note. If I was to ask you to close your eyes and describe the whole square, you would be able to do so with ease. There are not many occupations which train you to look on the world in that way.'

'Are you in the same game yourself?' Woodend asked.

'I was. Once.'

'What kind of policeman were you?'

'I was considered by many – myself included, I must say – to be the best homicide detective in Madrid. Then the Civil War

36

broke out...' Ruiz glanced quickly around him, '...and I chose to fight on the wrong side.'

'The war was a long time ago,' Woodend said.

'Not in the mind of our great and wise leader,' Ruiz told him. 'Those who opposed him then are still being punished even now.'

'Surely not.'

'Take the case of army officers as an example. Those who fought with Franco receive a generous pension. Those who stayed on the side of the democratically elected government – who upheld the oath they had sworn, to defend the Republic – get no pension at all, and live in poverty. I know a number of them who feel they would have been better off being executed – as so many of their comrades were – once the war ended.'

The waiter emerged from the bar. Ruiz held up two fingers to indicate that he should double the order.

'I should not complain, I suppose,' the Spaniard continued. 'My situation is considerably better than that of many.'

'An' why's that?'

'Long ago, I did the General a service of a sort.' He paused, as if remembering that service with an element of regret. 'I would have been shot if I'd refused, but that is not why I did it.'

'No?'

'No! A real man will always choose death before dishonour, and I like to think I am *enough* of a real man to have chosen the correct path.'

'So why *did* you do him this service?' Woodend asked, intrigued.

'Because, for once, the General's interests and the interests of Spain were the same. And so, despite my temerity in opposing almighty Franco, there is a little something in my credit column which allows me a small leeway. Besides, I have an American wife. True, she was forced to take Spanish nationality in order to marry me, but she is an American nevertheless. The Spanish authorities do not wish to do anything which might offend the Americans, especially one who has influential friends in the Spanish Section of the State Department, as my Cindy does.'

The waiter brought the beers. Woodend took a gulp of his. It was lighter and more gaseous than the best bitter he was used to, but having said that, it still wasn't half bad.

'So what do you do now?' he asked Ruiz.

'Officially, very little,' the Spaniard replied.

'And *unofficially*?'

Ruiz grinned. 'Unofficially, I am what, I suppose, you might call a private investigator.'

'An' what does that entail, exactly?'

'Where the Spanish police force is not

actually corrupt, it is at the very least inefficient. If people wish to learn the truth of what has happened, rather than merely accepting the official version of events, they sometimes come to me for help.'

'You're bein' very open an' frank for a man who lives in a police state,' Woodend said suspiciously.

'As I have already said, it is an *inefficient* police state,' Ruiz replied. 'It is possible that our meeting will have been observed – perhaps even noted down – but in all probability the report of it will be left to moulder in a filing cabinet somewhere. Besides, if I cannot speak openly with a brother officer, then who can I speak openly to?'

Woodend found himself warming to the other man. Ruiz had said that he'd been a very good detective, and Woodend could well believe that he had been. It was plain, too, that Ruiz had judged him to be in the same class of investigator as he was himself – and everyone is open to flattery.

He looked up, and saw the bald man in the new blue suit crossing the square and coming to a halt before the church.

'What do you make of him?' he asked on impulse.

Ruiz glanced across in the direction he had been looking. 'The pilgrim?' he asked.

'What do you mean by that?'

'Only that that is what he seems to me.'

'Because he's standin' by the church?'

Ruiz laughed. 'I did not mean that kind of pilgrim. I can tell nothing about his religious beliefs. But it is apparent that he cares deeply about something – and the something he cares about is connected to this place.'

'He's a foreigner,' Woodend pointed out. 'An Englishman.'

'That much, I could have guessed.'

'An' he says this is his first visit to Spain.'

'On that matter, at least, he is undoubtedly lying.'

Which is just what I thought earlier, back at the airport, Woodend reminded himself.

A second man of roughly the same age as the first was crossing the square. This one had thinning brown hair and was wearing a light jacket of red and black check.

'Another foreigner?' Woodend asked.

'Undoubtedly,' Ruiz replied. 'Though, from the way he is dressed, I would guess that this one is an American.'

'And is he another pilgrim?'

'Let us just say that he is doing all he can to appear not to be.'

The man in the check jacket was maintaining his pace, and heading straight for the bald man. Holloway appeared not to have noticed him, and it seemed that, if the man in the check suit did not alter his course, a collision was inevitable. At the last possible moment, the American swerved to the right.

40

The two men's bodies missed each other by inches, but their hands briefly brushed as the man in the check jacket slipped something into Holloway's waiting palm.

'Now what do you think of that?' Woodend asked.

Ruiz sighed. 'I think,' he said, 'that there are times when I wish I was a real policeman again.'

Four

There was a note taped to the dressing-table mirror, where he was bound to see it as soon as he entered the room.

'Took a pill,' it said. *'Should be spark out till breakfast time. Love, Joan. XXX'*

Just like Joan to remember to pack the sticky tape, Woodend thought, smiling and looking down fondly at his sleeping wife.

The smile soon changed to a frown. Joan was snoring loudly. Very loudly. She'd never snored at all during the first twenty-odd years of their marriage, but now she seemed incapable of closing her eyes, even for a second, without emitting a noise like a pig being suffocated.

He wondered if it was merely the onset of middle age which was causing this change in her, or whether it had anything to do with the disturbingly unspecified medical condition which the doctor in Whitebridge wanted to test her for once she'd had a good rest.

'You'll be all right, lass,' he said softly. 'Two weeks in the sun, an' you'll be as fit as a butcher's dog again.'

He heard the door open in the next room. So the mysterious Mr Holloway was back.

Through the wall came the sound of voices, low enough for Woodend to be unable to distinguish the words – or even the language – but loud enough to tell him that there were two of them, and they were both male. Perhaps, after pretending not to know each other on the square in front of the church, Holloway and the American had met up somewhere else and decided to return to the hotel together.

It was about time to turn in, Woodend decided, but before he did that it would probably be a wise move to empty his bladder of all that gassy Spanish ale. He opened the bedroom door as quietly as he could – not that there seemed much chance of waking Joan up – and stepped out into the corridor.

The toilet was four doors down the hallway, and Woodend was away from the bedroom for a little more than two minutes. When he returned, the sound of voices was still coming from the next room, but now those voices seemed to have grown much louder – and much angrier.

'Who'll look after Charlie?' Joan mumbled. 'Whoever will look after Charlie?'

She turned over, then twisted around in the bed to find a comfortable position. She was still asleep, but even with the pills working on her, there was a good chance that if the argument on the other side of the wall continued to rage at its present level, it would eventually wake her.

Woodend opened the door again, and stepped into the corridor. His impulse was to bang angrily on Holloway's door, but since the object of the exercise was to ensure Joan's continued sleep, he settled for tapping lightly.

He could still hear the voices, but they seemed further away than they had from his own room.

He knocked again, risking being a little louder this time, but there was still no response.

They were on the balcony!

That was why they couldn't hear him – because they were on the bloody balcony!

He sighed with annoyance, took a step back, and returned to his own room. Joan had shifted position in the bed again, and was mumbling soft, unintelligible words to herself. Much more of the racket from the next room and she'd be *wide* awake, he thought furiously, as he crossed the room to the balcony door.

Later, he would be able to reconstruct events as they must have happened in those few seconds before he stepped on to his balcony. At the time, however, all he saw was the tail-end of those events – the final few seconds before the death!

It was, in a way, almost balletic. Holloway was leaning heavily against the rail, as if he were looking down at the sea below. But he was positioning his weight wrongly. His legs, which should have been his anchor, were hardly touching the floor at all. His torso, in contrast, seemed to be concentrating the mass of his body at its centre.

'For Christ's sake, be careful!' Woodend gasped.

He didn't know – would never know – whether Holloway actually heard his warning, but even if he did, it went unheeded. The bald man slumped forward, so that his waist was pressing down even harder on the rail, and his upper body was actually hanging over the other side of the balcony.

The two balconies were about eight feet apart. Too wide to reach across and grab the other man. Too wide – given the drop below

– to even risk jumping the gap.

Holloway slumped even further forward. His nose was now touching the outside of the railing. The palm of his hand was brushing against the tiling that ran along the outer edge of the balcony floor.

'Do something, you bloody fool!' Woodend shouted. 'Push yourself backwards – while you still can!'

Holloway's legs left the ground. His trunk – working hand-in-hand with gravity – was now firmly in control, and would have its way.

The body rocked gently for perhaps a second, then the upper half took the plunge, and the lower half was forced to follow.

They would ask Woodend later if he thought Holloway had been conscious while all this was going on, and the Chief Inspector would answer, honestly, that he had no idea. But there was one thing he *was* sure of – that the moment he left the balcony, Holloway was all too terribly aware of what was happening to him.

His horrified scream – as he plummeted through the air – was ample evidence of that.

The policeman who always lurked somewhere in Woodend's large chassis was once more firmly back in the driving seat. The Chief Inspector rushed from his own room to the one adjoining it. Holloway's door was

45

wide open now, but even a cursory glance into the bedroom was enough to establish that the visitor he'd been arguing with was long gone.

Woodend took the stairs two at a time, his heavy footfalls giving the receptionist below ample indication that everything was far from as it should have been.

'Didn't you hear the scream?' the Chief Inspector demanded when he reached the lobby.

'I ... I hear something,' the receptionist admitted. 'I not know what it was. It was a scream?'

'Get on to the police,' Woodend told him. 'Say there's been a mu— ... an accident. One of your guests has gone over the edge of his balcony.'

'But that is...'

'How do I get down to the rocks?'

'There ... there are steps round the side of the hotel which will take you down the cliff. But please, *señor*, they are most treacherous in the dark, and I do not think you should...'

'Get on to the police!' Woodend repeated. 'Ask for an ambulance, as well. Not that I think it'll do much bloody good now!'

The receptionist had been right about the steps being treacherous in the dark. Woodend almost lost his footing twice on the way down. But finally, as much by luck as by judgement, he did reach the pebble beach below the hotel.

From the grotesque angle at which Holloway was lying, it seemed likely that he had managed to turn whilst still in mid-air, so that instead of landing on his head, he had hit the ground feet first. Not that that had made an ounce of difference to his fate. The impact had been hard enough to completely rearrange his skeleton. The legs would certainly be smashed. The spine, too. Organs would have been shifted around. Bones would have been thrust up into areas they had never been intended to penetrate, piercing and destroying with ruthless efficiency as they went.

At least it would have been quick, Woodend thought. After those few, terrifying seconds in mid-air, the shock of the impact would certainly have been enough to kill Holloway immediately.

He bent down beside the corpse. There was some light provided by the street lights at the top of the cliff, he discovered. Not much – but enough for a rough preliminary examination.

The look on Holloway's face was as chilling as Woodend would have expected on the face of a man who had known with absolute certainty that he was about to die. But it was not his expression the Chief Inspector was interested in. He ran his index finger gently across the top of the bald head, and was not surprised when he encountered a contusion on the right side of the skull.

The bruise wasn't caused by the fall. He'd already established that Holloway had hit the ground feet first. Nor had it occurred after the initial impact. The blow had been landed before Holloway ever went over the balcony. Indeed, the blow was what – indirectly – had *made* him go over.

For the first time since events had begun to unfold, Woodend began to consider the incongruity of the position he had allowed himself to blunder into. He was not a police-man here in Spain. He had no official stand-ing of any kind. And he certainly had no business examining the body of a man who had died in violent circumstances.

He heard two sets of footsteps descending the steps he had so recently come down him-self. He looked up. The two men were both carrying large torches in their hands, so all he could make out were a couple of black shapes behind the shining lights.

Woodend climbed to his feet, and waited. It seemed to take an inordinate amount of time for the men to complete their descent, but then, he thought, why *should* they hurry?

Finally they reached his level, and he could get a better look at them. They were both dressed in the same olive-green uniform as the policeman who had been watching from the hotel lobby earlier in the day, but while one of them was scarcely more than a boy, the other was in his middle thirties.

It was the older one who spoke. *'Qué pasa aquí?'*

'I'm sorry, but I'm afraid I don't know any Spanish,' Woodend said, apologizing for his ignorance of the language for perhaps the tenth time that day.

'Inglés?' the older policeman asked. 'English?'

'That's right.'

'You were touching the body!' the Spaniard said accusingly. 'I saw you do it! Why?'

'I wanted to see if there was any chance that he was still alive,' Woodend replied.

The Spanish policeman snorted contemptuously. 'You think a man can fall from such a high place and still live?'

'I didn't think it was likely, but I thought it was best to check.'

The policeman turned to his younger companion, and said something in very rapid Spanish. The younger man immediately reached down to his belt, withdrew his pistol, and pointed it at Woodend.

'Listen—' Woodend began, feeling his mouth start to dry out.

'No, *you* listen!' the older policeman interrupted. 'We are going to arrest you on suspicion of murder. If you try to resist us in any way, we will shoot you without hesitation.'

Five

It was a very small car for a big man like Woodend to be crammed into the back of, and the situation was certainly not made any easier by the fact that his hands were cuffed behind him. Most of the people he'd arrested in his time would have complained bitterly about the situation, but the Chief Inspector did not bother. He was uncomfortable because he was *meant* to be uncomfortable. It was all part of the older policeman's strategy.

The little car sped through the narrow streets until it reached the edge of the town. Neither of the policemen in the front of the vehicle said a word – even to each other – during the course of the journey, and Woodend was damned if he'd give them the satisfaction of him being the first one to break the silence.

The car slowed as it approached what looked like an army barracks, then came to a complete halt when it reached a stone archway blocked by a pair of heavy metal gates. Two uniformed men, both holding submachine guns in their hands, appeared out of the shadows. Though they must already have known who the occupants of the vehicle were, one of them still stepped closer – as if to make absolutely sure – before giving a nod to his companion. Then the guards opened the gates, and the car edged slowly into an enclosed courtyard. Once it was completely inside, the gates were closed again.

Two new policemen appeared from inside the building. One of them opened the back door of the car and half-assisted – half-pulled – Woodend into the courtyard. Taking an arm each, the men frogmarched him into the building, down a corridor, and into a room which contained only a table, three chairs, a large portrait of General Franco, and a very powerful desk light. Still without having said a word, the men led Woodend over to one of the chairs, slammed him down on to it, and left the room, locking the door behind them.

Woodend's wrists chafed against the handcuffs, but he had more on his mind than merely physical discomfort.

He did not know how the Spanish police operated, but he'd already seen enough to realize that when the metal gates had closed behind him, he had entered a world in which the rules of police interrogation, as he knew them, simply did not apply.

He wondered how he would handle the interrogation when it eventually got under way, and accepted that it was not up to him – that the initiative was in the hands of his captors, and all he could do was react.

How long would they keep him waiting?

Half an hour? An hour? Even longer than that?

Had he been in their place, he would have left it for about forty minutes – just long enough for him to become seriously concerned.

He calculated that around forty-five minutes had passed before the door opened again, and the older of the two policemen who had arrested him entered the room.

'I am Captain López of the Guardia Civil,' he said.

'And I am—'

'I know who you are.'

López sat down opposite him, and Woodend studied the face of the man who was to be his interrogator.

López was handsome in the way that the Latinate idols in the Saturday morning matinees of Woodend's childhood had been handsome. He was moustachioed, but his moustache was neatly trimmed and, unlike the ones sported by most of the other Spanish policemen Woodend had seen that night, did not resemble some fat hairy caterpillar which had fallen asleep above his lip. The

Captain's eyes were quick and cold, his wide mouth was edged with thin lips. He was what, in Lancashire, would be called 'a nasty piece of work'.

'I'd appreciate it if you'd take these handcuffs off me, Captain,' Woodend said.

'I'm sure you would,' López agreed. He reached into the pocket of his jacket, extracted a packet of cigarettes, and lit one up. 'Tell me about the man you killed tonight.'

Woodend knew he should have been expecting it – or something very like it – but the comment still knocked the stuffing out of him.

'I didn't kill anybody!' he protested.

López laughed scornfully. 'You are staying in the room next to the dead man's at the hotel,' he said. 'It would have been easy for you to go into his room, strike him on the head, and then throw him over the balcony.'

'So I murdered him, did I? An' what did I do next? I asked the receptionist to call the police, an' then I waited around for you to come an' arrest me!'

López raised an eyebrow. 'Is that a confession?'

'Of course it's not a bloody confession!' Woodend said exasperatedly. 'If I had killed him, would I have gone down to the body? Would *you* have gone down to the body, if *you'd* been the killer?'

'But I was *not* the killer.'

53

'An', as I've already said, neither was I. But let's pretend for the moment that I was. What would have been the point in my goin' to look at the body?'

'Perhaps you wished to make absolutely sure that he was truly dead,' López suggested.

'I want to see my consul,' Woodend told him.

'There will be plenty of time for that,' López said easily.

'I demand to see him now.'

The Captain laughed again, with more genuine humour to his tone this time. 'According to your documentation, you are a policeman. But you should not confuse your kind of policeman with my kind of policeman. Do you understand what I am saying?'

'I'm not sure.'

'Perhaps it would make things clearer for you if I told you two important things about the Guardia Civil. Shall I?'

'Why not? It'll help to pass the time.'

'The first thing is about our especial nature. We are not part of the community, as I believe the police in England are. We live in barracks, even when we are married and have families. And we never police the area in which we were raised. I was born in Leon, and the men who serve under me come from all parts of Spain – except this one. Then there is our motto – *Toda por la patria*. Do you know what that means, Señor Wood-end?'

'No.'

'All for the fatherland. Note the words carefully. All for Spain. Not for the *Spanish*, but for *Spain*. In this country, the state is much more important than the individual. Do you see the significance of that?'

'I'd have to be pretty thick not to,' Wood-end told him. 'You said there were two things. What's the second one I should know?'

'When the Generalissimo first attempted to seize power from the rabble of Jews, Free-masons and Communists who controlled this country in 1936, there were many who opposed him. But the Guardia Civil did not. It gave him its wholehearted support. The Generalissimo has a long memory – both with regard to his friends and with regard to his enemies.'

'So what you're sayin' is that you can do pretty much what you like. An' that if you don't want me to see my consul, then I won't?'

'Exactly.'

This time it was Woodend who laughed.

'Have I said something amusing?' López asked, puzzled.

'We're not as different as you seem to think, you an' me,' Woodend told him. 'Oh, I might have approached the interrogation from another angle entirely, but I'd still have had the intention of makin' the feller I was questionin' feel just as helpless an' friendless as you're tryin' to make me feel now.'

López smiled, ruefully. 'You seem to have seen through my game.'

'Now that's *another* trick I'd have used,' Woodend said.

'What is?'

'Lettin' the feller I was interrogatin' think that he understood exactly what I was doin' – an' *why* I was doin' it. Lettin' him believe that though I might not know it myself, he was really the one in control.'

López's smile was replaced by a frown. 'Why were you following this man Holloway?' he demanded.

'I wasn't followin' him.'

'Of course you were. You bring your wife along with you, to make us think that this is an innocent holiday. But the true purpose of your visit to Spain was to keep this man Holloway under observation. What had he done? What crime do you suspect him of?'

'You don't really think I killed him at all, do you?' Woodend said.

'I am asking the questions here.'

'That particular accusation – pretendin' to suspect me – was just part of the softenin'- up process, which also included the hand-cuffs an' the long silences. But it makes no difference. I never saw Holloway until today,

56

an' I've no idea who he is, or where he comes from. But why do you need my co-operation anyway? Why don't you simply get somebody in your Ministry of Justice to contact the Central Records Office at Scotland Yard, an' find out what *they've* got on him?'

'To do that, we would first have to know who the man really was,' López said.

Another trick? Woodend asked himself.

No, he didn't think so.

'So Holloway's passport was a forgery, was it?' he asked.

López nodded. 'And not a particularly good one,' he said. 'It should have fooled neither the official at the airport nor the clerk on duty at the hotel. Their incompetence will have to be investigated thoroughly, and action must be taken to ensure that such a mistake does not happen again.'

'So what do *you* think this feller who called himself Holloway was really doin' here?' Woodend asked casually.

'I do not...' López began. Then he pulled himself up short. 'You can save me – and yourself – a great deal of time by telling me all that you know immediately.'

What *did* he know? Woodend asked himself.

He knew that Holloway had been uneasy about being in Spain at all, yet had seemed to be on familiar territory. He knew that though Holloway and the man in the check jacket had pretended not to recognize each other, something – a message of some kind – had passed between them on the square in front of the church. And he knew that someone – possibly the man in the check jacket – had had an argument with Holloway which had come to blows, and that then Holloway had tipped over the balcony.

But how much of this information was he willing to share with the Captain? It was perfectly possible that the man in the check jacket had nothing at all to do with the murder. So would it be fair to surrender him to someone like Captain López? Woodend didn't think so.

'I heard an argument in the room next to mine,' he said. 'It was between two men, one of whom – I assume – was the man I know as Holloway. I went on to my own balcony just in time to see Holloway fall off his. An' that's about it.'

'You know, of course, that Holloway was attacked before he fell,' López said.

'Do I?'

'You were bending over the body for some time. Certainly long enough to discover that he had received a blow to the head.'

'You really do need to make up your mind what part I'm supposed to be playin' in this investigation, you know,' Woodend said.

'What do you mean?'

'Why am I here? Am I a suspect? Am I a

witness? Am I fellow officer who you want to consult about the crime? Or am I just another bloody foreigner, who you're havin' fun pushin' around? Make your choice, an' we'll see where we go from there.'

'You do not realize the seriousness of your position,' López said threateningly.

'Bollocks!' Woodend countered.

López frowned again. 'Bollocks?' he repeated. 'What does that mean? I do not know the word.'

'Try *cojones* then,' Woodend suggested helpfully.

'You told me you did not speak Spanish,' López accused.

'Nor do I. But I picked up a few words from the Spanish wife of one of my inspectors. Very fond of that expression, is Maria. Because in England – just like in Spain – there's a lot of *cojones* about.'

'If you were Spanish—' López growled.

'But I'm not,' Woodend interrupted him. 'Look, Captain, you tried to make me cave in an' tell you what you seem to think I know. Maximum points for effort, but it simply didn't work. So why don't you just cut your losses an' let me go back to my hotel?'

López glanced down at his watch, then looked as if he hated himself for having done so.

So he's working against the clock, Woodend thought. He knows he can only hold me for a certain amount of time, and that time's just about running out.

'Would you stand up, please?' López asked.

Woodend stood. The Captain walked around the table, and took up a position behind Woodend's back. There was a click, and the handcuffs fell away from the Chief Inspector's wrists.

'Your consul wishes to speak to you at the first hour of the morning,' the Captain said. 'Your hotel will be able to give you the address of his office.'

'So my consul's known all along that I've been here?'

'Of course,' López said innocently. 'You surely do not imagine that we would invite a senior English policeman to come to the barracks for a discussion without first informing his diplomatic representative.'

So that was the official version of what had happened, was it?

There had been a discussion – an interchange of ideas – between two experienced police officers.

'How will my consul feel about the fact that I was brought here in handcuffs?' Woodend asked.

'But you were *not* handcuffed,' López said.

Woodend held out his wrists for the Spanish policeman to inspect. 'So what's that?' he asked, indicating the reddening of the skin. 'A rash?'

'Ah yes, you *were* handcuffed,' López said. 'I remember now. The two officers I sent to bring you in were very inexperienced – and perhaps a little over-zealous. They should never have shackled you. It was all a misunderstanding, which we greatly regret.'

'You may be over-zealous, but I'd never have accused you of being inexperienced,' Woodend said.

'I'm sorry, I don't understand.'

'Those two officers who brought me in? One of them was you.'

'You are mistaken,' López told him. 'I have been here all evening.'

'An' I suppose you can produce half a dozen witnesses to swear to that, can you?'

López grinned. 'At least half a dozen,' he agreed. 'I will instruct one of my men to drive you back to your hotel.'

'An' will you let me ride in the front of the car this time – just like a grown-up?'

'If that is what you wish.'

'I'll walk,' Woodend said firmly.

'It is some considerable distance.'

'I'll still walk,' Woodend repeated.

López shrugged. 'That is your choice. But please do not fail to mention to your consul in the morning that transportation *was* offered.'

'Aye, I'll mention it,' Woodend agreed.

'After all, we wouldn't want him thinkin' the Guardia Civil had treated me unkindly, now would we?'

Six

'This is a bad business,' Ralph Featherington Gore, the British Honorary Consul tut-tutted. 'A very bad business indeed.'

As if it were my fault, Woodend reflected. As if I'd bloody well *wanted* to see that feller Holloway take a plunge to his death.

He'd suspected he wasn't going to like the Consul the moment he'd noticed that the man was wearing a silk cravat with a horse-head pin – and the fifteen minutes they'd so far spent together in the Consul's office had only confirmed that initial impression.

Featherington Gore was the sort of man who took himself very seriously and expected everyone else to do the same – the sort who believed that the main aim of the people who met him was to do all they could to win his approval. He didn't have to be efficient, his general air seemed to say. He didn't have to work hard at producing results. He was *Ralph Featherington Gore* – and that should have been enough for anyone.

'Using a fake passport, indeed,' the Consul said disapprovingly. 'Don't these people realize what damage they're doing to our reputation abroad when they indulge in such unsavoury activities? What is the point in me putting on a good show for the Generalissimo, when people like this Holloway chap then go and let the side down completely?'

'So you know Franco personally,' Woodend said. 'A drinkin' mate of yours, is he?'

Featherington Gore shot Woodend a look of intense dislike. 'I wouldn't put it in quite those terms,' he said, 'but I have certainly met the *Caudillo* on several occasions.'

You mean you've stood in a reception line while he's strode past you, Woodend translated.

'I take it you've seen the body,' he said aloud.

Featherington Gore wrinkled his nose in distaste. 'Yes, I performed my official duty in that regard,' he said. 'I can't say I was very impressed with his suit. Admittedly, it looked new – but the quality was shocking. Surely he could have made a little effort.'

'Maybe if he'd known in advance that he was goin' to snuff it, he'd have been a little more careful about what he wore,' Woodend suggested.

'At any rate, it is a complication without which I could well have done,' Featherington

Gore said, ignoring – or misunderstanding – the Chief Inspector's comment. 'We cannot even release the body, since – thanks to the dead man's deviousness – we have no idea to whom it *should be* released. And, inevitably, by dying in that manner, he has cast the British community here in a very bad light.'

'Aye, he certainly should have taken that into consideration before he decided to get himself killed,' Woodend agreed.

Featherington Gore looked puzzled. 'I'm afraid I'm not following you, old chap.'

'You don't seem to have given much thought to the implications of the murder.'

'What implications?'

'Well, for a start, if he was murdered, then somebody must have murdered him.'

'Oh, I see what you mean,' Featherington Gore said. 'From Her Majesty's Government's point of view, the most convenient outcome would be if it was discovered that he was killed during the course of a robbery.'

'Yes, I can see how that might be convenient. But in my experience, robbers an' their victims don't usually have long, intense discussions before they come to blows,' Woodend pointed out.

Featherington Gore frowned. 'You're sure that's what you heard from your room?'

'I'm sure.'

'It couldn't have been a case of Holloway saying, "Are you trying to steal my wallet?"

and the other man answering – in *Spanish*, of course – "Don't come any nearer, English-man, or I'll kill you"?'

'No,' Woodend said heavily. 'It couldn't have been that way at all.'

'Well, if that's the line you intend to adhere to...'

'It is.'

'You leave no interpretation open other than that Holloway knew his killer,' Feather-ington Gore said, miffed.

'Brilliant!' Woodend said. 'I wish I'd thought of that.'

'Of course, that doesn't rule out the possibility that his murderer could be a Spanish criminal. We already have the evidence of his passport and his poor taste in suits to suggest that Mr Holloway did not naturally mix with the better elements of society.'

'Then again, his murderer could just as easily turn out to be English.'

Featherington Gore shuddered. 'I sincerely hope that does not, in fact, turn out to be the case.'

'Have you been in touch with the Ambas-sador about this inconvenient little murder?'

'Indeed I have. I sent a telegram to His Excellency this morning. No doubt he will reply with instructions as soon as he is able.'

'An' in the meantime?'

'In the meantime, there is very little we can

do here on the ground, as it were. As I understand it, the investigation is being led by Captain López, who is a very sound chap – for a Spaniard. As far as you're concerned personally, having delivered your report to me, you now have my permission to continue with the rest of your little holiday.'

'I wonder if *you* could help *me*,' Woodend said.

The Consul did not seem very keen on the possibility. 'In what way?' he asked suspiciously.

'My missus isn't feelin' very well. I'm sure it's nothin' serious, but I'd be happier in my own mind if you could recommend a good doctor – preferably one who speaks English – to give her the once-over.'

'The "once-over",' Featherington Gore repeated, as if the term were completely alien to him. 'I'm not sure I can be of much assistance there. If I require a medical examination, I go to Madrid to see Don Carlos Muñoz, who is a very eminent physician, with an international reputation. However – ' he paused for a moment – 'I'm sure there must *be* competent doctors in this town, and no doubt my secretary – who has probably had reason to consult one herself – will be able to advise you on which to visit.'

Featherington Gore stood up and held out his hand across the desk. Clearly, he considered the interview to be over.

Woodend rose to his feet, too. 'If there's anythin' else—' he began.

'Yes, yes,' Featherington Gore interrupted impatiently. 'If there *is* anything else, I will certainly summon you.'

'Aye, leave a blue lantern in your bedroom window, an' I'll be there before you know it,' Woodend said.

And having delivered the best parting shot he could think of at that moment, he headed for the door.

He was already turning the handle when Featherington Gore said, 'Er ... Mr Woodend?'

Woodend turned. 'Yes?'

'Your passport says that you're a Chief Inspector. Is it accurate?'

'What, are you suggestin' I'm travellin' on fake papers as well?'

'No, no,' Featherington Gore hastened to assure him. 'I'm sure the passport is genuine. I merely wondered if the rank listed was correct.'

'Ah, you're wonderin' if I've been promoted since the passport was issued,' Woodend said.

But from the expression on his face, that was clearly *not* what Featherington Gore had been wondering at all.

'It's just that Chief Inspector is a quite senior post,' he said. 'And you don't seem to ... don't seem to...'

'Dress the part?' Woodend suggested helpfully.

'Yes, I suppose that is what I mean.'

'Well then, at least me an' the victim have got *somethin'* in common – even if it's only poor taste in clothes,' Woodend said.

The doctor's office was located on one of the side streets which led off the church square. The brass plaque on the door looked reassuringly professional, but Woodend still had his doubts.

'I'd be much happier if you'd let me come in with you, lass,' he said to his wife.

Joan sighed. 'If the doctor speaks reasonable English, I won't need you,' she said.

'An' what if he doesn't?'

'If he doesn't, you'd be no more use at makin' him understand what's wrong with me than I would.'

'I know that, but—'

'When men go to the doctor's, they take their wives along with them to baby them,' Joan said. 'We don't mind that. It's like all the other trials and tribulations that go with the marriage licence – just somethin' we have to put up with! But when we're not feelin' well ourselves, we've got enough on our minds without lookin' after you an' all.'

Woodend chuckled, then was serious again. 'You're sure?'

'I'm sure. Go an' solve this murder, Charlie – that's the sort of thing you're good at.'

Had he been in England, he'd have jumped at the suggestion – for though he would never have admitted it, going to the local police and offering his services was his idea of a perfect holiday. But this wasn't England. It wasn't even close. He had no idea how police officers in Spain went about their duties – and if they were all like Captain López, he suspected that he didn't really want to find out.

'Maybe I'll just wander over to the square, an' have a drink,' he said tentatively.

'You do that,' Joan agreed, ringing the bell. 'An' when I've finished with the doctor, I'll come an' find you.'

The door was opened by a girl in a maid's uniform. 'Señora VoooDend?' she asked uncertainly.

'That's right,' Joan agreed.

'Please to follow me.'

'I really don't mind comin' in with you, love,' Woodend said, as his wife took a step over the threshold.

Joan turned slightly. 'Oh, bugger off, Charlie!' she said – and then she laughed to take the edge off her words.

But it wasn't like Joan to swear under any circumstances, Woodend thought worriedly. It wasn't like her at all. Still, she was inside now, the door was closing, and there was

69

nothing more he could do for the moment.

As he walked towards the square, he realized that he was being followed. One of López's men? Probably! Well, he should at least let the bugger know he'd been spotted.

He came to a halt, and turned round. But it was not a Spanish policeman – either in plain clothes or in uniform – who was on his tail. It was an *ex*-policeman.

'Mr Ruiz!' he said. 'What an unexpected pleasure.'

Seven

Paco Ruiz's limp seemed more pronounced that morning, Woodend thought, as the Spaniard led him across the square to a bar which was just clearing away the evidence of workers' breakfasts and preparing itself for the first wave of assaults from the tourist trade.

'It's worse some days than others,' Ruiz said, as they sat down at one of the tables.

'What is?'

'My leg. There are times when it feels almost as strong as it did when I was a young man of twenty, but there are also times when I think I'm about to lose the use of it for ever.'

'How did you know I was thinkin' about your leg, when you were walkin' in front of me?' Woodend wondered.

'Only a fool pretends that his infirmity is not noticed by others. It is gout, you understand.'

'Is that right?' Woodend asked flatly.

Paco Ruiz smiled. 'You do not believe me, of course.'

Woodend returned the smile. 'From the way you walk, I'd be prepared to bet you're sufferin' from an old injury, rather than a creepin' disease. Of course, I could be wrong.'

'But you don't think you are?'

'No, I don't.'

'Then why have you not asked me *how* I acquired my limp?'

'Because it's none of my business.'

Ruiz's smile broadened. 'You would still like to know, though, wouldn't you?'

'I'm itchin' to know,' Woodend agreed. 'But I imagine that if you ever get to the point where you want to talk about it, you'll need absolutely no promptin' from me.'

The waiter arrived.

'Beer, Mr Woodend?' Paco Ruiz asked. 'Or is it still too early in the morning for you?'

'I'm on holiday,' Woodend said. 'An' when

71

I'm on holiday, there's no such thing as *too* early.'

Their discussion so far had not really been about Paco Ruiz's leg at all, Woodend thought. It had been more in the nature of verbal sparring – a testing process. Each of them had been trying to establish whether he could trust the other man – and whether the other man could trust him. And Woodend had decided that he *could* trust Ruiz. Not only that, but he found himself rapidly developing a tremendous liking for the man.

The beers arrived. They both took a sip.

'I have discovered something which you may find intriguing from a professional viewpoint,' Ruiz said.

'Professional viewpoint?' Woodend repeated – *sounding* intrigued.

'Yet I am not sure I should involve you,' Ruiz confessed.

'Why not?'

'What do you know of Spain? You perhaps read an article in your newspapers about a demonstration which has been broken up by the police, and you imagine it to be like one handled by the British authorities. I can assure you that it is not. People might sometimes get injured in a British demonstration, but here heads are broken on a regular basis.'

'Maybe you're right, but even so—'

'What do you *see* of Spain – even looking at

72

it with the trained eye of a detective? You see the people in the shops and bars, who are happy to have your custom and who treat you with traditional Spanish courtesy and hospitality. True, you also see policemen with guns, but you tell yourself that this is only the Continental way of doing things, and that it is nothing to worry about. But as I hinted previously, there is a darker side to my country.'

'I met a piece of the darker side after we parted last night,' Woodend said. 'His name was Captain López.'

Paco Ruiz shook his head. 'You have just made a mistake which is commonly made by people who do not know this country.'

'López isn't part of the darker side?'

'He's a pawn. Nothing! He is the man who handles the bloody meat. But to understand Spain fully, you must see further than the assistant at the front of the shop. You must seek out the butcher beyond.'

'Aren't you bein' a little melodramatic?' Woodend wondered. 'I know some terrible things were done in the Civil War, but—'

'You think you know about those times, but, in truth, you have no idea,' Paco Ruiz interrupted.

'Don't I?'

'No idea at all. What *kinds* of terrible things do you think were done?'

'Well,' Woodend began, already starting to

feel that he was on shaky ground, 'I know that a lot of civilians were killed during the war.'

'*Only* during the war?'

'I would assume so.'

'Then you would assume wrongly. The killing did not stop when the Nationalists won. In the summer after the war ended, tens of thousands were executed for no other crime than being on the losing side. In Madrid alone, up to two hundred and fifty people *a day* were led before the firing squad. After a while even Franco's strongest supporters grew sickened by all the bloodletting, and asked him to show a little mercy.'

'An' did he?'

'He made what he probably considered a concession. He said only eighty percent of those brought before the military tribunals *must* be found guilty. *That* was his definition of even-handed justice. And this man, with so much blood on his hands, still controls this country.'

'But it can't be anything like as bad as it was, can it?' Woodend asked.

'He no longer spills as much blood, but his grip is tighter than ever,' Ruiz said. 'No one knows how many people are in prison. You will not read any figures in the press – as you might do in your own country – because the press is not free.' He paused to light up a

74

black cigarette. 'Why do you think all foreign films are dubbed into Spanish, instead of merely having subtitles?'

'I don't know.'

'Because some of the audience may understand English.'

'So what?'

'The censor does not want their minds polluted by foreign ideas. If a woman is a man's mistress in an American film, she will become his niece in the Spanish version. Any scenes in which they make physical contact will simply be cut, in order to maintain that fiction. It will make a nonsense of the movie, of course, but at least it will keep our people pure.'

'You're jokin'!' Woodend said.

'I wish I were,' Ruiz told him. 'Even language is suppressed. The Basques and Catalans have their own languages, but they are not allowed to use them. Or to christen their children with Basque or Catalan names – the names they give them *must* be Spanish.'

'That's incredible!'

'It affects football, too. Real Madrid is the regime's favourite team. Barcelona is, for many, a symbol of Catalan nationalism. Once, when they were playing each other, the Guardia Civil visited the Barcelona team's dressing room, and told the goal-keeper that if he played well, his brother, who was in prison for his political activities, would be made to suffer.'

'Why are you tellin' me all this?' Woodend asked.

'Because a man should never enter a darkened room without at least having some idea of what to expect in there. If you and I are to conduct an investigation – even an unofficial one – I would rather you started out with a true picture of the Spain in which we live.'

'*Are* we goin' to conduct an investigation?' Woodend asked.

'That is entirely up to you, Señor Woodend. *I* shall certainly try to find out more, if I can.'

'About *what*, exactly?'

'The American who we saw contact Holloway is called Mitchell – or, at least, that is what it says on his passport. Holloway was not the only man he saw last night, either. Later – though before Holloway was killed – he had a meeting in a quiet bar with a whole group of men.'

'I don't see that's particularly significant.'

'Then consider this. All the men were roughly the same age as Holloway and Mitchell.'

'A feller's mates *do* tend to be the same age as he is.'

'And though the barman is convinced that they were all foreigners, they were talking to each other in *Spanish*.'

'Now that *is* interestin',' Woodend agreed.

'Was our friend Holloway at this meetin'?'

'What makes you ask?'

'Because it strikes me that the piece of paper Mitchell gave him could have had directions on it.'

'That is true. And perhaps he *was* there. One of the men at the table may have been bald, but he was wearing a hat, and so the barman is not sure.'

'So do you think that one – or all – of these men was involved in Holloway's death?'

'Not necessarily. But I certainly think Holloway's death is connected with the reason they are all here.'

Woodend nodded, then offered Ruiz a Capstan Full Strength. The Spaniard shook his head and reached for his own packet of black cigarettes.

'Before we go any further with this, I'd like to know what your interest in the case is,' Woodend said.

Ruiz took a long, reflective drag on his Celtas. 'It is a long time since I have investigated a real crime. I miss it. Besides...'

'Besides what?'

'Tourism has become very important to the Spanish economy. Four years ago, we had four million visitors. This year, we are expecting *fourteen* million. The death of a holidaymaker – even if he were only *pretending* to be on holiday – could damage the tourist trade.'

'And that bothers you, does it?'

'Not especially. There are times when I think we have too many tourists – that they are destroying the Spain which I love. But it *does* bother the authorities – and in order to minimize the damage, they will insist that an arrest is made soon.'

'But it doesn't really matter whether the feller who's arrested is actually guilty?' Woodend said, beginning to understand the way that Ruiz's mind was working.

'It does not matter at all,' Ruiz agreed. 'We do not have trial by jury in this country, and most of the judges will do what they are told without a moment's hesitation. So some poor man will be arrested. He will probably have a criminal record – but he will not be a serious criminal.'

'Why not?'

'Because serious criminals often have powerful allies – some of them in government – and the man who is to take the blame for Holloway's death must have no way in which he can defend himself. So he will be tried, found guilty, and executed. And everybody will be happy – except for his friends and family.'

'An' you,' Woodend said.

'And me,' Ruiz agreed. 'I have seen enough injustice in my lifetime. If I can prevent more, I will.'

'Can I tell you somethin' that's been

puzzlin' me?' Woodend asked.

'Please feel free.'

'When I was arrested last night, there were very few people around. In fact, the only person I actually saw, before López arrived, was the hotel receptionist. Yet by the time I talked to López in the Guardia Civil barracks, he had already been contacted by the British Consul. Now the question is, who contacted the Consul?'

'I suppose it's always possible that it could have been the receptionist,' Ruiz suggested.

'It could have been,' Woodend agreed. 'But he didn't look to me like a man with enough initiative to have done that. On the other hand, he might well have called somebody who *did* have the initiative.'

'Me,' Ruiz said.

'You,' Woodend replied.

Paco Ruiz shrugged. 'All right, I admit it. I heard you were in trouble, and I did all I could to get you out of it.'

'Because it was yet another example of the injustice of the Spanish authorities?'

'Of course.'

'It had nothing to do with the fact that it was in your own interest – or perhaps in the interests of the case you saw developin' – to get me released from police custody as soon as possible?'

'That could have played a part in it.'

Woodend grinned. 'About all those warnings you've just given about the kind of country this is?'

'Yes?'

'I don't think they were ever really meant to scare me off.'

'No?'

'No. In fact, I'm almost certain they were intended to have exactly the opposite effect. You think you've got the measure of me, don't you?'

A small, knowing smile came involuntarily to Paco Ruiz's lips. 'Perhaps I do,' he admitted.

'You've decided that the best way to get me interested in the case is to present it as a real challenge. As you see it, the more obstacles there are in my way, the more I'll feel the urge to try an' get round them. It's nothin' more or less than a classic con, Paco.'

Ruiz's smile became a grin. 'I apologize,' he said.

'For tryin' to con me? Or for bein' found out?'

'Possibly a little of both.' Paco's face grew more serious. 'I should never have tried it. I really *do* hope that you can find it in your heart to forgive me.'

'It'd be hard not to, when I know that if I'd been in your shoes, I'd have played it in exactly the same way,' Woodend admitted.

He looked up, and saw Joan walking across the square towards him. She was moving a lot slower than she used to, he thought. She'd said she was in no more than minor discomfort, but could he really believe her?

'Some creatures walk into a trap even though they know it's a trap,' Paco Ruiz said. 'They just can't resist it.'

'Meanin' that you've still got hopes I might agree to work on the case?'

'Exactly.'

'I'm goin' to have to disappoint you,' Woodend said, with genuine regret in his voice.

'Because I overplayed my hand, and succeeded in scaring you off after all?'

'Because my wife's here for a rest, an' my main concern has to be to see that she gets one.'

'That is your wife?' Paco Ruiz asked, following Woodend's gaze across the square.

'Yes, that's her.'

'She looks a very nice woman.'

'She *is* a very nice woman.'

'If my wife and I were to invite you and your wife out for dinner this evening, do you think she would enjoy it?'

'Yes, I think she would.'

'So will you come?'

'I can't promise, just at the moment,' Woodend said. 'You see, the way it works in my family is that I make the major decisions like whether the government should invade Russia or raise income tax.'

'Yes?'

'An' Joan makes the minor ones like where we should go for our holidays, an' whether we should have dinner with my new mate.'

'Is that a polite way of refusing?' Paco Ruiz asked.

'No, it's what we Northerners call "knowing who really wears the trousers in our house",' Woodend said. He smiled. 'Ask her yourself. I'm sure she'll be delighted.'

Eight

Jessica Medwin had decided to use her husband's temporary absence as an opportunity to do all sorts of things she didn't normally have the time for. Thus, she had risen early that morning and put in a solid three hours hard work in her rose garden. That task successfully completed – and feeling amazingly virtuous – she allowed herself the luxury of a long, sudsy soak in a deep bath. Then, smelling sweet and feeling silky, she drove into Lancaster to have lunch with an old friend.

It was at that point that her day started to go wrong.

'So where exactly has your Peter gone?' Miriam Thoroughgood asked Jessica over the rich and evil whipped egg and cream dessert.

Jessica – who was just raising a spoonful of the delicious concoction to her mouth – froze.

'He ... er ... didn't actually say,' she replied cautiously.

'Didn't say! What do you mean, he didn't say? You surely didn't let him get away with that!'

She hated it when her best friend made her feel like nothing more than a silly little girl, Jessica thought. She was beginning to wish that she'd never arranged this lunch.

'Goodness knows what he could be up to,' Miriam said.

'Up to?' Jessica replied, despising the fact that she was merely repeating her friend's words.

'Well, the pair of you have been married for over twenty years now, haven't you?'

'Yes, we have. So what?'

'And haven't you ever considered the possibility that he might have grown just a little bored with you – that he might, perhaps, have gone off somewhere with another woman?'

Jessica laughed. 'Not my Peter.'

'You wouldn't be the first woman, by a long chalk, to have ever said something like that and then found out she was completely wrong,' her friend cautioned her.

'Peter worships me,' Jessica said, and seeing the sceptical look on her friend's face, she continued, 'Look, he's probably off on some kind of official visit, that's all.'

'Then why didn't he tell you where he was going?'

Jessica waved her hands helplessly in the air. 'Oh, I don't know. Perhaps he thought his secretiveness would give him an air of mystery which would make him more attractive to me. As if he needed to do that! He might be a funny-looking little thing, but he's *my* funny-looking little thing, and I adore him just as much as he adores me.'

'Oh, I admit he doesn't look like much of a catch,' Miriam said airily, 'but he is quite an important man, you know, Jessica, and there's a certain kind of woman who finds that attractive in itself. At any rate, I certainly wouldn't trust him, if I were in your place.'

Jessica felt the embers of revolt which had been smouldering in her stomach suddenly – and unexpectedly – burst into flame.

'I know you wouldn't trust him, my dear,' she said sweetly. 'You didn't trust either of your own husbands, either. Perhaps that's why they're now both your *ex*-husbands.'

Though Don Antonio Durán was not strictly

his boss, Captain López was far too much of a political animal to ever cross a mayor – especially a mayor who was soon to be elevated to the post of Provincial Governor. So when, in the early afternoon following the murder, Durán rang to ask if he could see the Captain as soon as possible, López replied that 'as soon as possible' could be right away.

He drove up to the Mayor's villa, which was located on the edge of town. A servant led him into the west wing of the house, down a corridor laid with thick carpets, and into an office which was lined with pale oak panels.

The *Alcalde* was sitting behind his heavy mahogany desk, in a chair which must have been specially built to take his considerable bulk. Yet he probably hadn't always been a grotesquely fat man, López thought. The small sharp eyes, at least, hinted at the leaner and hungrier man who still lived inside the huge frame.

'I hear there's been a murder,' Durán said, without preamble – and without inviting the Captain to sit down.

'That's right, Your Excellency. It was—'

'A middle-aged Englishman who arrived here alone, yesterday.'

'You are well informed, Your Excellency.'

'It is my business to be well informed.' The Mayor paused. 'A murder is bad for the town – especially at the height of the holiday season.'

'I know that, Your Excellency. That is why I am pursuing my investigation with all the vigour of—'

'On the other hand,' the Mayor interrupted him, 'there is a distinct danger that the cure may be even worse than the illness.'

'I beg your pardon, Your Excellency?'

'Our visitors, with their pockets full of money, could find a full-scale murder inquiry very unsettling.'

'Yes, I agree they well might. But since we must face the fact that there *has* been a murder—'

'I have been imagining two possible conversations our visitors might have with their friends when they return home,' the Mayor cut in, 'two different conversations prompted by two entirely different police responses to the murder. Are you following me?'

'Yes,' López said dubiously.

'The first conversation takes place following a very low-level police investigation. "I hear there was a murder where you were staying," the friend might say. "That's right," the visitor would agree. "And did the police catch the killer?" "No, they didn't." What do you think the friend might say next, Captain López?'

'That it reflected very badly on Spain, and

86

on the honour of the Guardia Civil?' López hazarded.

'You see, that is where I think you are you wrong,' the Mayor replied. 'The way I imagine it, the friend would shrug and say, "Oh well, we have murders in this country, too, and not all of them are solved, either." But let us now move to the other possible scenario, the one in which the police have done all they could to track down the killer.'

'And have they caught him, in this scenario?'

'Perhaps they have, and perhaps they haven't. It really doesn't affect the argument. "What was your holiday like?" the friend asks. "Dreadful," replies the visitor. "There were police all over the place. I was questioned twice myself, but that wasn't even the worst of it. We couldn't get decent service in the restaurants because all the waiters were continually being interrogated by the law. It was impossible to get a taxi half the time, for much the same reason. There were queues in the shops, and if anything broke down in the hotel you had to wait forever to get it fixed. I certainly won't be going back there again." And his friend says, "I don't think I'll be going there, either." In other words, in an attempt to restore our good name, we may be doing no more than blackening it even further.'

'But—'

'As I see it, it is all a question of deciding which course of action will damage us the least.'

'There is a third alternative,' López said tentatively.

'And what might that be?'

'I have spent the morning looking through my records, and have found a man who could have committed the murder – or could certainly be made *to look as if* he had committed it.'

'And who is this man?'

'He is of no consequence in himself. We suspect that he is a radical. His brother is already in gaol for his anti-state activities. It will not be too difficult to construct a case against him.'

For a moment, Durán looked tempted. Then he shook his huge, fat head. 'Arresting someone will only keep the case alive in other people's minds,' he said. 'It would be far better to let it simply fade away.'

'But we must consider the reputation of the Guardia Civil!' Captain López protested.

Durán raised a quizzical eyebrow. 'The reputation of the Guardia Civil?' he repeated. 'Or your own *personal* reputation?'

'They are the same thing.'

'No, they're not,' the Mayor contradicted him. 'You are answerable to your Captain-General. As far as you are concerned, he is a giant whose opinion of you can make or break your career. True?'

'I would not put it quite like that.'

'Then you're a fool, because that is the way things are. But consider this; while you must gaze up at your Captain-General, there are others who are powerful enough to look him squarely in the eye. A provincial governor is one example which comes immediately to mind. And in a few weeks' time, *I* will be the civil governor of *this* province – which just happens to be the one in which you work.'

There was a knock on the door, and the servant entered.

'Yes?' Durán said, bad-temperedly.

'Your bitch is about to give birth, Your Excellency. You said you wanted to see it.'

'Quite right,' the *Alcalde* agreed. 'We should always take the opportunity to observe the miracles of nature.' With some considerable difficulty, he raised himself from his chair and waddled over to the door. 'Wait here,' he said to López, almost as an afterthought.

The Captain did not move from the spot on which he was standing until he was sure the Mayor had left the building, but then he stepped quickly over to the desk. The *Alcalde*'s papers and official documents were spread across the surface in a haphazard manner, but even so, López had spotted the glossy sheen of the corner of a photograph projecting from under a pile of reports.

Making a mental note of exactly where he had first observed it, the Captain pulled the picture free and held it up to the light.

It was a photograph he had seen before – the photograph which the official police photographer had taken of the dead Holloway.

So not only did Durán know the circumstances of the man's arrival in the town, but he had sent for his picture – and had done so in such a way as to make certain that the officer in charge of the case knew nothing about it.

That was not good! Not good *at all*!

López was on the point of returning the picture to the exact spot in which he had found it when he saw that lying beneath it were several other photographs. He strained his ears for the sound of approaching footsteps, then reached for his new discovery.

He laid the photographs on the desk. They were much older – and much less expertly taken – than the picture of the murder victim. And they fell into two distinct groups.

The first set contained shots of a group of men in an olive grove. They were wearing the baggy trousers and shapeless jackets of a much earlier era, and they were all carrying rifles. There was something about the composition of the pictures which suggested to López that the photographer had taken them hurriedly – and perhaps secretly.

90

The second set was quite different. Each picture contained only one man, and it was plain from the expressions on their faces that they – like Holloway – were dead.

López picked up one picture from each set, and began to compare them.

Were the men in the first set the same men as appeared in the second? he wondered. And if there were, how much time had elapsed between the two sets?

The faces, especially in the olive grove set, were fuzzy. What he needed was a magnifying glass. He wondered if the *Alcalde* kept one somewhere among the chaos of his desk.

There was the sound a door being opened, then he heard heavy footsteps as Durán plodded down the corridor.

López gathered up the photographs, replaced them where he had found them, and took two quick steps backward.

The *Alcalde* returned to his study, breathing heavily from his exertion. 'A false alarm,' he gasped. 'The bitch isn't ready yet.' He walked around his desk, and squeezed his huge frame back into his chair. 'Where were we?' he asked.

'I need more,' López said.

The *Alcalde* looked puzzled. 'More of what?'

'I need to have things clearly spelled out for me.'

'What has brought about this sudden need

of yours for me to be more explicit?'

The photographs! López thought. The bloody photographs which suggest that this matter goes much deeper than you would have me believe!

But aloud, all he said was, 'When you ask a man to walk through a swamp, you should at least mark out his path clearly for him.'

The *Alcalde* sighed heavily. 'Very well,' he agreed. 'Perhaps this will be clear enough for you. I will not hold it against you, Captain López, if you fail to solve this murder.'

'Good.'

'More than that – I will understand that your failure to solve it was due to your sensitivity to the needs of this town. That will make you a hero in my eyes – and heroes should be rewarded. If, on the other hand, you do solve the murder – but disrupt the tourist trade – it will be a black mark against you. And the next time I talk to your Captain-General, I will have some very unpleasant things to say to him. Do we understand each other?'

López nodded. 'Oh yes, Your Excellency. I think we understand each other *very well* indeed.'

Jessica Medwin had intended to shop with Miriam Thoroughgood that afternoon, but the other woman's comments at lunch had left a bad taste in her mouth, and so she told her 'so-called' best friend that she had a headache, and would go straight home. She hadn't. The shopping expedition had gone ahead, but without the poisonous Miriam by her side, and by the end of the afternoon – having been extremely frivolous and spent much more than she'd intended to – Jessica was feeling much better.

She arrived home at five to six. She called down the hallway to the maid that she would just love a gin and tonic, then went through to the lounge and switched the television on.

The Six O'Clock News was just starting. There was trouble over the question of civil rights for negroes in the southern states of the USA again. The Beatles had travelled up to Liverpool, their home town, for the premiere of their film *A Hard Day's Night*. The Prime Minister, addressing a businessmen's lunch in Manchester, had promised that the country could look forward to the future with a new and glowing confidence.

There was a knock on the door, and the maid entered the lounge. She placed the tray she was carrying on the small table next to Jessica's chair, then said, 'Will there be anythin' else, ma'am?'

'I don't think so,' Jessica said. 'In fact, I won't be needing you again until supper time, so why don't you put your feet up for a couple of hours?'

The maid gave a small bob. 'Thank you,

ma'am.'

When she'd left the room, Jessica picked up her drink. The glass felt deliciously cold against the palm of her hand, and she was already anticipating the soothing effect of the gin.

So bugger Miriam Thoroughgood!

The bulletin had moved on to coverage of the day's cricket at Lords. England had had an outstanding innings, and as Jessica watched the fielders chasing the ball she thought that it was a pity Peter would probably have missed it.

The newsreader's face filled the screen again.

'Spanish police are investigating the death of a man presumed to be English,' he said, in a suitably solemn tone.

How could anybody be *presumed* to be English? Jessica wondered idly. Either you were or you weren't.

'The man fell to his death from the balcony of his hotel room in a Costa Blanca resort,' the newsreader continued. 'The local authorities suspect that foul play was involved.'

A picture of the dead man was flashed up on the screen. He had a bald head, and an unnaturally pained expression in his lifeless eyes.

'Anyone recognizing the man is asked to contact Scotland Yard,' the voice-over continued. 'The number to ring is Whitehall One Two, One Two.'

Jessica didn't hear this last part. Her ears were filled, instead, with the sound of a scream.

It took her several seconds to realize that she was the one who was screaming.

Nine

The meal together was turning out to be a great success, Woodend thought. The location helped – a cosy restaurant with a sea view. And it certainly did no harm – from the point of view of service – to be dining with a man whom both the owner and the waiters treated like a visiting film star. But it was the company, more than anything, which was making the evening so enjoyable.

He'd already known he got on well with Paco, but he'd had slight misgivings about meeting Ruiz's wife. She could have been loud. She could have been opinionated. She could have been a drunk! The whole evening, in other words, could have become extremely uncomfortable.

He realized he had nothing to worry about

the moment he met Cindy Ruiz. She was no more than a few years younger than her husband, yet though she had made little attempt to disguise the lines that age had brought, she somehow managed to maintain the air of the fresh-faced research student she had been when Ruiz first met her. Her features had character written all over them. She was attentive when listening, witty and interesting when talking. And – best of all – Joan was getting on with her like a house on fire and had not looked so relaxed for months.

Talk had drifted – perhaps almost inevitably – on to the subject of the Civil War and its aftermath.

'So they actually arrested Paco for no other reason than that he'd been on the losing side?' Joan asked incredulously.

'That's right,' Cindy agreed.

'You must have had a terrible time while he was in prison.'

'It wasn't easy,' Cindy admitted, 'but it was even worse when they let him out.'

It was just the sort of dig at her husband that a Whitebridge woman might have made – 'At least when the bugger was banged up, he wasn't gettin' under my feet around the house all the time' – and Joan laughed as she would have done back home. Then, with growing horror, she sensed that Cindy had not been trying to be funny at all.

'Oh, I'm sorry,' she said.

Cindy smiled, understandingly. 'It's my fault. I wasn't expressing myself clearly. When I said they let him out of prison, I didn't mean you to get the impression that it was so he could come home to me.'

'It wasn't?'

'Not at all.' Cindy glanced across the table at Paco. 'You don't mind if I talk about it, do you?'

Ruiz shrugged. 'Why should I mind? It was a long time ago.'

But he wasn't being entirely honest there, Woodend thought. It might have been a long time *in years*, but from the shudder which he had only partly managed to disguise with his shrug, it was clear that it was as fresh in his mind as if it had all happened only yesterday.

'General Franco had the idea of building a monument to the fallen of the Civil War, you see,' Cindy told Joan. 'The site he selected for it was a granite mountain forty miles from Madrid.'

'What a strange place to choose,' Joan mused.

'Strange?'

'Such a long way away from everythin'. Most of our war memorials are in the local churchyards, where people can get to see them easily.'

Cindy laughed. 'You mustn't think of the Valley of the Fallen as the kind of memorial

97

you might see in England or America,'
she said. 'The basilica, where Franco will
eventually be buried, is nearly three hundred yards long and has a seventy-yard-
high dome – all of it blasted out of solid
rock.'

'Good heavens!' Joan exclaimed.

'But even that seems modest in compari-
son to the cross which stands outside the
entrance,' Cindy continued.

'That must really be big, then,' Joan said.

'Huge! Its a hundred and seventy-five
yards high, and its arms are so wide that two
double-decker buses could pass each other
on them.'

'If anyone could work out how to get the
buses up there, in the first place,' Paco said,
in what Woodend thought was an attempt to
lighten the mood.

But Cindy was not to be deflected. 'Can
you imagine how expensive it was to build?'
she asked. 'How many resources were
poured into it? And remember, this was at a
time when the Spanish people were so poor,
as a result of the war, that they were almost
starving.'

Paco Ruiz smiled. 'Stop being so outraged
and get on with the story, Cindy,' he said.

'Obviously, such a gargantuan project
would require huge amounts of labour,'
Cindy Ruiz continued. 'But fortunately for
Franco and his cronies, such labour was

readily available. And not just cheap, but free.'

'Free?'

'That's right. The gaols were crammed to bursting point with political prisoners. Why not make them earn their keep, somebody suggested. In other words, Joan, why not use those prisoners as slave labour? And my Paco was one of those slaves!'

'How terrible!' Joan said.

'Oh, I was one of the lucky ones,' Paco Ruiz said in a self-denigratory tone. 'I worked in the valley for less than a year.'

'That was only because one of those huge blocks of granite they were building the cross with slipped – and crushed your leg!' Cindy said, her outrage returning.

'I was *still* lucky,' Paco said. 'I escaped with no more than a limp, which some days hardly bothers me at all. We will never know how many of my comrades actually died during the construction of that monstrosity.'

'How can you still live here, after all that's happened to you?' Joan wondered.

'I love my country,' Paco Ruiz said sincerely. 'I would feel more of a prisoner outside it than I would in any gaol. Besides, Franco is not Spain, and Spain – however much the *Caudillo* tries – will never be rebuilt in the image that he desires. However hard he can make our lives at the moment – however much we have to struggle against him – one day he *will* be gone. And I predict that ten years after his death, it will be as if he had never existed.' He paused, and looked slightly embarrassed. 'Enough talking about politics and past history. Let's order some more wine, and then I can offend your delicate English sensibilities by proving to you that a bullfighter is every bit as much of an artist as a ballet dancer.'

'Is he indeed?' Woodend asked innocently. 'An' how many handbags does a bullfighter normally own?'

'I don't understand,' Paco Ruiz said.

'Well, up North, where I come from, most men think all ballet dancers are nancy boys,' Woodend said.

'Charlie!' Joan said sharply.

'Not that I subscribe to that particular view in any way myself,' Woodend added, with mock haste.

'He doesn't,' Joan said hotly. 'He *really* doesn't. He may come across as bein' about as tactful as a sledgehammer, but he's the most tolerant an' understandin' man I know.' Then she saw that the Ruizes were laughing – that they hadn't taken her Charlie's statement seriously in the first place – and she continued, 'Yes, he's very tolerant an' understandin'. In fact, now I think about it, it's his only redeemin' feature.'

The laughter continued, the talk flowed as easily as the wine, and they would probably still have been there at the table when the restaurant finally closed its doors for the night, had it not been for the arrival of the woman.

She was middle-aged and slightly harassed-looking. Woodend recognized her immediately as the Consul's secretary, and noted that she seemed very relieved to have found him.

'I've been looking for you everywhere, Mr Woodend,' she said, confirming his initial impression. 'Mr Featherington Gore says that it's very important he talk to you.'

'When? In the mornin'?'

'Now! Immediately! He was most insistent.'

'Did he say what it was about?'

'No. I'm only a secretary. Mr Featherington Gore hardly notices I exist until he wants something done. And he certainly never tells me anything important. But I'm not as stupid as he seems to think I am, and I imagine that what he wants to see you about is the murder that happened yesterday.'

Woodend glanced quickly around the table. Cindy had an expression of interest on her face, Joan one of resignation. Paco Ruiz merely looked envious.

'It can't be a legal certainty until the next of kin has seen it, but we think we've identified the body,' Featherington Gore said.

101

We've identified the body, Woodend noted. People like Featherington Gore always used 'we've' when something had been achieved. It was only when things went wrong that they slipped into 'you've' or 'they've'.

'So *you've* identified him,' Woodend said. 'I still don't see why that's any reason I should have been dragged away from a perfectly delightful dinner with my friends.'

Featherington Gore frowned. 'My secretary said that the people you were dining with were Spanish.'

'They were. Well, one of 'em, at least.'

'Are they on the Embassy list?'

'An' what's that, when it's at home?'

The Consul sighed at his ignorance. 'It's a list of the people who are deemed to be acceptable to invite to Embassy functions – the Queen's Birthday and similar events.'

'In that case, I'd be rather more than surprised if they *were* on it,' Woodend said.

Featherington Gore's frown deepened. 'If I were you, I'd be very careful about the company you keep while you're in Spain.'

'I'm doin' my best – but it's not always easy.'

'I beg your pardon?'

'Well, you're my consul, aren't you, so whatever my personal feelin's on the matter, I felt pretty much obliged to come an' see *you*.'

'I'm afraid I'm not following you,' Featherington Gore said.

No, you wouldn't, Woodend thought.

'You said you wanted to talk about the dead man,' he reminded Featherington Gore.

'Ah yes. His name is Peter Medwin. He's the Northern Region Manager of the National Coal Board.'

Woodend whistled softly. 'Quite an important feller, in his own way, then,' he said.

'*Very* important. He was what you might call a captain of industry. And from what I've been hearing, he seems to have had some influence within government circles.'

'Aye,' Woodend agreed. 'As a boss in one of the biggest employers in the country, he probably would have had.'

'Which, of course, puts an entirely different complexion on the matter of his death.'

'You're sayin' that now you know who he was – an' how much pull he had with the government – it's finally become worth findin' out who killed him?' Woodend asked.

'Since he was a British citizen, it was *always* important to find out who killed him,' Featherington Gore responded, but without much conviction. 'However, now his identity is known, it has become necessary for Her Majesty's Government to become involved in an official capacity.'

'Official capacity,' Woodend repeated.

'Hang on, just exactly where is all this leadin'?'

'As I understand it, the Foreign Office has been in contact with both the Spanish Ministry of Justice and with your chief constable in ... in...'

'In Lancashire,' Woodend supplied, since it was plain from his floundering that Featherington Gore lived in blissful ignorance of any geography which existed north of London.

'Exactly! In Lancashire,' the Consul agreed. 'And as a result of these consultations, it has been decided that the investigation into Mr Medwin's death will be a joint operation.'

'What!' Woodend exploded.

'Captain López will, of course, be in command of the Spanish side of things. And while I will admit that you would not be *my* first choice for the job, you are, apparently, the only high-ranking British officer within a thousand miles of Benicelda, and so are to represent British interests.'

'You seriously expect me to work with that snake López?' Woodend asked, astounded.

'That is correct.'

'There are people I'd trust with the family silver, but he's not one of them,' Woodend said. 'Bloody hell, now I come to consider the matter, I'd think twice before I handed my plastic picnic set over to his care.'

'The matter is not open to debate,' Featherington Gore said coldly.

'Is it not?'

'No. It has been decided at the highest levels of both our governments that you will work with Captain López on the investigation – and work with Captain López you will.'

'An' when's this ill-matched joint effort of ours supposed to kick off?' Woodend asked.

'Given the serious nature of the inquiry, it will, of course, commence immediately.'

'Right, I'd better get up to the Guardia Civil barracks as soon as possible,' Woodend said. 'You couldn't lend me your push-bike, could you?'

'This is no time for frivolity,' Featherington Gore said haughtily. He waited for Woodend's apology, and when it became apparent that none would be forthcoming he continued, 'A Guardia Civil vehicle and driver have been placed at your disposal. They are waiting for you at the back door.'

'The *back* door,' Woodend repeated thoughtfully. 'Well, it's certainly nice to know just how important I've suddenly become.'

Ten

Captain López strode agitatedly up and down his office, occasionally stopping to take a generous – though necessary – swig from the excessively large glass of brandy which sat on his desk.

'It's all gone wrong,' he told himself in a voice which was not quite a moan. 'It's all turned to shit.'

It hadn't looked that way earlier in the day. After his discussion with the *Alcalde* – after the warning he had *been given* by the *Alcalde* – he had carefully mapped out a course of action which he thought would satisfy nearly everyone.

His first step would have been to order his men to question possible witnesses to the crime – though he would have made it plain that they should not find *too* many of these witnesses, nor question them for too long. Having thus established at least the appearance of a normal investigation, he would have written up his first report for Madrid, a report which he'd already decided would be

106

as imaginative as *Don Quixote* – and probably almost as long. It would have been followed by a second report, then a third and fourth, each one a little thinner and a little less optimistic. His final report – submitted around the time Durán became Provincial Governor – would have been as slim as a slice of *jamón serrano*, and the implicit assumption it contained would have been that there was now very little possibility of making an arrest.

The Captain-General, he'd calculated, would have been displeased, but not overly so. The new Governor, on the other hand, would have been both delighted with the outcome, and no doubt very willing to reward the man who had caused it to come about.

It had taken a single dispatch from Madrid to bring this carefully constructed plan tumbling down.

'*This is a delicate matter with international implications,*' the dispatch had said. '*In order to resolve the problem, you must give Chief Inspector Woodend your fullest co-operation. It is vital that the British Foreign Office be satisfied that we are doing all we can to bring the perpetrator of the crime to justice. His Excellency, the Minister of the Interior, will be gravely displeased with any other outcome.*'

López held out his hands in front of him, as if attempting to balance his choices. On

107

the one hand, he still did not want to cross an *alcalde* who would soon be Governor. On the other, he did not want to bring the wrath of Madrid down on his head – and the dispatch made it clear that it *would* be wrath – because even Durán would not be prepared to protect him from a Captain-General who was eager to have his balls served up on a silver platter.

Perhaps he could appear to co-operate with the English policeman while, in fact, leading Woodend on a wild-goose chase. In that way, he could contrive to make it look as if the failure of the investigation was not his own fault, but that of the Englishman.

But what if that didn't work?

What if Woodend turned out to be as smart as he looked – and started to make real progress?

Madrid would be happy enough if the case were solved – but Antonio Durán would be furious, and a furious *alcalde* was the very last thing he wanted to have to deal with.

He needed a power base of his own, López told himself. He needed leverage which did not depend on the influence of other people. But where could he pluck that power – that leverage – from?

He reviewed his meeting with Durán. The *Alcalde* had said that he was worried about the effect of his investigation on the tourist trade, but even at the time – even before he

108

had seen the photographs on the desk – that had seemed to López to be a very weak argument.

So why had he gone along with it?

Because that was the way things worked under the Dictatorship. Because individual progress was made not by showing initiative, but by learning to bend with the wind.

He thought back to the case which had made his name – which had allowed him to first put his foot on the ladder of success.

He had been home on leave in Leon when the local captain had called him into his office.

'Your uncle has a printing press,' the captain had said.

'Yes,' López admitted. 'That's because he is a printer.'

'We suspect he is using the press to produce radical pamphlets,' the captain told him, 'but the old man is being very cunning about it, and when we raid his workshop there is nothing there.'

'What has this got to do with me?' the young López wondered.

'You are family,' the captain told him. 'You have access to the workshop day and night. Perhaps you can find something we have missed.'

There *hadn't* been anything in the workshop – at least, not when López had searched it on his own. But by the time he led members of the local Guardia Civil into the place, there had been evidence aplenty.

And that was how things were done, López reminded himself. You found out what your superiors wanted, and you gave it to them. Thus, rather than questioning the *Alcalde*'s aim, he had turned his mind to ways of *implementing* that aim. But now, trapped between the *Alcalde*'s 'devil' and Madrid's 'deep blue sea', he began to wonder just what Durán's game *really* was.

'Why should the *Alcalde* wish to see the murderer escape?' he asked the empty room. 'What's in it for him?'

And then, in a blinding mental flash, he had what he could only have called an inspiration.

The Alcalde already knew *who the killer was, and for devious reasons of his own, had decided to protect him.*

He began to follow this new insight through to its logical conclusion.

If Durán knew who the murderer was, then Durán was implicated – at least on the fringes – in the murder itself.

And if he himself could find out the killer's name, then he would also come to understand the motives behind the *Alcalde*'s involvement.

Then he would have Durán by the balls!

It wouldn't matter, under those circumstances, what Madrid did or did not choose to do. The Captain-General could hang him out to dry for all he cared, because the new Provincial Governor would look after him. The new Provincial Governor simply would not have any choice.

What a difference his flash of insight had had on his total view of the situation, López thought. A few minutes earlier he hadn't known whether he wanted the crime solved or not. Now he *did* want it solved. But only by him – and for his private use alone. Which meant that while seeming to work with Woodend, he must ensure that the other man was kept well away from anything which might lead him to a solution.

It was going to be a delicate balancing act. But then, he reminded himself, his whole career had been nothing but a balancing act.

He looked out of the window and saw that the gates had been opened and an official car was entering the compound. The *hijo de puta* of an English Chief Inspector had arrived.

Woodend looked around López's office – at the expensive desk, at the deep leather armchairs, at the huge and imposing picture of Generalissimo Francisco Franco on the wall.

'It doesn't have quite the same kind of feel about it as the last room we met in, does it?' he said.

'Yes, I must apologize for that unfortunate occurrence last night,' López said. 'You must understand that, at the time, I did not know we were going to be colleagues.'

'We were both policemen then, an' we're both policemen now,' Woodend said dryly. 'We've *always* been colleagues, at least in theory. The difference is that then you didn't know you were goin' to have to extend any professional courtesy to me, an' now you do. So why don't you stop pussyfootin' around an' say what you really mean?'

'The truth?' López asked.

'The truth,' Woodend agreed.

'We are like two polecats that have been put in a sack together,' López said. 'We do not like it – we do not like *each other* – but, given our situation, it would be pointless to fight.'

Woodend grinned. 'That's better,' he said. 'Now we've got things out in the open, we can start to establish some sort of workin' relationship. What have you got on the case so far?'

I have selected the man I was going to arrest for the murder, but now that Madrid has decided to take a closer interest in the case that option is no longer open to me, López thought.

'I have questioned the hotel receptionist,' the Captain said aloud. 'He did not see Holloway enter the hotel in the company of the man who was to be his murderer. But that tells us very little, since the receptionist

112

admits that he left his post to visit the toilet, roughly ten minutes before the murder took place.'

'Very convenient,' Woodend said dryly. 'Have you carried out a house-to-house?'

'A what?'

'Have you had your men out on the streets, lookin' for witnesses who may have seen Holloway an' the other man together?'

'Yes.'

'An' have they come up with any leads?'

'No.'

'Can I see their reports?'

'They are in Spanish.'

'Can you get them translated for me?'

'It will take some time.'

'Are there *any* reports for me to see?'

'We do not do things in Spain in exactly the same way as you do them in England.'

'In other words, no,' Woodend said. 'Have you questioned the American who spoke to Holloway a couple of hours before he died? Have you questioned any of the other men the American met – again, just before Holloway died?'

'I know nothing of that.'

'Do you know, I rather thought you wouldn't.'

'Do you have the names of these people? Do you know where I can find them?'

'I know the American's name, but before I tell you what it is, we'd probably better lay down a few ground rules,' Woodend said. 'These men will have to be questioned – you can even call what happens an "interrogation", if you feel more comfortable with that – but they're not to have any accidents.'

'I don't understand,' López said.

'Oh, I think you do,' Woodend countered. 'It's strange how many prisoners all over the world – includin' some in England – seem to have this tendency to fall down stairs. Well, I don't want anythin' like that to happen durin' this investigation. If there's stairs for them to go down, I want somebody with them, holding their hands, when they do it. If there's doors to "accidentally" walk into, I want your officers to ensure that they don't. In other words, before I set you on the trail of these men, I want your promise that no physical harm is goin' to come to them.'

'I would not come to your country and tell you how to do your job,' López growled.

'An' I won't tell you how to do yours – as long as you do it properly,' Woodend said. 'Do we have a deal? Or do I have to tell the Consul that I can't work with you?'

'We have a deal,' López answered reluctantly.

Woodend stepped through the big wooden gates of the Guardia Civil barracks, and out on to the cobbled street.

Strange that a police force which was

entrusted with protecting the public should feel the need of so much obvious protection itself, he thought.

Or maybe it wasn't. The Guardia Civil's main interest, after all, was to guard the state, rather the *people* who constituted that state – López had made that quite plain during their first meeting – so seen from that angle the Guardia wasn't really a police force, as he understood the term, anyway. What it actually was, he decided, was no more and no less than an army of occupation.

He had gone just far enough down the street to be out of sight of the barracks when the headlamps of a parked car flashed at him. He was not really surprised. Truth to tell, he had been half expecting it.

'I'll drive you back to your hotel,' Paco Ruiz said, as he opened the passenger door.

Woodend squeezed his large frame into the tiny car.

'This is very kind of you,' he said, though he was well aware that if kindness was one of Ruiz's motives, it was – at best – a very secondary one.

'Are you willing to tell me about your meeting with Captain López,' Paco asked, as he pulled the car away.

If there'd been room in the small vehicle to shrug, Woodend would have shrugged. As it was, all he said was, 'There's not much

·to tell.'

'I wouldn't trust López,' Paco cautioned.

'I don't. I've seen snakes I'd rather go into partnership with. But whatever my personal feelin's on the matter, the Captain an' I are still goin' to have to work as a team, because that's what the powers that be want to happen.'

Behind the wheel, Paco stiffened. 'And where does that leave me?' he asked.

'Out in the cold, I'm afraid.' Woodend sighed. 'Look, Paco, I know you really wanted to work on this case, but you have to see that it's just not possible any more. I've got to use the Guardia Civil in my investigation – there's simply no choice in the matter. An' you know the way they work – if you get in their way, they'll stomp on you. They might even lock you up. You don't want Cindy to go through all that again, do you?'

'You talk about Cindy, but what about Joan?' Ruiz countered. 'You're supposed to be on holiday *together*, yet now you'll abandon her while you go chasing a killer.'

'She's used to it,' Woodend said awkwardly.

'And Cindy is used to living with the possibility that one day I will do something which will cause the police to take me away again. She knew what I was like when she married me and – just as with you and Joan – she accepted me for what I was.'

'I'm really sorry, Paco,' Woodend said.

There was a difficult silence for a few seconds, then Ruiz said, 'Well, I suppose I must be philosophical about these things. Can you at least tell me what stage the investigation has reached?'

'It doesn't seem to have gone very far at all,' Woodend admitted. 'López says he's had his men out on the streets lookin' for possible witnesses, but I don't believe him.'

Paco shook his head, wonderingly. 'That is very strange,' he said. 'López is an ambitious man. This case could quite make his reputation. And yet you say he seems to have made very little attempt to solve it?'

'That's how it looks to me.'

'Politics!' Paco said decisively.

'What?'

'In this country, everything is down to politics, in one way or another,' Paco said. 'If López is being lethargic, it is because he has been told—'

He stopped, suddenly, as if he had just decided that to say more would be a very bad idea.

'Go on,' Woodend encouraged.

Paco laughed. 'Franco grabbed power through a conspiracy, and conspiracies have been endemic to government here ever since. But that is not to say that *every* action of *every* man who works for the government is driven by his involvement in some conspiracy. No doubt I have misjudged López.

117

No doubt his apparent laziness is no more than *real* laziness.'

'I'd still very much like to hear what it was that you were goin' to say,' Woodend told him.

Paco slowed the car down to a halt. 'Here is your hotel,' he said, pointing to the main entrance. 'In your situation, I would go straight up to my room. Because, as the old proverb says, only a fool – or a man of great courage – dares to keep his woman waiting.'

Woodend smiled. 'Is that really an old proverb?' he asked. 'Or did you just make it up as a way of changin' the subject?'

'The truth of a saying is not to be tested only by its antiquity,' Paco said enigmatically. 'Go to your wife, because – God knows – she will be seeing very little of you in the next few days.'

Woodend struggled out of the car. 'I'm truly sorry things turned out the way they did,' he said.

'Think no more of it,' Paco Ruiz replied.

'Really?'

'Really. It was a disappointment, naturally, but part of being a man is learning to live with disappointments.' Ruiz paused. 'I would still like to see Joan again. Perhaps the four of us can get together before you leave for England, and have another meal.'

'I'd like that,' Woodend said. 'An' I'm sure that Joan would like it, too.'

'Well, then, we must stay in contact,' Paco Ruiz said.

He closed the door and slammed his car into reverse. As Woodend watched the tail lights disappearing down the street, he found himself wondering again exactly what it was that Paco had been about to say.

Eleven

There were two police officers sitting opposite the still-distraught Jessica Medwin in her sunny lounge that morning.

One of them was a man – handsome, early thirties, with an air about him which seemed to suggest more of the high-flying business-man than a detective inspector. The other, the woman, was blonde, a little younger, and had a slightly larger than average nose which hinted at her Central European origins but in no way detracted from her obvious appeal.

They seemed to know each other very well, Jessica thought, even through her grief, yet they did not look entirely comfortable about being together.

She was right. They did know each other

very well. They had once, in fact, been lovers – but now were trying to put all that behind them.

'What I don't see is why I should be talking to officers from Whitebridge,' Jessica said to the man. 'Surely, if I needed to speak to anyone, it should have been a local policeman.'

'Normally, that would have been the case,' Bob Rutter said gently. 'But it's *our* Chief Inspector who's in Spain, you see.'

'He's flown out already?'

'No. He's – he *was* – on holiday in the place where your husband met his tragic death...'

'Where my husband was *murdered*!' Jessica Medwin said firmly.

'Where he was murdered,' Rutter agreed. 'And *because* Mr Woodend was already there, it's been decided that he'll be the one who conducts the investigation on behalf of the British government.'

'Is he good at his job?' Jessica asked, her lower lip trembling slightly as she spoke.

'He's better than that,' Rutter assured her. 'He's the best I've ever worked with, and the best I *will* ever work with. But he's going to need your help. Can you think of any motive for his murder?'

Jessica Medwin suppressed a sob. 'I've been racking my brains to think of anyone who might have wanted to kill Peter,' she said. 'And I can't come up with a single name. He was a lovely man. Ask the people who knew him. Ask the people who worked for him.'

'We will,' DS Monika Paniatowski promised. 'But you must realize that there are some details we can get only from you.'

Jessica Medwin nodded. 'Of course.'

'How long were you married?'

'How long *were* we married?' Jessica asked, as if she thought she'd slightly misheard. Then she nodded sadly. 'Yes, it is "were" now that he's dead, isn't it? We were married for nearly twenty years.'

'So you must have been childhood sweethearts.'

Jessica Medwin managed a small smile. 'It's kind of you to say that, but I'm older than I look,' she told Paniatowski. 'We were both well into our twenties when we started going out together.'

'So you're not the one we should talk to about his early years,' Bob Rutter said.

'Why should you want to talk to *anybody at all* about Peter's early years?' Jessica Medwin wondered. 'How can that possibly help you to find out who killed him?'

'It probably won't,' Monika Paniatowski said. 'But we're asking the questions because that's the way we work.'

'I'm not sure I understand.'

'We collect all the information we can, even though most of it is eventually rejected as irrelevant.'

'I see,' Jessica Medwin said. 'Well, even though I didn't know him then, I can tell you something about Peter's youth, if you think it might be helpful.'

'As I said, we won't know until we've heard it.'

'Peter comes – came – from a mining family. His father was a miner, and so was his grandfather. When they were old enough, both Peter and his two brothers followed the family tradition, and went down the pit.'

'But he didn't *stay* down the pit.'

Jessica Medwin smiled again, this time with a kind of sad pride. 'No, he didn't. He started going to evening classes as soon as he could. He wanted to better himself, you see.'

'So by the time you met him, he wasn't actually a miner any more,' Rutter said.

'What makes you think that?' Jessica Medwin asked, an abrasive note entering her voice.

Rutter looked confused. 'Well, I...'

'Is it that you can't imagine someone like me ever falling for a man who spent half his life covered with coal dust?'

'No, I ... I didn't mean to suggest—'

'Of course you did,' Jessica interrupted. 'That's exactly what you meant to suggest.' Her mouth suddenly lost some of its tightness. 'But don't feel *too* guilty about it,' she continued, softening a little. 'You're not the first person to see things in that way – not by a long chalk. All my friends were horrified when I started walking out with Peter. "You're a manager's secretary," they reminded me. "You've got a good job. You shouldn't be associating with a grubby little miner." I didn't argue with them. Why should I have? If *they* couldn't see what *I* saw in Peter, then there was really very little point in continuing our friendships any more.'

'What *did* you see in him?' Paniatowski asked.

'People thought he was timid. But he wasn't. He was gentle. And strong! God, he was strong. I came from a background in which compromise and hypocrisy were the norm. Getting on with people – being *acceptable* – was all that mattered to most of the people I knew. Peter wasn't like that at all. If he believed in something, there was no power in the world that could have talked him out of doing what he thought was right.'

'Why was he in Spain?' Rutter asked.

'I don't know.'

'Didn't he give you an explanation before he left?'

'No. He didn't even say he was *going* to Spain.'

'Then what *did* he say?'

'He said there was something important he had to do, and he would only be away for a few days.'

'And you accepted that?'

'Why shouldn't I have? If it was important to him, I knew he had to do it. And if he didn't want to tell me what it was he was doing, or where he was going to do it, that was fine with me. I trusted him. I always have, and I always will. Whatever his reason for being there, it was a *good* reason.'

'Had he been to Spain before?' Rutter asked. 'Perhaps you'd taken a holiday there together.'

'I used to travel to the Continent quite a lot, with my family. But I haven't been abroad since we got married. Neither of us have.'

'And why was that?'

'Peter didn't want to travel. He seemed to have an aversion to it.' Jessica Medwin frowned. 'Which was strange – in a way.'

'Why?'

'He had no prejudices of any kind. He was the first Coal Board manager to employ coloured people in his mine. Some of his superiors really didn't like that at all.'

'Why not?'

'There's too much prejudice even now – God knows – but if you think back, you'll remember there was even more in the fifties. Some people simply didn't want to employ coloured folk. But my Peter was having none of that. He said a man shouldn't be judged by the colour of his skin – especially since

124

the mine turned everybody black anyway.' Jessica Medwin paused. 'That was just his little joke.'

'We understand,' Monika Paniatowski said.

'He had to fight damned hard to get his own way on that particular issue. In the end, he even threatened to resign. And he meant it, you know! He really would have gone through with it, at whatever the cost to himself. And the coloured people weren't the only ones he went out of his way to help. He was the same with the Eastern Europeans – the Poles and the Romanians. He said they'd had quite enough of a tough time already, and it was his duty to help them. Yet when it came to the question of holidays abroad, he was adamant. Said he didn't trust foreigners. I could never quite understand that. But there you are, that's how he felt, and I wasn't going to argue with him.'

'We'd like to talk to other people who knew him,' Monika Paniatowski said. 'You wouldn't mind if we did that, would you?'

'Why should I mind? You're not going to find out anything unpleasant about him, because there's nothing unpleasant for you to find. Peter's life was an open book.'

Except that nobody – not even you – has the slightest idea what he was doing on the Costa Blanca, Paniatowski thought.

Twelve

If this had been an English police station rather than a Guardia Civil barracks, Woodend thought, there would have been a two-way mirror through which to look at the men in the next room. As it was, he found himself peering – like a voyeur – through a grille in the party wall.

There were five men in all, sitting side-by-side on an uncomfortably narrow bench. But though their shoulders were – of necessity – touching, they didn't speak. In fact, they didn't even look at each other.

'Who are they?' Woodend asked.

'You do not recognize any of them?' Captain López asked, a slight smile playing on his lips as if Woodend's ignorance amused him.

'I've seen the Yank before,' the Chief Inspector admitted. 'He was on the church square on the night of the murder. But the other four are complete strangers to me.'

'Then allow me to enlighten you,' López said, the supercilious smile still lingering. 'The fat man next to the American is a German by the name of Schneider. The one with the small moustache is a Frenchman called Dupont. The last two are both English. The tall one with grey hair is Sutcliffe, the shorter one with the thin face is Roberts.'

'An' they're here because they're the ones who had the meetin' on the night Medwin was murdered?'

'Partly. But there is much more to it than that.'

You're really goin' to make me work hard for whatever titbits of information you feed me, aren't you, you cocky young bugger? Woodend thought.

But aloud, all he said was, 'Would you care to be a little more explicit?'

'Of course,' López agreed. 'Despite the fact they are from different countries, they seem to have a great deal in common.'

Woodend waited for López to say more, and when it became obvious the Spaniard was not about to, he sighed heavily and said, 'For example?'

'They are all roughly of the same age.'

'I can see that for myself.'

'They all arrived here within the last three days.'

'A lot of people must have done that.'

'They are all travelling alone.'

'Yes, that is unusual.'

'And though they were all at first staying in different hotels, last night Schneider, Sutcliffe, Roberts and Dupont all moved out of

127

their own hotels and into the one at which Mitchell had been staying.'

'So what does that prove?'

'That they were all in it together.'

'In *what*, together?'

'I have no idea,' López admitted. 'But I have always found interrogation an excellent way of finding out what I do not already know.'

Close to, Mitchell looked rough, Woodend decided. He must once have been a vigorous, healthy man – the sort who thought nothing of a thirty-mile hike – but now he seemed to be almost melting away as he sat there.

'Tell us about Mr Medwin,' Woodend said.

'Who?' the American asked. The tone was just about perfect, but the rapid blinking of his eyes gave him away.

'Medwin,' Woodend repeated. 'The man who was killed.'

'I thought his name was Holloway.'

'How long have you known him?'

'I didn't know him at all, in any real sense of the word. I met him – briefly – on the night he died.'

'Where did you meet him?'

'In a bar somewhere.'

'Was that before or after your meeting on the church square?'

'We never met on the church square.'

'Of course you did. You didn't look at each other, but you slipped a note into his hand as you walked past him.'

'No, I didn't.'

'I saw you with my own eyes, for God's sake!'

'You're mistaken.'

'Tell me about the meeting you're willing to *admit* that you had with him.'

'Like I said, we met in a bar.'

'Just the two of you?'

'No, there were some other guys there.'

'The same "guys" who are in the room next door?'

'Maybe.'

'Maybe?'

Mitchell coughed. It was a heavy cough – one which, from the pained expression on his face, seemed to be tearing his insides up.

'To ... to tell you the truth, I can't remember,' he gasped. 'I was pretty drunk at the time.'

No, you weren't, Woodend thought. The state your body's in, it couldn't *tolerate* being 'pretty drunk'.

'You can't remember who any of the other men were, yet you remember Medwin was there,' Woodend said. 'Why do you think that is?'

'Who knows what tricks the brain plays on you when you've drowned it in booze? Maybe I remember him because he got himself killed shortly after we'd split up?'

'What brought you all together in the first place?' Woodend wondered.

'Pure chance. We were all strangers in a strange place. It seemed kinda natural for us to decide to have a drink together.'

'Why did the others all move into the same hotel as you? Was it for mutual protection?'

'Mutual protection? From what?'

'From whoever killed Medwin.'

'What has his murder got to do with any of us?'

'I don't know,' Woodend admitted.

'On the question of hotels, I remember now that we talked about them when we met in the bar that night. The other guys said they were not happy with their hotels, and I said that mine was pretty good. I didn't know that they'd checked into mine, but I can certainly understand why they might have done.'

'So you remember discussing hotels?'

'Yeah.'

'But you don't remember the names and faces of the people you were discussing hotels with?'

'I plead the Fifth,' Mitchell said. 'The Fifth of bourbon.' He laughed at his own joke, and the laugh quickly turned into another attack of coughing. 'Or maybe it was the Fifth of Spanish brandy,' he continued, when he could speak again. 'I really don't remember.'

'When was the last time you were in Spain?' Woodend asked.

'I've never been to Spain before.'

'Yet the waiter from the bar where you were drinking is willing to swear that you were speaking to each other in Spanish.'

'He's mistaken.'

'It seems that a lot of people are mistaken. I'm mistaken about the note I saw you pass to Medwin, the waiter from the bar's mistaken about the language you spoke, and probably—'

'People do make mistakes. Nobody's perfect.'

Mitchell was finding it all an effort, Woodend thought. And not just a *mental* effort. All his brain power should have been focused on the interrogation, but it couldn't be – because he was using a large part of it to combat the *physical* pain he was experiencing.

'Medwin was an old friend of yours, an' now he's dead,' the Chief Inspector said. 'Don't you want to help us catch his murderer?'

'I've said nothing at all to lead you to believe he was *any* kind of friend.' Mitchell winced as he fought back a fresh onslaught of pain. 'And as for his killer, we'll...'

'Yes?'

'Nothing.'

'You were just about to say that you'll deal

131

with the killer yourselves, weren't you?'

'Of course not.'

'You may think you *know* who the killer is,' Woodend said. 'And perhaps you do. But can you ever be sure? Say you did take justice into your own hands, an' killed the wrong man. You'd never even know it, would you? An' all the time, the real murderer would be laughin' up his sleeve at you, Mr Mitchell. Laughin' at you – and laughin' at the memory of your friend. You don't want that. Nobody would. So why don't you help us? We're the professionals. We'll make certain the right man is brought to book.'

He was getting somewhere! Woodend thought. True, he was groping in the dark. True, too, he was making big assumptions, and leaping across wide speculative gaps. *But he was still getting somewhere.* The look of indecision on Mitchell's face was all the proof of that he needed.

And then, just as it looked as if real progress was about to be made, Captain López chose to break the spell.

'Shall I tell you what I think, Mr Mitchell?' the Guardia Civil Captain asked aggressively.

Mitchell shrugged. And in that shrug there was clear evidence of relief; relief that something had happened to make him back away from a course of action he hadn't wanted to take – but had suspected that he well might;

relief that López had saved him from himself!

'I couldn't care less whether you tell me what you think or whether you don't,' he told the Captain.

'I think that the six of you were all part of a gang, here to commit a serious crime,' López said. 'I do not know the exact nature of the crime – maybe you are smugglers or bank robbers, or perhaps gunrunners – but the exact details do not matter.'

'Preposterous!' Mitchell replied.

He wasn't putting on an act, Woodend thought. He had no need to. Because it *was* preposterous!

Whatever Medwin had been planning to do in Spain, it wasn't to rob a bank or run guns. Medwin had been a National Coal Board regional manager, a man with no need to turn to crime – and López knew that as well as he did.

'So we're international criminals now, are we?' Mitchell asked, unconcernedly. 'And I suppose Medwin was our leader?'

'Perhaps,' López agreed. 'Or perhaps not. What is important is that two nights ago you had an argument with him. Maybe Medwin wanted a bigger share of the money. I don't know, and it doesn't matter. But whatever caused the quarrel, the other five decided he had to die.'

'Pure fantasy!' Mitchell said.

'Who pushed him off that balcony, Mr Mitchell?' López demanded. 'Was it you? The German? The Frenchman?'

'This is insane!'

'My English colleague here may be fooled by your protests of innocence, but I am not,' López warned him. 'You should remember, Señor Mitchell, that you are not in the United States of America now. Here, we do not need one quarter of the evidence to convict that would be necessary in your own country. You will all be found guilty of the murder. Make no mistake about that. And there is no Supreme Court to slow matters up. Once the verdict is given, execution quickly follows.' The Captain paused for a moment. 'But not all of you have to die. If one of you were to give evidence against the others, he would be spared and would probably be released after only a few years in prison. And one of you *will* give evidence, I am certain of that. So why shouldn't it be you? Why should you choose to be executed, when you have the power to save yourself?'

'Am I under arrest?' Mitchell demanded.

'We are the ones who ask the questions here,' López snapped.

'*Am I?*' Mitchell asked, looking directly at Woodend.

'No,' Woodend said. 'No, you're not.'

'So I can leave any time I wish to?'

'Yes, you can.' Woodend agreed. He turned

to López. 'That's correct, isn't it?'

'If he were a Spaniard...' the Captain said.

'But I'm *not* a Spaniard,' Mitchell counter-ed. 'I'm an American citizen, and I demand that my rights as such be respected. Am I to be allowed to leave, or am I to report to my consul later that I was held here against my will?'

López looked distinctly uncomfortable. 'An innocent man would not *wish* to leave,' he said. 'An innocent man would have the strong desire to stay and help us all he could.'

'But you don't think I *am* innocent,' Mitchell said. 'That's the whole point. You think I'm guilty, and nothing I say is going to change your mind. Under those circum-stances, I can see nothing to be gained from remaining in these barracks any longer than I have to. Which means that I would like to leave now.'

Throughout the whole interrogation two privates had been standing at the door, as still as statues. Now López turned to one of them and spat out a few words in very rapid Spanish.

'What did you say?' Woodend asked.

'He said I was to be shown out through the back door, so the others wouldn't see me go,' Mitchell told him.

And immediately the words were out of his mouth, he looked as if he would gladly have bitten off his own tongue.

'You told me you didn't speak Spanish,' Woodend reminded him.

'No, I didn't,' Mitchell replied, making what – under the circumstances – was a very quick recovery. 'All I *actually* said was that we weren't speaking Spanish at the table that night.'

'You also said this was your first visit to Spain.'

'And so it is.'

'Then why is your Spanish so good?'

'You may not know this, Chief Inspector, but there is a large country called Mexico which borders my own. They speak Spanish there, and that is where I learned mine.'

'I don't believe you,' Woodend told him.

'I don't care *what* you believe,' Mitchell replied.

Woodend waited until the first constable had escorted Mitchell from the room before asking López if he would dismiss the second one as well.

'Why should I?' the Captain asked.

'Because we need to talk.'

'We can talk as much as you wish. My constable does not understand any English.'

'Maybe not. But he'd probably learn more than you'd care to have him learn from the *tone* of our conversation.'

López ran the index finger of his right

hand through his moustache. There were times when he looked *just* like a matinee idol.

'Is that a threat you have just made?' he rasped. 'Because I am good at making threats, too. Probably much better than you are.'

Woodend sighed. 'It's no threat. We just need to be able to have a frank discussion.'

López thought about it for a moment, then signalled to the constable that he should leave the room. 'Let us begin this "frank discussion" of yours, then,' he suggested.

'I'd appreciate it if you didn't interrupt my interrogation the next time we have someone in for questioning,' Woodend said, keeping his voice as level as he could.

'*Your* interrogation?' López responded. 'This is *my* country and *my* police station.'

'I understand that, but we're supposed to be workin' on this case together,' Woodend said, using an amount of tact and diplomacy which would have left Rutter and Paniatowski open-mouthed with amazement. 'I was gettin' somewhere with my questionin' of Mitchell. I know I was.'

'I disagree,' López replied.

'An' do you think *you* were gettin' somewhere?'

'Perhaps not. But I will.'

It was hopeless, Woodend thought. Totally bloody hopeless.

'Have you contacted the FBI yet?' he asked.

López shook his head. 'No. I have not contacted them. Why should I have done that?'

'Because there's a distinct possibility they might be able to give us some information on Mitchell.'

'Perhaps Mitchell is not his real name,' López suggested. 'Perhaps, if he has a criminal record, it is under another name entirely.'

'Why should you assume he's usin' an alias?' Woodend wondered. 'Because of his passport? Is it a fake, like Medwin's was?'

'I do not know. It has not yet been established. His passport is being examined by our experts.'

'Then how is it that within an hour or so of Medwin's death, you *already* knew that his passport was a forgery?'

'It was a very clumsy attempt at forgery. I knew immediately that it was not genuine.'

'So you're sayin' that if Mitchell's passport is a fake, it's a *better* fake than Medwin's was?'

'Yes.'

'What about the passports the others are usin' – the German, the Frenchman an' the two Englishmen. Are they real?'

'They, too, are being examined.'

'So Medwin, who – accordin' to you – may well have been the brains behind this criminal enterprise of theirs, was the only member of the gang to have a passport which was an obvious fake?'

'So it would appear.'

'But that doesn't make any sense.'

López shrugged. 'What can I tell you? You are a detective, I am just a local policeman. I can only deal with the facts which are given to me.'

Bollocks! Woodend thought. 'How long will these examinations by your experts take?'

López shrugged again. 'Who can say?'

'Well, for a start, *you* should be able to – because you're supposed to be in charge of the bloody investigation.'

'Must I remind you again, Mr Woodend, that you are not in England?' López asked.

'At the very least, you could send Mitchell's *description* to the FBI,' Woodend pointed out.

'Telexing and phone calls abroad are very expensive, and this is still a poor country.'

'But it's what you might have to do anyway – if Mitchell's passport turns out to be a fake.'

'We will leap that ditch when – and if – we encounter it.'

Woodend had worked with some bobbies in the past who were not particularly bright. In fact, he'd worked with some very stupid ones. But López – whatever other faults he might have – wasn't stupid. So just what game was he playing with all his bloody obstructive tactics?

Thirteen

As Paco Ruiz's little Seat 600 valiantly struggled up the steep slope which led to the *Alcalde*'s villa, Ruiz himself was reminded of those long-ago days when, as a young policeman, he had occasionally been landed with the duty of providing security at society weddings.

Some of the weddings had been less of a love match than a financial alliance. Old money married old money, and thus augmented the family fortune, rather than depleted it. Not that such mercenary considerations showed themselves on the surface. Far from it. The nuptials had had a stiff dignity about them which could be traced back through four hundred years of courtly behaviour, and Paco – fresh from the country – had hardly been able to avoid laughing at such ritual and posturing.

But it had been at the other kind of weddings – the ones of the *nouveaux riches* –

where he had found it hardest to keep a straight face. Everything about them had to cost a great deal – simply to show that the family could afford it. There were so many carriages that the guests virtually had one each. There were so many flowers that the air was almost clogged with their perfume. And the wedding cakes! The wedding cakes – the product of many hours of labour by a large team of skilled confectioners – were so brash and hideous that Paco had had to restrain himself from jumping on to them as if he were acting in a slapstick comedy film.

It was the *Alcalde*'s villa which had brought back the memories of those long-gone weddings. Its setting was undoubtedly magnificent. Sitting on his front terrace, the Mayor could look down on the town and the sea, while if he chose to move to the back of the house he was presented with an uninterrupted view of the mountains. But the villa itself completely let the scenery down. It was pink, sprawling and over-ornate, and if it had been just a little smaller – and covered with marzipan – it would have looked quite at home on one of those lavish wedding tables he had provided security for as a young man.

The guard on the gate – wearing a suit rather than a uniform, but undoubtedly armed – waved him into the courtyard. A second man, dressed in a slightly smarter suit and wearing a better class of hair oil, had reached the car before he'd even had time to climb out.

'Ruiz?' the second man asked.

Not Don Francisco, Paco noted. Not even *Señor* Ruiz. His place in the order of things was being established right from the start.

'Yes, I am Paco Ruiz,' he said.

'You are punctual. That's good. His Excellency the *Alcalde* does not like to be kept waiting.'

'I imagine he has many demands on his time,' said Paco, playing the diplomat with his tongue firmly in one cheek.

'Don Antonio is, indeed, a very busy man,' the flunky said. 'You must follow me.'

He led Ruiz into the west wing of the villa and down a corridor. Durán was sitting at his desk, his corpulent body looking almost as if it were imprisoned in his chair.

'You asked to see me,' Durán said.

'Yes, Your Excellency.'

'We have not met before, have we?'

'No, Your Excellency.'

'But that is not to say that I know nothing about you.'

'I imagine Your Excellency is kept well informed of everything that goes on in his town.'

Durán nodded, and the three or four chins he had developed wobbled almost hypnotically. Leaning forward as far as his corpulence would allow, he consulted one of the documents which lay on the desk before him.

'Before the Generalissimo rose up and saved our beloved Spain from the Communists and the atheists who wished to destroy it for ever, you were a policeman in Madrid,' he said.

'That is correct.'

'But then you allied yourself to the wrong side in our struggle for national survival?'

'Yes.'

It was no betrayal of his past to agree with that, Paco told himself. He had unquestionably been on the wrong side, because whichever side loses always *is* the wrong side.

'You were imprisoned for a time, then given the opportunity to work on the construction of the magnificent monument to our glorious dead in the Valley of the Fallen.'

Put that way, it sounded like a privilege, Paco thought.

'That is correct,' he said again.

'Eventually, in 1943, you were released – and sent to Vichy France.'

Vichy! The part of France which the Germans had allowed the French collaborators to run as a puppet state for them, while their jackboots trampled on the rest of the defeated country. Vichy! Where the air had been filled with the stink of defeat, humiliation and corruption.

'*Why* did you go to Vichy France?' Durán

143

demanded.

Why was I *ordered* to go? Paco thought. Or why did I *agree* to go?

I was *ordered* to go because the government wanted to know what had happened to all the gold that had been stored in the Spanish treasury before the Civil War. And I *agreed* to go because I needed to find out who was killing all my old comrades who were living in exile there. But if I'd known then that my mission would be indirectly responsible for saving Franco's life, I'd have cut my own head off rather than go.

Aloud, all he said was, 'The mission was sanctioned by the *Caudillo* himself. I cannot talk about it, even to you, Your Excellency.'

Durán nodded again. 'Whatever your mission was, it must have been successful,' he said, 'because once you returned to Spain, you were set at liberty. And where does that leave you now? You have been forgiven – to some extent at least – for your past transgressions. But you are still not trusted enough – even after all this time – to be embraced by the Movement. You do not have an official position, nor are you ever likely to have one. So what *do* you do?'

'I—'

'I will tell you what you do,' the *Alcalde* said, cutting him off. 'You do whatever you can! You use the skills you learned as a policeman in a purely private capacity. You

144

track down thieves who the authorities cannot be bothered to track down themselves. You trace missing persons, though, of course, you immediately drop those investigations if you discover that the person you are tracing has gone missing for reasons of state.'

For reasons of state! Paco repeated silently to himself. That was an interesting way of saying that they had been spirited away by the secret police.

'Yes, I immediately drop those investigations,' he agreed.

'It is a fairly miserable way to make a living, is it not?'

But at least my hands are clean, Paco thought. At least they are not stained by either blood or dirty money, as the hands of all those in the government are.

'It is a fairly miserable living,' he admitted, 'but it is still a living of sorts, Your Excellency.'

'So now we come to the point of your visit,' the *Alcalde* said. 'Why did you want to see me?'

Paco steeled himself. He had a suspicion which was based on López's apparent reluctance to pursue the murder investigation with vigour, and in order to confirm that suspicion, he was going to have to risk telling one huge lie.

'The Englishman who was killed,' he said.

145

'What about him?'

'I talked to him just a few hours before he died.'

'Why? What was your reason?'

'It was pure chance. I happened to be sitting at the table next to his in a bar. I heard him speak, and thought it might be a good opportunity to practise my English. So I struck up a conversation.'

Durán sneered. 'You mean you realized he was a foreigner, and decided that if you could perform some small, demeaning service for him, he might give you a little money,' he said.

Paco tried to remember if he'd ever killed a fat man at close quarters. He didn't think he had. Given the shortages and deprivations during the war, there hadn't been many fat men around *to* kill. Still, he could imagine what it would be like to plunge a knife into Durán's huge gut – the sound it would make, the way all the layers of blubber would close in around the blade.

'I said, you realized he was a foreigner and decided that, if you could perform some small, demeaning service for him, he might give you a little money,' Durán repeated.

'There was that as well,' Paco agreed, picturing Durán looking like a stuck pig as he gasped for air.

'There had better be some point to this dismal little tale of yours,' the Mayor said threateningly.

'There is,' Paco assured him. 'The English-man said that he knew you. He said you were one of the reasons he was in Spain.'

'That is ridiculous.'

Paco said nothing. The *Alcalde* stared at him.

'I said that is ridiculous,' Durán barked.

Paco shrugged. 'Perhaps you are right, Your Excellency.'

'Perhaps?'

'Undoubtedly you are right. But I can do no more than tell you what the Englishman said.'

Another silence followed, even longer than the last one, then the *Alcalde* said, 'Did he ... er ... did he say any more about me?'

Paco wondered just how much further he could push things – how much more play there was left in his lie.

'Well?' Durán demanded.

'He ... er ... imparted no more actual infor-mation, but I got the distinct impression that he held some kind of grudge against you.'

The *Alcalde*'s piggy eyes narrowed sus-piciously. 'Why are you telling me this?'

'You are my *alcalde*. It is my duty.'

'Duty! What do you know about duty? The truth is that you imagine that doing me a favour – however inconsequential that favour may be – could be one small step towards your final rehabilitation. Isn't that right?'

Paco bowed his head. 'Your Excellency sees right through me.'

'Why now? Why should you suddenly start to ingratiate yourself after all this time?'

'I'm getting old,' Paco said, doing his best to sound thoroughly ashamed. 'I'm getting old and it would be nice to think that when I can no longer work, I can at least look forward to a small government pension.'

His suspicion allayed, the *Alcalde* relaxed a little. 'This man Holloway was obviously deranged,' he suggested.

'I am no doctor, as you know. But that is certainly the opinion I would give to anyone who asked me what I thought of him.'

The *Alcalde* nodded. 'Even though you were motivated mainly by self-interest, you have performed a service of sorts. I will instruct one of my people in the town hall to pay you a small fee.'

'That is most generous of you, Your Excellency.'

Durán waved his hand magisterially. 'You may go now. But don't forget, the man Holloway was obviously deranged.'

'He was as mad as a hatter,' Paco agreed.

Fourteen

It was only twelve miles from the house that Peter Medwin had shared with his wife to the one in which his brother Reginald lived, yet from the change in the landscape it was almost as if they had crossed a continent.

Peter's house was large and detached, with a view of the golf course and the rolling countryside beyond it. Reginald's home was a grimy pit village, in which streets of squat terraced houses clung desperately to steep hillsides and the cobbled streets proved themselves booby traps for old ladies' ankles.

The man who answered the door was perhaps a couple of years older than the murder victim, but was about the same height, the same build and had the same shiny bald head.

'Mr Medwin?' Rutter asked. 'Mr Reginald Medwin?'

'That's right.'

'We're detectives from Whitebridge. I'm DI Rutter and this is DS Paniatowski. We're investigating your brother's death.'

'I talked to Jessica on the phone not twenty

minutes past, so I was expectin' you,' Medwin said. 'I suppose you'd better come inside.'

He led them into the front parlour which, despite the smallness of the house, was probably reserved for christenings, weddings – and funerals. It was a neat, cheerful place. The brass ornaments around the fireplace were all polished to a dazzling shine. The windows gleamed, despite the dust in the air outside. The walls looked as if they were stripped and re-papered every second year – whether they needed it or not.

Medwin invited the two detectives to sit down. 'I'd offer you a cup of tea,' he said, 'only the missus is out shoppin', you see, an' I'm not entirely sure where she keeps everythin'.'

'Don't worry about it, Mr Medwin, we've only just had a cup,' Monika Paniatowski lied.

Medwin did not sit down himself. Instead, he remained standing, with his backside to the empty fireplace.

'How can I help you?' he asked.

'We'd like to know everything that you can tell us about your brother,' Rutter said.

Medwin looked confused. 'I don't rightly know where I should start,' he confessed.

'Just say whatever comes into your mind first,' Paniatowski advised.

Medwin nodded gratefully. 'He were

150

always different, our Pete,' he said. 'There seemed to be a lot more goin' on in that head of his than there was in the heads of the rest of us – though, to be honest with you, none of us had any idea quite what it was.'

'So he was secretive?' Rutter asked.

'Private, more than secretive,' Medwin told him. 'I mean, he never told any of us that he wanted to win a scholarship to the grammar school, but he didn't exactly hide it from us, either. Still, I'd never have known just how much it mattered to him if I hadn't caught him in tears the day our dad got the letter to say he hadn't been accepted.'

'He was very upset, was he?' asked Rutter, who was a grammar-school boy himself.

For a moment it looked as if Medwin didn't understand him. Then the miner said, 'I wouldn't call it "upset". He wasn't cryin' like a girl, if that's what you're thinkin'.'

'I'm sorry, I thought you said—'

'Them were tears of *anger* in his eyes. He said to me, "I were good enough to get in, our Reg. I were more than good enough. The only reason I've not got accepted is 'cos they've given it to some toffee-nosed lad who speaks as if he's got a plum in his mouth." An' he were right. The powers that be didn't want folk from here educated. They wanted to keep us in our place, so they'd have enough poor buggers to send down the pit.'

'Which is where Pete went,' Paniatowski said.

'Which is where Pete went,' Reginald Medwin agreed. 'The day he left school, our dad signed the agreement bindin' him to be an apprentice mechanical engineer. Fancy title, isn't it? *Mechanical engineer!* But the mechanical engineers still ended up down the bloody pit, bent double or else up to their knees in water, just like the rest of us.'

'But Peter didn't stay down the pit, did he?' Rutter asked.

'Depends what you mean by that,' Medwin said. 'If you mean that he found a magic carpet to waft into a management position, then you've got it all wrong. It took years of hard graft at night school before he was ready to make the leap. He was twenty-four when he come out of his apprenticeship, an' nearly thirty before he got to wear a collar an' tie at work. So don't go thinkin' our Pete didn't know what it was like to get his hands dirty.'

Rutter knew too little about industrial life to see the need to do any calculations. He'd been brought up in a leafy London suburb where apprenticeships were not something anyone ever went into. Paniatowski, on the other hand, had been raised in the shadow of the Whitebridge mills and engineering works, and she latched on to the discrepancy immediately.

'Did you say he was twenty-four when he finished serving his time?' she asked.

'Aye, that's right,' Medwin agreed.

'Why so late? He started work when he was fourteen, so he should have been a craftsman by the time he was twenty-one.'

'Normally, yes,' Medwin said, with some reluctance.

'Then why wasn't it true in Pete's case?' Paniatowski continued.

Medwin shifted his weight from one foot to the other. 'We've never been ones for washin' the family's dirty linen in public,' he said.

'He didn't go to prison, did he?' Rutter asked.

Medwin flushed angrily. 'Go to prison! No!' he said. 'It was nothin' like that.'

'Of course it wasn't,' Paniatowski said hastily. She turned to Rutter. 'There's times when you can make even a Tory member of parliament seem almost intelligent, you know.'

Medwin laughed, and Rutter tried not to resent Paniatowski for pulling him out of a sticky situation.

'He went away, did he?' Paniatowski asked.

'Aye, that's right,' Medwin agreed. 'One day he come home from work an' when he'd had his bath he told our dad that he was goin' to go south an' seek his fortune. Well, our dad was furious, just as you might expect, considerin' how it was goin' to reflect on him.'

Rutter looked blank.

'Mr Medwin had signed Pete's indenture documents,' Paniatowski explained. 'He'd given his word that Pete would serve his full apprenticeship. He lost a lot of face by Pete backing out like that.'

'You're right there,' Medwin agreed. 'They had a blazin' row, the two of 'em. Dad even hit Pete a couple of times, an' he'd never raised his hand to any of us before. I couldn't understand why Pete was doin' it to him. I had a go at Pete myself. Asked him what it was he wanted to do that was so important he'd make a liar of our dad.'

'And what did he say?'

'He said he was sorry, but he just had to go. An' he went. I spent three years hatin' him. I thought I'd never forgive him. But when he did come back, an' I saw the state he was in, I just had to.'

'What was wrong with him?'

'Nothin' you could put your finger on, but he looked like a complete wreck – as if he'd been to hell an' back. Even our dad couldn't stay angry at him, an' he wasn't a man who found it easy to forgive an' forget.'

'Do you have any idea what had happened to him while he was away – what *made* him look like he'd been to hell and back?'

'I didn't at the time, but I think I do now.

We know more than we used to, you see. We've got a television set nowadays, an' we can see what's goin' on in the rest of the world.'

'How do you mean?' Paniatowski asked.

'I saw this documentary on the down-an'-outs in London. A terrible life they lead. Worse than bein' a miner. Anyway, it was the look in their eyes that got to me. They were full of despair. That's how Pete's eyes looked when he come back home. Full of despair.'

'So you think he was a down-and-out himself?'

'I do. The way I see it, he went off to London thinkin' the streets were paved with gold, but soon found out that it wasn't like that at all. He'd have been too proud to come back home at first, you see, but in the end he must have realized he didn't have any choice. An' credit where credit's due, once he had decided to pull himself together again, he made a bloody good job of it. Within a week he was up at the pit office, askin' if they'd take him on again. I wouldn't have said he'd have a cat in hell's chance myself, but somehow he managed to talk them into it. An' he's never looked back from that day to this.' Medwin's jaw quivered a little. 'At least, not until ... not until...'

Paniatowski stood up. 'We'd better go,' she said.

'Our Pete was a wonderful feller,' Reginald

155

Medwin said. 'He never forgot where he come from, an' he'd time for anybody who needed it. He's helped half this village, in one way or another. Only last year, he offered to buy me a bigger house in a nice area – out of his own pocket, mind – but I'm too set in my ways to think of movin' now.'

There were tears forming in the corners of his eyes – the tears of grief that he probably thought no man should ever display.

Paniatowski urged Rutter to his feet. 'We really do have to go,' she said. 'We're running very late.'

'Catch him, will you?' Medwin pleaded. 'Catch the bastard who did that to our Pete.'

'We'll catch him,' Paniatowski promised. 'And don't bother about seeing us out. We can find our own way.'

The two detectives were already by the front door when Rutter stopped and turned around again.

'Can I ask you one more question, Mr Medwin?' he said.

The miner sniffed. 'Aye, you might as well.'

'Your brother Peter was away for three years. Could you tell us roughly when that was?'

'It were a bit less than three years, actually,' Medwin said, with a choke in his voice. 'He left the village in the autumn of 1936, an' he come back in the late spring of '39.'

Fifteen

In his time, Woodend had watched hundreds of men enter dozens of interrogation rooms, and knew that Roberts would look around him just as all the others had done. But it was *the way* he looked around which was particularly telling. He didn't look into any of the corners of the room, as if he thought he might find some clue as to what was about to happen to him hidden there. He didn't search for some unguarded exit through which it just might be possible to make a dash for freedom. Instead, he looked *coolly* around, assessing the place as if he were considering buying it.

'Why don't you sit down?' Woodend suggested.

'Might as well, now I'm here,' Roberts said jauntily, lowering himself into the chair opposite the English inspector and the Spanish police Captain.

'What is it?' Woodend asked.

'What's what?'

'What's the question you're just burstin' to ask?'

157

Roberts grinned like a naughty schoolboy who's been caught out cheating in a test.

'Oh, I was just wondering what's happened to Ham-'n'-Eggs,' he said. 'We all saw him come in, but nobody saw him come out again. Haven't thrown him in a deep dark dungeon, have you?'

'Ham-'n'-Eggs?' Woodend repeated.

'Yes. You know – what's-his-name – Mitchell.'

'Why do you call him that?'

'Ham-'n'-Eggs? It's a nickname, isn't it?'

'But where does it come from?'

'From the fact that he likes eating ham and eggs so much. You see, back in the old...'

'Go on,' Woodend said.

'Nothing.'

'What you were about to say was that *back in the old days*, all he ever talked about was ham-'n'-eggs. Isn't that right?'

'Didn't know him in the "old days", whenever they were. Only met him the night before last.'

'I've been responsible for lumberin' a few people with nicknames in my time,' Woodend said. 'But I don't think I've ever done it after I've known them for less than two days.'

'You would have done if you'd been with Mitchell, like I was. He spent half the night talking about ham-'n'-eggs. You can just imagine it, can't you?'

'Can I?'

'Of course you can. Now what was it exactly he said?' Roberts pursed his brow for a second, and then began talking out of the corner of his mouth. ' "I don't like this Spanish muck." Spanish muck! He hadn't even tried it. "Wish I had some ham-'n'-eggs." "What I wouldn't give right now for a plate of ham-'n'-eggs." He couldn't seem to stop going on about it.'

Roberts was making a pretty poor job of trying to cover up his gaffe, Woodend thought. His American accent was unconvincing and – more importantly – his tone of his voice carried no conviction with it. Besides, Mitchell didn't look as if he had the appetite for much food any more – especially anything as rich and fatty as ham and eggs.

'You don't seem to be overly concerned about being here, Mr Roberts,' Woodend said.

'Why should I? The police might pull you in if they don't like the look of your face – happens all the time – but if you haven't done anything wrong they never keep you for long.'

'You sound like you're talking from personal experience, Mr Roberts,' Woodend said. 'What is it, exactly, that you do for a living?'

'Me? I'm what you might call a gentleman of leisure.'

'Which means?'

'That I pursue the sporting life.'

'So you're a habitual gambler?'

'I'm certainly not averse to placing the odd bet on the gee-gees or the dogs, if that's what you're implying.'

'Where do you live?'

'Here and there. Hither and thither.'

'Tell me about a few of the "thithers".'

Roberts grinned. 'During the flat season, you'll as like as not find me in comfortable digs near one of the major race-courses. Goodwood! Ascot! Somewhere my name counts for something. Then again, once in a while I get sick of the old English weather, and when that happens I'll slip across to Monte Carlo for a spot of roulette.'

'And what are you here in Spain to bet on?'

'Absolutely nothing. I had a bit of a win on a rank outsider, to tell you the truth, and I thought to myself: Rodney, that money's burning a hole in your pocket, and if you don't take yourself off to somewhere there's absolutely nothing to tempt you, you'll have wagered it away in no time. So here I am.'

'Why don't you tell us about the last time you were in Spain?' Woodend suggested.

'Haven't got a clue what you're talking about, old sport.'

'The last time the old gang was together,' Woodend said patiently. 'You know who I'm talking about. You, Ham-'n'-Eggs, Sutcliffe, the Frenchman, the German – and Peter Medwin.'

Roberts' mouth fell open in surprise, but only for a second. 'Don't know any Peter ... Peter ... What was his other name again?'

'Medwin,' Woodend repeated.

'The name still doesn't mean anything to me, I'm afraid. Maybe Holloway knew him.'

'He *was* Holloway!' Captain López exploded angrily. 'I am tired of listening to this *mierda*. I will make the same offer to you that I made Mitchell. Confess to the murder, give evidence against the others, and I will do all I can to save your worthless neck.'

'You don't think we killed Medwin, do you?' Roberts asked, sounding genuinely shocked this time.

'You mean *Holloway*!' Woodend pointed out.

'I thought you said his real name was Medwin.'

'I will count down from five,' López said. 'Once I have reached One, your chance is gone. Anything you say about your part in the murder after that will be of no interest to me.'

'Now just a minute!' Roberts protested.

'Five,' López began. 'Four ... three ... two ... one...'

Woodend listened with increasing rage and a growing feeling of impotence. If López had been one of his subordinates, he'd have chewed the man's balls off. As it was, he could only sit there as another promising line of interrogation disintegrated into dust.

Sixteen

The old man sitting at the table outside the bar wore a grey suit, and a grey felt-brimmed hat. His shirt was open at the neck, and thick white hairs sprouted out from over the top button, like weeds seeking the sun. When Paco Ruiz sat down on the chair opposite him, the old man looked up. The expression on his face said that he was more used to being ignored than to being sought out, and that though he suspected Ruiz had made a mistake and would quickly stand up again, he rather hoped the new arrival would stay.

A waiter arrived and placed two glasses of *vino blanco* on the table. Ruiz looked down at his watch, then flashed the fingers on his right hand three times. The message was clear to the old man – his new companion had just ordered fresh drinks every fifteen minutes. When the waiter nodded and walked away, the old man gave Ruiz an almost toothless grin, to show his appreciation.

'You certainly must have seen a lot of changes in your time,' Ruiz said, as though the two of them were already deep in the middle of a conversation.

The old man nodded. 'Many, many changes.'

'First the war, now this,' Paco said, indicating a group of obviously foreign tourists who were just walking past the bar. 'Tell me, what do *you* think of all these foreigners?'

'The women have no modesty,' the old man said. 'They flaunt their bare arms and bare legs in public. And on the beach, it is even worse. They prance about in their underwear – an underwear so revealing that no decent Spanish woman would ever think of wearing it even *under* her clothes.'

'And the men?'

'The men have no sense of pride. When I was younger, I would never have allowed my wife to dress in that manner. And if I had seen another man look at my wife – fully dressed – in the way these *extranjeros* allow other men to look at their women half-naked, I would have killed him.'

Paco nodded. 'And no court in the land would ever have convicted you,' he said.

'I wouldn't even have been *arrested*,' the old man said. 'The Guardia Civil back in those days were just as much *hijos de putas* as they are now, but even they would not have dared to interfere in a matter of honour.'

'What was life like in the old days?' Paco asked.

'It was hard, but we were content,' the old man said. 'We are not blessed with good land around this town, but at least it allowed us to grow a few olives. And then there was the fishing. When we had a good catch, it was a cause for celebration throughout the whole village.'

'So you had nothing to complain about?'

'We had *plenty* to complain about. And we did complain. If the bulls were the national sport, then complaining was the local one. But we never expected things to change and, in truth, being men, we did not really *mind* them as they were.' The old man paused. 'Does what I am saying make sense? Or do you, like my children, think I have gone soft in the head?'

Paco laughed. 'I can only hope that when I reach your age I can still see things as clearly as you can,' he said. 'But tell me, what do you think of the young men you see around you nowadays?'

The old man spat reflectively on to the pavement. 'They want to wear silk next to their bodies,' he said. 'They sob themselves to sleep at night because they cannot afford to buy a motor car. They are men only because of what they have swinging between their legs – and even in that respect, they put on a pretty poor show.'

'How was this allowed to happen?' Paco wondered aloud.

'It is all the fault of the foreigners.'

'The foreigners?'

'Of course. Our people look upon them, and want to be like them. I hope I am wrong about this, but I do not think it will be too long before Spanish girls are exposing their flesh just as the foreigners do.'

'When did all this start – this dilution of Spanish manhood, this erosion of the proper female modesty?' Paco asked.

'About eight years ago now. When Don Antonio Durán was made the *Alcalde* of Benicelda. It was all *his* idea to encourage the invasion. I still don't know why he did it. It can't have been for the money they would bring, because he was rich even then.'

'Was he?' Paco asked. 'I didn't know that. How did he make his money? Did he inherit it?'

The old man gave a hoarse cackle.

'Inherit it?' he repeated. 'If you can think that, you must not have known his father. Roberto Durán was so poor he couldn't afford an arsehole to shit through. And as for *Don* Antonio himself...'

'Yes?'

'He was a good-for-nothing – an idle was-trel.'

'Still, the money he has now must have come from somewhere,' Paco reflected.

165

The old man looked cautiously around him. 'When the Civil War broke out, we were all on the side of the government in this town,' he said, almost in a whisper. 'And why shouldn't we have been? We knew that the other side favoured the church and the rich landowners.' He paused, as if suddenly worried that he had said too much. 'I mean...'

'I piss on the rich landowners,' Paco said. 'And I piss on Don Antonio Durán, as well.'

The old man looked reassured. 'We raised a militia to fight at the front,' he continued. 'I did not go myself – even then, I was too old for fighting – but many of our young men did. When Antonio Durán disappeared, we thought that was what he had done, too. We said to ourselves that war had finally made a man of him, and that if he ever returned alive, we would give him the hero's welcome that he deserved. How little we knew.'

'He hadn't gone to join the Republican militia?'

'Just the opposite. We did not see him again until March 1939, when he entered the town at the head of a *fascist* militia. He summoned us all to the town hall square. I can see him there even now, standing at the top of the steps, as proud as a peacock. Franco's army would reach the town soon, he told us. But until it did, he would be in control, and his decrees would have the force

166

of law. I wanted to scream that he was a traitor to the Republic. I wanted to pull him off those steps and beat him within an inch of his life. And I was not alone in that. Yet I did nothing – and neither did anybody else.'

'There was nothing you could do,' Paco said sympathetically.

'True,' the old man agreed. 'There was nothing we *could* do. He knew our struggle was over, and so did we. Those units of the Republican Army which had not already surrendered had fled. Franco had won. He is *still* winning.'

'So you think that Durán made his money by plundering the town?' Paco asked.

The old man cackled again.

'There was nothing *to* plunder,' he said. 'We had been through nearly three years of war. Anything of value we had ever owned had been sold or melted down to support the war effort.'

'Then where do you think he ... ?'

'He must have marched through other towns before he got here – towns which, perhaps, had more that was worth looting. I think that he and his militiamen stole from them.'

A new group of visitors walked past the café. The women, as the old man had already pointed out, were exposing more flesh than even a Spanish prostitute would be willing to put on public display. The men accompanying them were wearing shorts that no one but a *maricón* – and then only in the safety of a secret, forbidden homosexual club – would ever dare to show himself in.

It was a strange and exotic world which was now being revealed to the Spanish people, Paco thought – and it must be even stranger for the old man than it was for him.

'But for the tourists, you might have gone to your grave without even seeing a foreigner,' he said.

'You are wrong there,' the old man told him. 'Even without these new arrivals, I would still have seen the others.'

'The others?' Paco repeated. 'What others?'

'The ones who came before.'

'I'm not sure I know what you're talking about.'

The old man sighed, as if he had just realized that he was talking to an imbecile.

'The men with guns,' he said, speaking so slowly and carefully that even his dull-witted drinking companion should be able to understand. 'The ones who arrived in the town in March 1939, shortly after Antonio Durán had taken over.'

Seventeen

The Miners' Welfare and Social Club was located on the edge of the village, framed by a slag heap on one side and the pit winding gear on the other. When Rutter and Paniatowski arrived, it was already full of pit men swilling back pints of best bitter in a futile effort to wash the taste of thick black coal dust from their throats.

The bar steward saw the two police officers the moment they entered the door, and made a bee-line for them.

'This is a members-only club,' he said in a voice which indicated that he felt under no obligation to be welcoming to strangers. 'An' even if it wasn't, we still wouldn't serve ladies in the bar.'

Paniatowski smiled sweetly at him. 'Lucky for me I'm not a lady then, isn't it?' she asked, producing her warrant card.

The steward instinctively glanced up at the clock on the wall. 'We're well within our rights to be servin' alcohol at this time of day,' he said, having satisfied himself that – on this occasion at least – they really were.

'We're not here looking for trouble,' Rutter assured him. 'We just want to talk to one of your members – a man called Jim Stoddard.'

The bar steward hesitated for a moment, then said, 'He's over there – at the far end of the bar.'

Rutter and Paniatowski strode over to where the miner was standing. 'Could we have a quick word, Mr Stoddard?' Rutter asked.

Stoddard turned slowly round towards them. His face was not old, Paniatowski thought, but it was certainly battered. His nose was slightly off kilter, as it had once been broken. A broad blue scar ran above his right eyebrow. And though his skin was pink from a recent vigorous scrubbing, there was still a hint of the all-pervasive dust in his wrinkles.

'What can I do for you?' he asked.

'We're police officers,' Rutter said.

'Well, I know that,' Stoddard said. 'It's stamped all over you. An' even if it wasn't, my hearing's not quite so gone that I couldn't hear you talkin' to the bar steward. So what do you want? To ask me about Pete Medwin?'

'That's right.'

Stoddard nodded thoughtfully. 'A great loss,' he said, and there was an intensity to his voice which gave new meaning to the old platitude.

'You used to be his best friend, didn't you?' Rutter asked.

'I still *am* his best friend – or, at least, I was until he got himself killed,' Stoddard said, with unexpected ferocity. 'Whatever led you to think that I wouldn't be?'

'Well, I suppose...' Rutter began.

'Did you think that I'd have had to say goodbye to our friendship when he went up in the world? That once he'd started wearin' a suit an' tie to work, he'd forget all his old mates?'

'No, not that *exactly*—' Rutter continued, digging himself further into the hole.

'Of course that's what we thought,' Paniatowski interrupted. 'Why wouldn't we? There's not one man in a hundred who can resist the temptation to turn his back on his roots once he's started to get on in life. If Pete Medwin was different, why don't you tell us about it?'

An admiring smile spread across Stoddard's lips. 'You speak your mind, don't you, lass,' he said.

'I've found it's the best way to get other people to speak theirs,' Paniatowski replied. 'Why don't you tell me about the Pete Medwin *you* knew?'

'Success *did* change him,' Stoddard said. 'Of course it did. But he didn't forget his roots. He could be a tough boss, but he was always a fair one – because he remembered

171

what it was *like* to work down the pit. An' once we'd left work behind us, he was the same with me as he'd always been. Even when he was promoted to Regional Manager, he still made the time to come back to the village an' have a drink with his old muckers.'

'So you were as close to him as a brother?'

'Closer, in some ways.'

'Then perhaps you can tell us something about him that even his brother Reginald doesn't seem to know.'

A wary look came into Stoddard's eyes. 'An' what might that be, exactly?' he asked.

'We want to know about the missing years,' Paniatowski said.

'The missin' years?'

Paniatowski smiled. 'Come on, Mr Stoddard! You know what we're talking about.'

'Pete went away in 1935—'

'1936,' Paniatowski corrected him.

'Aye, that's right,' Stoddard said.

And Paniatowski knew that the slip had been deliberate.

'He went off to seek his fame and fortune in London, didn't he?' Rutter asked.

'That's what they say,' Stoddard replied.

'But what do *you* say, Mr Stoddard?' Paniatowski wondered. 'What does his *best mate* say?'

'The same as everybody else.'

Paniatowski looked disappointed. 'Then he

can't have been much of a best mate,' she said regretfully.

'If Pete didn't want to tell anybody about what he did in them years, what right have I to?' Stoddard asked, stung.

'He's dead,' Paniatowski reminded him.

'Not to me!' Stoddard told her. 'He'll never be dead to me.'

'I think I'm beginning to get the picture now,' Paniatowski said thoughtfully. 'You're covering up for him.'

'What?'

'You're trying to save his reputation. You don't want anyone to know about the truly shameful things he did while he was away.'

'You little bitch!' Stoddard exploded.

Rutter stepped between them, and squared up to Stoddard. 'Outside!' he said angrily.

'That won't be necessary, Bob,' Paniatowski said.

'He doesn't talk to you like that – not while I'm here,' Rutter told her.

'I shouldn't have talked to her like that whether you were here or not,' Stoddard said. 'If you want me to step outside so you can beat the shit out of me, then I'll go willingly enough. But before I do, I want to apologize to this lass, here.' He had to stand on tiptoes to look over Rutter's shoulder. 'I'm sorry, miss. That was unforgivable.'

'Apology accepted,' Paniatowski said, easing Rutter out of the space between them. 'And I should apologize, too. I should never have gone out of my way to provoke you like that. But I thought that provoking you was the only way I was going to get at the truth.'

Stoddard nodded thoughtfully. 'Aye, perhaps you're right,' he agreed. 'Pete didn't do anythin' wrong, you know. Anythin' *dishonourable*. It wasn't in his nature. But he still had his way to make in the world when he got back here, an' he knew that certain of the things he'd done can count against a man. That's why he kept quiet about them.'

'But he *did* tell you?'

'Yes.'

'Then tell us.'

'I can't. He didn't swear me to secrecy or owt like that – there was no need for oaths between us. But he expected me not to tell anybody. I still can't, without his permission– ' Stoddard gulped – 'an' I'm never goin' to get that now, am I?'

Paniatowski sighed. 'People can get murdered anywhere – but they usually don't,' she said.

'What does that mean?'

'Unless it's a random killing – and this one wasn't – there has to be a reason why someone gets murdered in a particular place and at a particular time. Now it doesn't make sense that Pete should have been killed on the Costa Blanca – unless he'd had some

174

previous connection with either the place itself or with some of the people who were there at the same time he was. And if we're ever going to find his killer, we have to know what that connection was.'

'I can't help you,' Stoddard said regretfully.

'Maybe you can, if I can find a way to help you help me.'

'I'm listenin'.'

'My drink's vodka,' Paniatowski said.

'I don't understand.'

'In a minute or two, I'm going to make a statement. It won't be a long one. In fact, it will only be...' she counted it out on her fingers, '...it will only be thirteen words. Now after I've made that statement, there's one of two things you can do. If I'm wrong, just say nothing. If I'm right, I'd like you to buy me a drink. All right?'

'Maybe,' Stoddard said dubiously.

Paniatowski took a breath. 'Of course, we already know that Pete Medwin went to *Spain* in 1936,' she said.

For a moment, Stoddard did not move so much as a muscle. Then he turned and faced the barman. 'I know you don't normally serve any foreign muck in here, Sid,' he said, 'but there's no chance you've got a bottle of vodka stashed away somewhere, is there?'

Eighteen

The fisherman had been watching Paco Ruiz ever since he had emerged from between the shacks and begun to make his way across the beach. Now, as the ex-policeman drew level with him, he put down the net he had been mending and rose slowly to his feet.

'You are Ramón Jiménez?' Paco asked.

'I am.'

'When I was told you were the one I should talk to, I did not recognize the name. But we have met before, haven't we?'

The fisherman nodded. 'You helped my cousin. Another man laid claim to his boat. This man had documents which said that it was his. You proved that those documents were false, and my cousin kept his boat. You did not take payment for the work you had done.'

Paco grinned. 'How could I? Your cousin had been denied the use of his boat for many weeks. He didn't have any money to pay me *with*.'

'And now you want something in return for your kindness?'

'Perhaps.'

'Then if it is in my power to give you what you need, you shall have it. What do you require?'

'Not a great deal,' Paco said. 'Just a little information. I want to know about something which happened in the spring of 1939.'

'Happened where?'

'On the beach. Do you know what I'm talking about?'

The fisherman nodded again. 'There is only one thing which happened on this beach in the spring of 1939 which could possibly be of interest to you,' he said.

The collapse of the Republic had long been expected, yet it was still a shock when it finally came. On a single day – the 26th of March – General Yagüe took thirty thousand prisoners and two thousand square kilometres of territory in the south. The next day the resistance around Madrid all but melted away and General Espinosa de los Monteros entered the city.

On the coast, the situation was equally chaotic. The fascists who had been in hiding for nearly three years now openly paraded on the streets of Valencia and Alicante, and fifty thousand Republican soldiers rushed down to the sea in the desperate hope of finding a boat which would provide them with an escape route from Franco's legendary vengeance.

'There were perhaps forty-five of them,' Ramón Jiménez said. 'Possibly even fifty. They were hiding in the hills outside the town – in an olive grove just behind where the *Alcalde*'s villa stands now. They were waiting for the ship they had been promised would arrive.'

'You're sure there were that many of them?'

'Yes, I saw them with my own eyes.'

'When?'

'When I went up to the hills myself.'

'Why did you go?'

'I took them food. We could not truly spare it – we were starving ourselves – but they had fought for us, even though they were not our countrymen, and now it was only right that we should give them all the help we could.'

'Were they all foreigners?'

'Yes, though some of them spoke good Spanish.'

'Tell me about the night the ship they were waiting for eventually arrived offshore.'

'It was a terrible, terrible night.'

The fascist militia which had taken over the town did not scare the men coming down from the hills. Why should it? The militia had only been able to seize control because there was no one left to resist it. It hadn't seen the fighting they had. It hadn't battled against a large, well-equipped enemy, using only rudimentary

178

weapons – and won! If the militia tried to stop them, the militia would lose.

They knew it would have been a different story if they had had to wait another day. In one more day, the full might of the victorious army would descend on the area, and if they were still there, it would flatten them without even breaking step.

But they wouldn't be there! The ship was already waiting for them, out in the darkness. The fishing boats were on the beach, ready to ferry them out to it. It required only one last small effort – after so many great ones – and they would be safe.

They covered their route with a military precision which none of them would have been able to conceive of three years earlier. They used cover where it was available, and moved quickly when it was not. They were carrying very little – only their canteens, their weapons, and the four small packing cases which had been entrusted to their care by the dying government in Valencia.

They left the open country and crossed the road which ran parallel to the beach. To the right they could see the town itself, illuminated by a thousand oil lamps, and – to some of them at least – it looked like a fairytale castle. Ahead of them were the fishermen's shacks, where they knew they would find friends.

They could hear the sound of the water lapping against the shore. It was almost over. The crusade which had turned into a nightmare – the voyage of discovery on which they had waded through rivers of blood – was almost at an end. They wanted to go – and it broke their hearts to leave.

They reached the shacks – and found them in darkness.

'Where is everybody?' Medwin asked nervously.

'Perhaps they thought it wiser to be somewhere else tonight,' Ham-'n'-Eggs said.

'But a few of them should have stayed, if only the ones who are going to take us out to the ship,' Medwin countered.

'They're probably waiting for us down by their boats,' Moses said.

Yes, Medwin agreed – more from hope than from conviction – they probably were.

'You weren't waiting down by the boats, were you?' Paco asked.

'No,' Ramón Jiménez replied. 'We were not. As soon as darkness had fallen, the fascist militia appeared. They told us they were taking us to the town. They said that if we resisted, we would be shot.'

'And there was no way you could have warned the *brigadistas*?'

'No way at all. That was why it had been planned as it had – so that the *brigadistas* would have no idea of what was waiting for them.'

They were getting closer to the sea. They travelled in a column – as they had so often done in the *past – with scouts at the front and a rearguard behind. At the centre of the column were the eight men whose turn it was to carry the four packing cases between them.*

He couldn't see the fishermen, Medwin thought. And that was wrong! Even if they'd been in hiding, they should have emerged by now.

He felt the heavy weight of responsibility pressing on his shoulders. There were no leaders. Not any more. And that was the simple truth. Yet he knew that because of his experience and the stories which had grown up around his exploits, many of these men were following him *– putting their trust in* him. *And it was not just the men he was worried about. It was the boxes, which were weighed down heavy with expectations. Which were weighed down heavy with* hope.

'We have to retreat,' he said.

'Retreat?' Ham-'n'-Eggs repeated. 'We have nowhere to retreat to!'

'We'll regroup,' Medwin promised. 'We'll regroup and come up with another plan.'

'It's too late for that,' Moses said.

There was a sudden blinding flash of light to their left. And Medwin realized that Moses was right. It was too late to retreat. It was too late for anything!

'They could have locked us in the town hall while they carried out their bloody business,' Ramón Jiménez said. 'But they did not. They made us stand on the esplanade overlooking the beach. They made us watch. That was part of our punishment.'

'And what did you see?' Paco asked.

'The flares went up, and it was as bright as day. We saw them – those brave men – caught like rats in a trap. And we saw the machine-gun pits which the fascist militia had dug as soon as it went dark.'

There were cries of confusion, and cries of despair. They had not been expecting this. They had all thought, deep in their secret hearts, that God – or luck, or fate, or whatever else they believed in – would grant them at least this one chance. Now they realized that even this final hope was gone.

The flares, coming out of the darkness, blinded them for a few seconds, and even when their vision returned, they still saw the world through a red film.

'Get down, you idiots! Get down!' Medwin shouted.

But his words were drowned by the rattle of machine-gun fire.

Medwin, following his own instructions, hit the ground himself. The sand was damp against his skin.

'We have to get out of here,' said a voice by his side, which he recognized as belonging to Ham-'n'-Eggs.

'I can't desert the lads,' Medwin said.

'You've no choice,' Ham-'n'-Eggs gasped. 'This isn't a battle. It's a rout. And it's every man for himself.'

'What about the boxes?' Medwin asked.

'To hell with the boxes. They're lost, whatever you do. You have to try and save yourself.'

'In the morning, they took us down to the beach to clear away the bodies,' Ramón Jiménez said. 'We buried them in a mass grave. We asked if we might send for a priest, but Durán said no. He told us that these men had killed too many priests in their time to have their own burial sanctified by one now.'

'The International Brigade did not kill priests,' Paco said. 'I know, because I fought beside them.'

'I know that now, and I knew it then,' Jiménez said. 'But Durán would not be convinced. I think he hated them for their courage and nobility – hated them because they showed him more clearly than a mirror what he was himself.'

'What happened next?'

'Once we had filled in the grave, he ordered a concrete mixer to be brought to the site. Then he stood there and watched as we cemented over the whole area. It is something I will never forgive him for.'

'How many men did you bury that day? Do you know?'

'Of course I know. We counted them. We wanted to be sure we knew the full extent of Durán's crime.'

'So how many were there?'

'Thirty-four.'

'Which means, according to your earlier calculations, that some of them escaped.'

Jiménez nodded. 'A few,' he said mournfully. 'A pitiful few.' There were tears in his eyes. 'I sometimes wake up in the night wondering what happened to them. I would like to think that they returned safely to their own countries, but I cannot really bring myself to believe that they did.'

'They made it,' Paco said.

'How can you be so sure?'

'Because a few of the few have finally come back!'

Nineteen

A policeman was often a hunter, Woodend thought as he looked across the table at the heavy metal cross which hung around Sutcliffe's neck, but he was also – more commonly than most people ever imagined – almost a priest. And there was something of the priestly function about each and every interrogation. Crack one of a man's secrets – however small and insignificant that secret may be – and he soon comes to believe that you can crack them all. Catch the smallest glimpse of that same man's soul, and he will soon lay the whole soul bare before you.

'Shall we begin?' Woodend asked.

Captain López, who was sitting next to him, merely nodded.

'I was just wonderin' what nickname the group gave *you*, Mr Sutcliffe?' the Chief Inspector said.

'I am Jacob. I am Esau. Men know me as Elijah,' Sutcliffe replied in a voice that was almost a chant.

'Oh, I don't think it was ever anythin' as

fancy as that,' Woodend told him. 'They called Mitchell "Ham-'n'-Eggs", didn't they, because he was forever goin' on about how he could fancy a fry-up? Roberts, I imagine, was known as somethin' like "The Gambler". So I was wonderin' which of *your* little peculiarities they would have latched on to.'

Sutcliffe ran his hands through his shock of grey hair. 'As the mighty and terrible God on High is my witness, I knew no Mitchell. Nor did I know any Schneider or Dupont.'

'Funnily enough, I never asked you about Schneider or Dupont,' Woodend pointed out. 'An' I couldn't help noticin' that when you swore an oath to your "mighty an' terrible God", you acted as if I hadn't brought Roberts's name up at all. But here's the interestin' question. You say you didn't know them.'

'Yes?'

'*When* didn't you know them?'

'You make no sense,' Sutcliffe said.

'That's where you're wrong,' Woodend told him. 'Mitchell's a common enough name, so the chances are you've come across at least a few fellers called that. I know I certainly have. So you were lyin' when you said you knew no Mitchell. Lyin' – and usin' your "mighty an' terrible God" to back you up. Unless...'

Sutcliffe struggled to keep silent, but despite what his brain ordered it to do, his mouth was already forming the words.

'Unless what?' he asked.

'Unless you were playin' games with me. Unless you were addin' a silent qualification to your words, so that when you said, "I knew no Mitchell," what you really meant was "I knew no Mitchell *back in the days when we were all here in Benicelda.*" Because then Mitchell was goin' by his real name, wasn't he? Just as Holloway was goin' by his real name of Medwin, an' Schneider an' Dupont were goin' by whatever *their* real names are. But Roberts was *always* Roberts, an' that's why you excluded him from your oath.'

Sutcliffe closed his eyes. 'For the Devil is a great tempter, and we must heed not his words,' he intoned.

'Don't think I've ever been confused with Old Nick before,' Woodend said easily. 'But let's move on, shall we? We've already established that you *were* here with the others, but we still don't know what your nickname was.'

'Why should you want to know it?' Sutcliffe demanded.

'So there *is* one to know, is there?' Woodend countered.

'No, I...' Sutcliffe began. Then he closed his eyes again and said, 'Yea, though I walk through the valley of the shadow of death, I will fear no evil: for thou art with me; thy rod and thy staff comfort me...'

'I suppose it all depends when you first came down with an attack of Godliness,' Woodend mused. 'If it's recent, then chances are you were a bit of a hellraiser before. Is that what they called you? Hellraiser?'

'Thou preparest a table before me, in the presence of mine enemies...'

'No, I don't think it was that,' Woodend said. 'I think you'd been bitten by the bug before you ever came to Spain. So what was the name they gave you? Holy Joe? Bible Billy? Or were you just "The Lunatic"?'

'They called me *Moses*!' Sutcliffe said angrily.

'Moses!' Woodend repeated. 'Now that's an interestin' choice. What comes into *your* mind when you think of Moses, Captain López?'

If Paniatowski had been sitting beside him, she would have responded immediately.

Because she'd have known that it wouldn't really matter *what* she said, since her only real function was to remind the suspect that there were two of them – and only one of him.

Because she'd have appreciated the fact that one of the keys to a successful interrogation is rhythm, and her silence would have shattered the rhythm that Woodend had been working so hard to build up.

López should have known those things too.

López should have said something – anything – no matter how meaningless it had been.

But López didn't.

López kept silent.

Let down by the man who should have been acting as his partner, Woodend turned his attention back to Sutcliffe, and continued to press on with his reluctant one-man show.

'Moses was a leader of his people,' he said. 'You're not a leader, Mr Sutcliffe. You're a follower. So I don't think they called you Moses at all. I think you just *wished* they had.'

'God called on me to deliver his people from the heathen,' Sutcliffe said. 'To save them from the Whore of Babylon.'

'Moses led his people out of Egypt,' Woodend said. 'He never led them *back* again. So why did you – if you really are the leader you claim to be – lead your people back to Spain?'

'The wicked shall not go unpunished,' Sutcliffe said. 'The dead shall not go unavenged. Yea, though the Whore rules in this land once more, yet did God call on us to enter it and serve as His powerful right hand.'

'What exactly was it you came back here to do?' Woodend asked.

Sutcliffe looked at him with genuine

amazement in his eyes. 'Are you a fool?' he demanded. 'Have you not listened? Do you not understand?'

'I've almost got it,' Woodend said soothingly. 'Perhaps you could explain one more time – in simple terms, so that even an idiot like me can finally understand.'

Sutcliffe nodded. 'We came back because we were called,' he said. 'Because in this town there still lives—'

'Confess!' López exploded – almost screaming the words. 'Confess to the murder, and I promise you that you will be the one who escapes the death penalty!'

And just as Mitchell had done earlier, Sutcliffe shut down.

Twenty

Dusk was falling. The foreign visitors, who had basked in the sweltering heat on the beach for most of the day, now wandered the narrow streets of the old town, grateful for the gentle coolness which nightfall brought with it.

They all looked so relaxed, Woodend thought enviously, as he watched them walk past his table. And why wouldn't they be? They had left the stresses and strains of having to work for a living behind them, whereas he had merely transferred his job to a new –and more difficult – location.

He took a sip of his beer – the third he had ordered from the waiter since he sat down – and wondered just what he was going to do about the fix he found himself in.

Though he still had no clear idea why López was trying to sabotage the investigation, there was no doubt in his mind that that was exactly what the Captain was doing. Disrupting Mitchell's interrogation could just have been a mistake – an error of judgement. But he had done it again – not once, but four times. And if anything, his interruptions had only got worse with each session. Schneider, for example, had barely had time to sit before López was screaming at him to confess to the murder!

Woodend took another sip of his beer. He seemed to be completely boxed in, he thought. The investigation was getting nowhere, but appealing to López had proved a waste of time, and complaining to the Consul would achieve nothing, except perhaps gaining him a reputation for awkwardness. Nor was he willing to let López take over – it simply wasn't in his nature to sit back and watch an investigation being run into the ground.

There was something else he could do, he thought. He was sure of that. His only problem was that he had no idea what it was!

'Joan!' shouted a voice.

He looked up. The woman who had shouted the name was in her early thirties, as was the woman who turned round in response.

Nothing to do with *his* Joan at all, then.

Woodend felt a sudden shudder of guilt run through his whole body. They were in Benicelda for Joan's benefit. She needed to relax, and it was his job to see that she did. Yet he could not honestly say that he had thought about his wife – even for a second – since he had started to wrap his mind around the case that morning.

Captain López looked up at the picture of General Franco on his office wall – at the hard eyes and the disapproving down-turn of the mouth. The Generalissimo was not a man who was easily pleased. He did not tolerate failure, whatever the reason. And it was this attitude which had set the standard to be followed by anyone and everyone who held power in the Generalissimo's Spain.

'There is no excuse for failure, and I have failed,' López told the image of the grim-faced *Caudillo*.

And not just on one front, but on several!

He had failed to stop Woodend asking questions which might eventually lead the

English detective to a solution to the crime – whatever that solution *was*.

He had failed to learn why it was so important to His Excellency Don Antonio Durán, the *Alcalde* of Benicelda, that the crime should be covered up.

He would certainly be judged to have failed by his Captain-General in Madrid.

However he examined it, the future looked bleak.

The knock on his office door sounded like nothing less than a summons to defeat and disgrace, and he ignored it. It was only when the caller outside knocked a second time – with more insistence – that he found the strength to say, 'Come on, damn you!'

The man who opened the door and walked into the office was a constable called Luis Alonso. He did not look like a policeman. Policemen did not sport a three-day growth of stubble on their chins. Nor did he live in the barracks, or wear the olive-green uniform and the three-cornered hat. There was no record that he was even based in the Benicelda barracks of the Guardia Civil, and his wages came not through the usual channels but out of a special fund which was administered from headquarters in Madrid.

There were a number of people rotting away in prison who wished they had never met Alonso – and certainly wished they had never confided in him. There were others who did not even know he was responsible for their condition – who never suspected that light-hearted, free-spending Luis might be the one behind their incarceration. His job was to infiltrate – to uncover trouble-makers even before they had even thought of making trouble – and as his record of arrests showed, he was very good at it.

His work that day had been of a more private nature. He had not been searching out people who had the occasional bad word to say about the General, or people who might express the view that – just once in a while – it might be nice if they could actually believe what they read in the newspapers. That day, he had been working exclusively on behalf of Captain López.

'What do you want?' López demanded.

'You asked me to report to you if I had discovered anything interesting, my Captain.'

'And have you?'

Alonso hesitated, as if there were two things he could say, and he had not yet decided which one to choose. 'I might have something interesting,' he said finally. 'It all depends.'

'It all depends! On what?'

'On what's in it for me.'

López felt a mixture of rage and hope bubbling up inside him – rage that a mere constable should even think of trying to strong-arm him; hope that maybe what

Alonso had learned would be well worth whatever it cost.

'If you have found out anything of use to me, I will see that you are amply rewarded for it,' he said cautiously.

Alonso rubbed his hands together. 'Oh, it will be of use, my Captain,' he said confidently. 'I've uncovered a deep, dark secret. And that kind of secret, if handled properly, can be worth a small fortune.'

'Then tell me what it is, you *hijo de puta*!' López said, thinking, even as he spoke, that his words sounded more like a plea of a desperate man than an order from a captain in the Guardia Civil.

Alonso quickly outlined what he had learned. 'Well?' he asked when he had finished.

'It might possibly be of use,' López said. 'On the other hand, it could lead to nothing.'

But he was finding it almost impossible to keep the excitement out of his voice. Only minutes earlier, he had been worried about landing in the shit. Now the prospect no longer bothered him, because he had just learned that at the bottom of the shit heap was the entrance to a gold mine.

Twenty-One

Mitchell looked around the room at the others. Dupont and Sutcliffe were sitting on his bed, and Schneider on the only chair. Roberts was leaning against the wall in the corner.

Mitchell would have liked to sit down himself. Hell, he'd have liked to *lie* down. But he couldn't, because he had to show the others that he was stronger than he looked.

No, he corrected himself – he had to *fool them into thinking* that he was stronger than he looked.

Because the truth was, he wasn't strong at all. The truth was that however hard he fought it, the illness that was eating away at his body was also sapping away what little strength he had left.

It was strange to be Ham-'n'-Eggs again, after all these years. He wondered how the others now regarded their old names.

Did Sutcliffe still think of himself as Moses? It was more than likely, from the way he talked.

Did Schneider ever look in the mirror and

see Magic Fingers staring back at him? Did he even *play* the accordion any more?

And what about Dupont? The Catalan socialists had called him Whistling Death, because nobody they had ever met before could handle a throwing knife like he could. Was it a name he still felt comfortable with? Did he feel proud when he thought of it?

And finally there was Roberts. The Gambler. He'd bet on anything – from the turn of a single card to how long it would be before the sun emerged from behind the clouds. He'd *risk* anything – his last peseta, *his own life* – without a second's thought. Roberts's recklessness had landed them in danger more than once, but it had also saved them from certain death in several tight spots. They all owed Roberts, and they knew it, but the only debts he'd ever attempted to collect from any of them had been *gambling* debts.

Mitchell cleared his throat. 'The reason that I've called this meeting—' he began.

'*You've* called this meeting?' Roberts said, with an amused smile playing on his lips. 'Who died and made you leader?'

'Pete Medwin did,' Mitchell said.

Pete Medwin really *had been* their leader. He'd been a funny little man who, even in his twenties, had been starting to lose his hair – but they'd have followed him anywhere.

Roberts looked uncharacteristically stricken by the reminder. 'Yes, of course,' he said.

'I'm sorry ... I didn't mean to ... It's just so hard to think of Pete Medwin as really...'

'It's all right,' Mitchell assured him. 'If you'd like somebody else to take charge instead of me...'

Roberts shook his head. 'No. You're the obvious choice. You're the one Pete would have chosen himself.'

The others nodded.

'This is going to be a bit like the old days,' Mitchell said. 'There are two things we need to do. The first is to assess our current situation. The second is to decide how that assessment will affect our plans. Firstly, our current situation. What do López and Woodend actually *know*?'

'They know, despite our protestations, that we are not strangers to one another,' Dupont said, speaking in Spanish – the only language they had all once shared with any degree of facility. 'They know we are bound together by ties which are stronger than steel.'

'Do you think they know about the Brigade?' Schneider asked.

Dupont shook his head. 'Not yet. But it is only a matter of time before they do.'

'What else?' Mitchell asked.

'They may suspect that we are not who we claim to be, but they have no idea of our real identities,' Schneider said.

'And since they do only *suspect*, that must mean that they do not yet *know* that our passports are forgeries,' Dupont pointed out.

'How can you be sure of that?'

'Because using fake travel documents is a crime in itself, and we are not yet in gaol.'

'But again, it is only a matter of time before they find out,' Schneider said.

'Which is why we must take a decision *now* about our future plans,' Mitchell told his comrades. 'We came here as representatives of the group who survived the massacre on the beach. We had a mission – to try Durán for his crimes and, if we found him guilty, to execute him. We are now faced with two choices. We can leave like curs – with our tails between our legs – or we can go ahead with the operation as planned. Which is it to be?'

'I vote we leave,' Roberts said.

Mitchell was stunned. He had expected some opposition – but not from Roberts. Never from Roberts.

'I can't believe what I've just heard,' he said. 'Your whole life's been a gamble. Why won't you take a little gamble now?'

Roberts smiled again, though perhaps a little sadly this time. 'There are two kinds of gamblers,' he said. 'There's the one who relies on blind chance – on random happenings. He will bet on the first bird to leave the tree, because neither he nor the man he is betting against has any real idea which bird it will be. Then there's the other kind – the one who will hold back until he's done his research. When he bets against a man in poker, it's because he knows how that man thinks. When he puts his money on a horse, it's because he has studied its form.'

'And which one are you?' Mitchell asked.

'I have been both in my time,' Roberts said. 'You all know that.'

'Well, then?'

'Both kinds of gamblers would tell you what I'm about to tell you now. We can't rely on blind chance, because our opponent has foreknowledge. Durán knows we are here – Pete Medwin's death is all the proof we need of that. And if we weigh up the odds, what do we find? Durán probably has a private army he can use against us if he needs to. But he probably won't even have to – because he has all the apparatus of the state on his side. The pack is stacked against us, my friends. The odds against us succeeding are astronomical.'

'What do you think, Magic Fingers?' Mitchell asked – using the old name deliberately, to try to conjure up the old spirit.

'We came here because of crimes left unpunished,' the German said. 'We came to see justice done. And now there is more blood on Durán's hands than there ever was. Are we to let him get away with that? Is that the lesson we are to leave him with? That the

200

mistake is not to murder – it is not to murder *enough*?'

'So you'll stay?'

'I will stay.'

'Dupont?'

'Me, also.'

'Sutcliffe?'

'For the Lord my God is a mighty God!' Sutcliffe said. 'He will not be mocked, nor will He be denied!'

Mitchell coughed awkwardly. 'Does that mean that you're with us?' he asked.

'I am with you. For am I not His right hand – the sword with which He will wreak His revenge?'

Mitchell breathed a small sigh of relief. 'Then it's still possible,' he said. 'With four of us, it's still possible.' He turned to Roberts. 'Perhaps you're right, old friend. Perhaps our enterprise is doomed, as you calculate. You may be the only wise one amongst us.' He gestured towards the door. 'Leave now. There's no one here who will hold it against you.'

Roberts's smile had turned wistful. 'I remember a visit I made to a dog track, years ago,' he said. 'I was desperate for money, and if I lost my stake that night, I would have nothing. But there was no reason why I should lose, you see.'

'Why not?' Mitchell asked.

'Because I knew in advance that the race

201

was fixed, and a certain dog was going to win. Then, as I was standing there in the paddock, I saw this other dog being led round. He was smaller than the rest, and even at a distance I could see he didn't have the right build to ever become a true champion. Even if the race hadn't been nobbled, he wouldn't have won. But I could tell, just by looking at him, that once the traps were open, he would put his heart and soul on running as fast he could. I placed all my money on him.'

'And you won – against all the odds?' Dupont asked.

Roberts laughed. 'What a romantic fool you can be, sometimes,' he said. 'No, of course I didn't win. I lost – just as I'd expected to.'

'Then I do not see...'

'But I felt better for having bet on that dog – for backing his spirit with my cash. And now I look at you four. You won't win the race – but when you lose, I want to be there supporting you.'

They slapped him on the back. They told him he was the bravest of the whole bunch of them. It was a good feeling they had, sitting around in that small hotel room. It was almost like being back in the old days.

Twenty-Two

The *Alcalde* knew that something had gone seriously wrong the moment López entered his office. There was a swagger in the way the man walked – a look of insolence in his eyes. Only that morning, the Captain would have got down on his knees and licked the boots of the future Provincial Governor if he had deemed that to be necessary in order to get on. Now there was no evidence at all of his former subservient attitude. Now he looked very much as if he thought he was the man in charge.

López strode over to the visitor's chair, and sat down on it without being invited to.

A bad sign, the Mayor thought. A very bad sign.

'I think you forget yourself, Captain López,' he said aloud.

'And I'm sure there are a lot of things *you'd* rather forget, Your Excellency,' the Captain replied. 'It is a strange system which governs us, is it not? The Generalissimo is reputed not to take bribes himself – why should he, when he can have all he needs simply for the asking? – but he is not averse to others doing so. Government ministers accept millions of *duros* worth of such "gifts". I myself can be bought for a few hundred. You, I would think – as someone who is less important than a minister, but more important than a humble police captain – fall somewhere in between.'

'This is outrageous!' Durán said, though his heart was sinking too fast for him to be able to infuse the comment with any real anger.

'Most people would never dare to order a captain in the Guardia Civil out of their houses,' López said, 'but you are the *Alcalde*, and you have the power to get away with it. So if you're as outraged as you claim, why *don't* you tell me to go? Better yet, why don't you have me *thrown* out?'

Durán felt a chill run through his corpulent body. 'I will hear what you have to say,' he told López.

'The point about the corruption in our country is that it is *permitted* corruption,' López continued. 'The *Caudillo* does not sanction every bribe that a captain takes, but he *knows* that we do take bribes, and he does not mind. But Franco is still a soldier down to his bootstraps, and disobeying orders is the worst crime he can conceive of. His men raped in the war – but only when he said it was all right for them to rape. His men stole

204

in the war – but only with his approval.'

'Get to the point,' Durán said.

But López was enjoying himself too much to do that quite yet. 'This morning, you were visited by a Francisco Ruiz,' he said.

'You have been watching my house?' Durán demanded.

'That much is obvious. How else could I have known that the man came to see you? But to continue. Ruiz was a homicide detective before the war. Now he makes a sort of living as a private detective for the poor and downtrodden. You are neither poor *nor* downtrodden, so what did he come to see *you* about?'

'That is none of your bloody business!' the *Alcalde* protested.

'But it is,' López contradicted him. 'You made it my business – you made *everything* you do my business – when you started telling me how I should conduct my murder inquiry.'

'The course of action I suggested was for your own good,' Durán said weakly.

'The course of action you *ordered* was for nobody's benefit but your own, Your Excellency. But in the light of my recent discoveries, none of that really matters any more.'

Durán felt himself start to tremble, though he was still not quite sure what it was he had to be afraid of. 'What do you mean?' he asked.

'After Ruiz left your house, I had him followed. I fully expected an ex-detective like him to spot his tail eventually, but he didn't. Perhaps Ruiz has lost his edge. Or maybe he was simply so intent on his investigation that nothing else seemed to exist for him. Which do you think it was, Your Excellency?'

López paused, as if he expected some response to his question.

'I don't know, and I don't care,' Durán said. 'I have no interest at all in the man.'

López grinned. 'You should have,' he said, 'because Ruiz obviously has a great deal of interest in you. He talked to several people during the course of the day, and though most of them were far too lowly to have anything at all to do with such an eminent man as yourself, it was you they discussed. And here is the important point, Your Excellency – after Ruiz talked to them, my man did, too.'

'I see,' Durán said heavily.

'What they had to tell him – these people of no apparent consequence – was very illuminating. So illuminating, in fact, that I – unlike that fool of an English policeman – have almost a complete picture of what has been going on. Why don't you show me the photographs?'

'What photographs?'

'The ones which you carelessly left lying around on your desk yesterday, and which you have since, no doubt – now that it is far too late – locked away in a drawer.'

'I don't know what you're talking about,' Durán protested.

'Show me the photographs!' López repeated.

Durán opened a drawer, took out the pictures, and handed them across the desk.

López examined one of them closely. 'A group of men in an olive grove,' he said. 'I would guess this was taken in March 1939, just before Alicante fell to the Generalissimo's victorious army. Would I be right?'

'You'd be right,' Durán agreed.

'The faces are not very clear, but it is certainly easier to distinguish them when you know what you're looking for.' López pointed to the head of one of the figures. 'I would say this is Medwin. Am I right?'

'Does it matter?'

'This one looks like Sutcliffe. And here is Mitchell, the American. How did you know they had returned? Were you still watching for them – even after all these years?'

'It is always wise for a man in my position to take precautions,' Durán said.

'Yes, I can understand that,' López agreed, 'because if I'd been in *their* position, I'd certainly have done all within my power to pay you a return visit. So, they came back – and you were faced with a real dilemma. You could not have them thrown into prison, because you were afraid that once they were locked up they would start telling stories you would much rather have left untold. So what did you do? You killed one of them, in the hope that it would panic the others into running away.'

'I did no such thing!'

'Oh, not personally. You are too old and too fat to do your own killing any more. But you *arranged* for him to be killed. The problem was, they didn't run away, did they? And now you were facing an even worse problem. They were the natural suspects for the murder, and you were afraid that if I arrested one of them, he would tell me all about what happened in March 1939.'

'I swear I did not order Medwin's death,' Durán said.

'Medwin's death is not really important one way or the other,' López said. 'He was a *brigadista*, which in the Generalissimo's eyes makes him a war criminal. It could never be openly acknowledged that you had him killed, but it certainly would not have done your career any harm. What *would* have harmed you – and can *still* harm you – is the secret which you hoped Medwin's death would bury for ever.'

'I do not know what you are talking about,' Durán said – but he did not sound convincing, even to himself.

'In March 1939, the *Caudillo* issued a

directive that anything of value which was captured from the fleeing enemy was to be handed over to the new military authorities,' López said. 'Do you remember that directive?'

'No. I never saw it.'

'You're lying. But even if you weren't, it makes no difference. Ignorance of the *Caudillo*'s orders had never been any excuse for not obeying them.'

'What do you want?' Durán asked dully.

'Ruiz is a problem, but he is only *one* of the problems you could face over this matter. In exchange for making all these problems go away, I will require a considerable sum of money immediately – though it will be nothing you can't afford – and a fairly generous share of the pie once you are Provincial Governor.'

Durán said nothing.

'You're wondering if I'm bluffing, aren't you?' López said.

'So far you have put on a good show, but you have said nothing to show me that I need to fear you as much as I fear the *brigadistas*,' Durán said, with unusual candour.

'Then why don't you let me ask you two questions?' López suggested.

'Why should I?'

'Because if you can answer them honestly – and without fear – then I have no hold on you at all.'

'Ask them.'

'The first question is this: what was in the boxes the *brigadistas* were carrying when they were ambushed on the beach?'

Durán gulped. 'And what is your second question?' he asked.

'The second is: what happened to those boxes after most of those *brigadistas* had been killed?'

Twenty-Three

'What would you like to do tonight, lass?' Woodend asked his wife.

Joan, who had been sitting by the window and looking out to sea, turned slowly, and with great care, to face him. 'What would *you* like to do, Charlie?' she replied.

Woodend shrugged. 'It's not really up to me. It should be your choice, after I've been forced to leave you on your own all day.'

A slight smile came to Joan's face. 'Forced?' she repeated. 'Is that what you were?'

'It wasn't my decision, one way or the other,' Woodend said awkwardly. 'The order came directly from the Home Office. Or from the Foreign Office. From some bloody office in London, anyway.'

'But it didn't exactly spoil your holiday, did it?'

'You've got it all wrong,' Woodend protested. 'I don't *want* to work on this case.'

'Don't want to work on the case? Or don't want to work *with that Captain López* on the case?'

'He'll never find the killer,' Woodend said, all the exasperation of the day coming out in a burst of emotion he knew he should never have allowed to be released. 'I don't even think he *wants* to find him!'

'So it is *him*, rather than *the case*, that you object to?'

Woodend sighed. 'Look, love, if you want me off the investigation, you've only to say so.'

'What about your orders?'

'Sod the bloody orders! I'm on holiday. They can't make me work if I don't want to. An' if I get a bollockin' when we get back to Whitebridge, well, it won't be the first bollockin' I've ever had, will it?'

Joan was silent for a moment. Then she said, 'They've been talkin' about the case on the wireless.'

'The wireless. But how could you understand what they were sayin', when you don't speak Spanish?'

'I was listenin' to the BBC World Service.'

211

'However did you manage that?'

'I was listenin' on the short-wave radio we brought with us. Why do you think the case was so heavy?'

'I didn't even know that we owned a short-wave radio,' Woodend admitted.

'There's a lot of things that go on in our house you don't know about, Charlie Woodend,' Joan said. 'A vast amount of things, if truth be told. But we're gettin' off the point I was about to make. They seemed to think on the wireless that this Medwin was a nice feller.'

'Accordin' to what Monika told me when she rang up – an' what I've found myself – that's just what he was. When he was a lad, he risked his life fighting for a decent life for other people. When he became a boss, he was a *good* boss who never forgot his roots. There aren't many workin'-class heroes about, but I think Pete Medwin was one of them.'

'An' you really do think there's no chance that López will find his murderer?'

'Not a cat in hell's chance.'

'So what are you goin' to do about it?'

'I beg your pardon?' Woodend said.

'López won't find the killer, and you won't find the killer either, as long as you're workin' *with* López. So what are you goin' to do about it?'

'I don't know.'

Joan's eyes narrowed, as they always did when she was looking right into his mind. 'You don't *know* – but you've had some thoughts on the matter, haven't you?' she said.

'Well,' Woodend replied cautiously, 'since López doesn't seem to be playin' it by the rules, I don't see the need to stick to them myself any longer.'

'An' what does that mean, exactly?'

'It means, I suppose, that I've been considerin' havin' a talk to a man who *does* seem to care about the case.'

'Paco Ruiz?'

'That's right.'

'An' where do you think Paco might be right now?'

'I don't know.'

'Guess!'

'It's more than likely he'll be havin' a drink at one of the bars near the church.'

'Then you'd better get your skates on, hadn't you?' Joan said. 'Otherwise, you might miss him.'

Luis de la Vega sat alone in the kitchen of the *Alcalde*'s villa. He had a perfect right to be there – or in any other part of the house, for that matter – because although in theory he was no more than the chauffeur, in practice he performed a number of other significant roles.

He was the bodyguard, which was why he always carried the pistol now lying on the table in front of him. He was the butler, supervising the ordering of the wine and instructing the cook what to prepare for the *Alcalde*'s meals. He helped the Mayor to dress and get out of the bath. And – though neither of them would have dared to admit it in a country run by a dictator who paid at least *lip service* to all the teachings of the Catholic Church – he had, for the previous two years, been Durán's lover.

It would not have been true to say that de la Vega relished the thought of visiting the *Alcalde*'s bed, but he did not *particularly* mind it either, and if half an hour or so of discomfort was all it took to attach himself to a man who was going places, then it was a price he was perfectly willing to pay.

What he *did* mind was the arrival to the villa of Pedro Trujillo, another young man with slim hips and a knowing look in his eye.

'We do not need this man, Don Antonio,' he had protested.

'He's is not here to take your place, my dear Luis,' the *Alcalde* had said soothingly.

'Then why *is* he here?'

'To assist you – to take some of the weight off you.'

And what sort of weight was he talking about? de la Vega wondered. The weight of the *Alcalde* pressing down on him in the bedroom?

'I do not need an assistant,' he'd said sulkily.

'He will only be here at night.'

'At night!' de la Vega exploded. 'At *night*.'

'Night is when there is most danger,' the *Alcalde* explained. 'There are bad men in town, men who wish me harm. I would be happier if I had two of you protecting me.'

'And that is all he is here for? To protect you?'

'Yes.'

'Not to supervise your meals? Not to help you dress? Not to—'

'Just to protect me.'

Well, if that really *was* all it meant, no real harm could come from it, de la Vega supposed. After all, the *Alcalde* could not betray him with a man who was on constant guard duty.

That was where Trujillo was at that moment. On guard duty. Checking the grounds.

I'll keep the bastard busy, de la Vega thought vindictively. So busy that even if Don Antonio gives him the eye, he'll be too tired to respond.

There was a sudden urgent tapping on the grille which covered the kitchen window. De la Vega first reached for his pistol, then asked, 'Who is it?'

'It's me!' a voice said, almost in a whisper. 'Pedro!'

'You should be on patrol.'

'I have been. That's why—'

'This is inexcusable! You leave me no choice but to report to Don Antonio in the morning that you have been negligent in your duties.'

'You must come outside, Luis!' Trujillo said urgently. 'You must come now!'

'But why?'

'I cannot explain. You must see for yourself.'

The man was not so much a rival as a fool, de la Vega thought. His weapon still firmly in his right hand, he stood up and slid back the bolts on the door with his left.

'Come in,' he said, opening the door.

'I cannot come in,' Trujillo said desperately. 'You must come out.'

'But why ... ?'

'Please!'

De la Vega sighed heavily. He would certainly tell Don Antonio all about this is the morning, he thought, and then perhaps the *Alcalde* would realize that the new boy was more of a hindrance than a help.

Nevertheless, he did step outside. Trujillo was standing close to the door, but in the shadows. And there was something wrong with him, de la Vega thought. He seemed much broader than he had earlier. And while his two arms were clearly hanging by his sides, he seemed to have developed a third arm which he had somehow managed to wrap around his own throat.

Trujillo made a sudden gurgling sound, and collapsed. Only to reveal that he had not been alone! Only to reveal that another man had been standing right behind him!

The hand containing de la Vega's pistol had been hanging loosely by his side. Now he started to bring it up so that he could take aim at the intruder. But he had left it too late. Far too late. He had scarcely begun to bend his elbow when he felt a sharp stabbing pain in his chest, and knew that he was finished.

Twenty-Four

Paco Ruiz had a glass of white wine in front of him, and was staring thoughtfully in the direction of the beach.

Woodend, feeling a little awkward and a little embarrassed, sat down opposite him. 'I don't suppose you could ask the waiter to bring me a beer, could you?' he asked.

Paco looked up. 'Of course I could ask. It is a very small request. I would do it for anyone.'

'You're angry with me, aren't you?' Wood-end said.

'I am ... disappointed,' Paco replied, choosing his words carefully. 'But not so much with you as with the predicament we both find ourselves in. I have been telling myself that if I had been in your position, I would not have rejected the help of a man who obviously had so much to contribute to the investigation.'

'I thought I explained that—'

'Yet there is at least a part of me which suspects that if I had found myself in your shoes, I would have done exactly as you did – because I would have felt there was no other choice.' Paco paused, and took a sip of his wine. 'Of course, *given* the situation as it is, I feel under absolutely no obligation to tell you what *I* have discovered.'

'The situation's changed,' Woodend said.

Paco raised his right eyebrow, but so slightly that Woodend might almost have missed it. 'In what way?' the Spaniard asked.

'I can't solve this case alone,' Woodend admitted. 'I'm probably doomed to failure even with you – but without you it's a dead certainty.'

Paco smiled. 'I lied earlier.'

'You mean, when you said you weren't angry with me?'

'Perhaps that was a lie, too. But only a small one. The *big* lie was that I felt under no obligation to tell you what I'd found out. I'm only an *ex*-policeman on paper. In my head, I'm still a cop, and I couldn't withhold information from a brother officer. It simply isn't in my nature.'

Woodend grinned. 'Well then, you'd better tell me what you've come up with, hadn't you?'

'You told me López was making no effort with the case,' Paco said. 'Coming from outside Spain, you had no idea why that might be. But I live here, and I knew immediately. If López was giving up the opportunity to make a name for himself by solving the crime, it had to be because someone much more powerful was ordering him not to. And the most powerful person in this town is the *Alcalde*. I went to see him this morning. I acted a little, I lied a little, and I learned that Durán not only knows about Medwin and his friends, but he is afraid of them.'

'I spoke to my sergeant this evening,' Woodend said. 'She told me that Medwin was in Spain from 1936 to 1939. He was a member of the International Brigade. He fought against Franco's fascists.'

He had expected Ruiz to be impressed – and perhaps even surprised – but the other man merely nodded and said, 'Yes, that is exactly what he did. He must have seen many of his comrades die, but I don't think he expected to see any of them die on that beach just down there.'

'What!' Woodend said.

Paco Ruiz smiled again. 'Ah, so you are unaware of that particular black event from our recent history,' he said.

'You know I am, you cocky bugger,' Woodend said, without rancour. 'But I'd certainly bloody like to find out!'

Paco told him about the ambush, and about the boxes which the *brigadistas* had been carrying.

'I don't think they were killed as an act of war,' he concluded. 'I think they were killed for the boxes.'

'An' what was in them?'

'I don't know, but it must have been something valuable. I talked to an old man who told me that Durán had nothing at the start of the war, yet by the end of it he was a rich man. I think he *became* rich that night on the beach. He killed around forty men to get what he wanted, but he didn't kill Medwin. Not then. He had to wait nearly another thirty years to do that.'

'So there's no doubt in your mind that Durán either killed Medwin himself, or else had him killed?'

'None at all.'

'And do you have any idea as to how we'll go about proving it?'

'Again, none at all.'

Durán had gone to bed, but sleep had eluded him. Now he was back in his office, staring gloomily at the mountain of files he had piled up on his desk.

He'd got away with a great deal in his time, he thought. Or rather, he had been *allowed* to get away with a great deal. But if he was once found guilty of this one big thing, then all the blind eyes which had been turned to him in the past would suddenly be open – all the understanding nods in his direction quickly denied.

They'd crucify him!

'See what we've done?' those responsible for his prosecution would say to the foreign press. 'You write that we are corrupt, but we are not. Doesn't the very fact that we have punished this man for his corruption prove just how honest the rest of us are?'

So the secret of the boxes must *never* come out. It must be hidden at all cost. And that meant, did it not, that he would be forced to give Captain López whatever he asked for?

Or did it *really* mean that?

López was safe enough for the moment – he was still too valuable for any harm to come to him – but once he had done what was necessary for the cover-up, he would be about as useful as a stomach ulcer. And there was only one way to deal with stomach ulcers!

Many men – even important men like

captains in the Guardia Civil – had been known to have accidents. If López's car should happen to crash into a stone wall and burn up, who would think to examine the driver's charred remains for bullet holes?

Durán heard the door to the office click open.

'Not now, Luis,' he said. 'I'm busy. Come to my bedroom when it's light again, and then we'll spend a little time together.'

His visitor laughed – but it did not sound like Luis's laugh. With an effort, Durán twisted round, so that his huge body was facing the door.

'What are you doing here?' he demanded.

'What do you think I'm doing here?' the visitor asked.

It was then that Durán noticed the knife in his visitor's hand, and the panic began to set in.

'We had a deal,' he said.

'Yes, we did,' the visitor agreed. 'The only problem is, I'm not sure I can trust you not to go back on it.'

'I ... I ... You have my word.'

'The word of a man who would gun down nearly fifty men for the sake of the treasures they were carrying with them?'

'That was war!'

'It was *greed*, Don Antonio.'

'And are you any less greedy?'

'No, but I am wiser. I would certainly not

leave myself as exposed to my enemies as you have.'

Durán nervously licked his thick lips, which were suddenly as dry as the desert sands.

'Our deal is not set in stone,' he said. 'If you are not happy with the terms, I'm sure we could renegotiate it.'

'Oh no, it's far too late for that,' his visitor told him.

Twenty-Five

He is lying on his front, his face pressing down on something soft and friable – and he doesn't know why. Around him are the sounds of loud explosions and men screaming – and he can't explain them, either. He sticks out his tongue and licks the earth, as if that, in some strange way, will explain to him where he is and what he is doing there. But it isn't earth at all. It is something altogether stickier and more cloying. It's ... it's sand!

'Are you all right, Sarge?' asks a desperate voice somewhere to his right.

Since the question has nothing to do with him, he decides to ignore it. His task – his only real concern – is to work out why he's in a children's sand pit when there is obviously something very important going on beyond the bounds of the playground.

'Sergeant Woodend, are you all right?' the voice asks again.

Sergeant Woodend! His name is Woodend. Maybe the voice is talking to him after all.

It's all coming back to him. The landing craft. Being up to his knees in water. The hail of bullets which greeted him as he waded to the shore. The explosion, once he was on the beach, which threw him into the air, twisted him round, and made him bellyflop on to the sand.

He is in Normandy. This is D-Day and the Allied Armies, of which he is one small part, are invading France.

Palms flat against the sand, he raises his trunk off the ground. 'I'm fine, Hawkins,' he says.

'Thank God for that!' Lance Corporal Hawkins says – and sounds as if he really means it!

Woodend climbs shakily to his feet – and almost wishes he hadn't. Men who had been alive only minutes earlier are now sprawled out dead on the sand. Limbs, which until recently had been part of entire bodies, now lie useless and alone.

There is even a complete head – jaggedly severed at the neck – resting on the sand like a ball left over from a game of beach football. Woodend recognizes the head as having once belonged to the lieutenant in charge of his platoon.

224

Even without the noise – even playing as a silent movie – the scene would be enough to convince those on the beach that they had landed in the very jaws of hell. But there is noise enough, and more. The explosions, the screams, the swearing, the praying and the whimpering – they all swirl together to create a soundtrack that even the Devil himself would have been hard pushed to create.

Woodend looks up to the cliffs. He can see the gun emplacements which are causing all the damage – all the death and destruction. He even thinks he can see – though he must surely be imagining it – the looks on the faces of the men manning those guns – terrified faces, faces as full of a sense of horror as the faces of the men on the beach. And it gives him new strength – gives him the will to fight back.

'Regroup the men,' he shouts at Hawkins. 'We have to knock out some of them bloody batteries before they can do any more soddin' damage.'

It never even occurs to him that he'll live through this nightmare, but he will. It never enters his mind that he'll be awarded a medal for his part in it, but that will happen, too.

They are halfway up the cliffs, and the explosions seem even louder than they were on the beach. Woodend is convinced the noise will burst his ear drums, that even if he does survive – as by now he thinks he just might – he will be stone deaf for the rest of his life.

He urges his men ever onwards – and the sounds change. Now it is not so much detonations he is hearing, it is simply a loud banging. It puzzles him. It is almost like ... almost like knuckles being rapped against wood.

Woodend opened his eyes. 'Wait on!' he half-shouted, half-mumbled, as he climbed out of bed. 'Wait on, I'm gettin' there as quick as I can.'

There were two Guardia Civil privates standing in the hallway.

'Come!' one of them said.

'What?'

'Come! Now!'

'Where?'

'*Capitán* López. He want see you.'

López was sitting at a table in the bar next to Woodend's hotel. He had a glass of brandy in front of him, and from the flushed look on his face, the Chief Inspector guessed that it was not his first.

Woodend sat down. 'Is there a problem?' he asked.

'The *Alcalde* is dead,' López said in a shaky voice. 'Murdered.'

'When did this happen?'

'Some time early this morning. His bodyguards are also dead, but that does not matter.'

'It doesn't?'

226

'Of course not. Madrid does not care about the fate of two nonentities from the provinces. But the *Alcalde* – a man who was to be Regional Governor – is a different matter. Unless I arrest the killers, my head is on the block.'

'In that case, I'm surprised you've not fitted up some poor bastard for the murder already,' Woodend said.

'You're not listening,' López replied bitterly. 'Since the *Alcalde* was *so* important, this is no longer merely a little local murder. The international press will be following the case.'

'So you'll have to have some *real* proof before you make an arrest,' Woodend mused. 'Which means that, for once, you'll be forced to do some proper detective work.'

'Exactly,' López agreed, and if he noticed the implied insult at all, it did not really seem to bother him.

Woodend stood up. 'Well, all I can do, now that it's a purely Spanish matter, is to wish you good luck,' he said.

'But it is *not* purely a Spanish matter,' López said.

'The victims are Spanish.'

'But all the main suspects are foreigners. And two of them are English.'

'You don't know for sure that one – or several – of those foreigners actually committed the murders,' Woodend pointed out.

'Don't I? Do you doubt it yourself?'

Woodend remembered the dream he had been so rudely awoken from by the arrival of the two Guardia Civil constables. The *brigadistas* who had been ambushed on the beach in Benicelda must carry similar memories around in their own heads – must dream similar dreams – and, unlike the soldiers involved in the Normandy landing, they could put a name and a face to the man responsible for the hell they had been forced to live through.

'Do you doubt it?' López repeated.

'No, probably not,' Woodend said reluctantly.

'So you see why I need your help – the help of a man who has risen through the ranks not by influence, but because of his own brilliance?'

'Flattery doesn't wash with me, especially when it comes from your lips,' Woodend said. 'Besides, the British Embassy would never wear it. An' even if it did, the Spanish authorities wouldn't countenance me pokin' around in the investigation.'

'You are wrong,' López told him. 'Both your embassy and my masters in Madrid are eager that you should be involved.'

'Why? Because they also know what a "brilliant" detective I am?'

'Yes.'

'Or could it be that the international press

are more likely to accept the evidence if I'm the one who produces it?'

'There is that, as well,' López admitted.

'In other words, you need me to *legitimize* your investigation.'

'It would be legitimate because it was *your* investigation.'

'I won't do it,' Woodend said firmly.

'You cannot resist the challenge.'

'Just watch me!'

'You would let me flounder around like a fish out of water?'

'It would be a pleasure.'

'And what about your conscience?'

'*What* about it?'

'Would your conscience allow you to stand back, knowing that there is a risk I might arrest the wrong man – and perhaps even get him convicted?'

No, it wouldn't, Woodend thought. An' you bloody *know* it wouldn't!

'Before I agree to help, there are some conditions that have to be met,' the Chief Inspector said heavily.

'Anything,' López agreed.

'You'd better hear them first,' Woodend advised him. 'This will be a very different investigation to the one into Medwin's death. I need freedom to go where I like, and to question whoever I want to. An' I don't want you by my side, buggerin' things up in the way you have so far.'

'Agreed.'

'Also, since I'll be talkin' to a lot of Spaniards, I'll need to have a translator.'

'But why should you wish to talk to any Spaniards when it is plain that the murderers—'

'As I said, I need freedom to go where I like, and to question whoever I want to.'

'All right. I will provide you with a translator. I have a lieutenant who has done a course at the University of Salamanca, and could probably—'

'I choose my own translator,' Woodend interrupted.

'But you do not know anyone who could do the job.'

'Yes, I do.'

'Who?'

'Paco Ruiz.'

He'd had other plans for that particular pain in the arse, López reminded himself. Ruiz had learned the *Alcalde*'s secret, and thus had been due to suffer a fatal accident – laid on by two of the Captain's best men – that very morning. But now Durán was dead, and there was no one left to blackmail anymore, Ruiz might as well be allowed to live.

Even so, López was reluctant to let Ruiz anywhere near the case – because while it was going to be difficult enough to pull the wool over one seasoned detective's eyes, it would be even harder if there were two of them.

'You must understand that Ruiz is not reliable,' the Captain said. 'During the Civil War, he was a—'

'I know all about that. He's still the one I want. In fact, he's the *only* one who's acceptable to me. If I can't have him, then I don't want the job.'

'I see,' López said.

'So do I get him, or not?' Woodend asked.

'You get him,' López replied, with bad grace.

Twenty-Six

The two bodies lay just outside the kitchen door, where they had died the night before. They were about twelve feet apart, and had been draped with thick woollen Guardia Civil blankets.

'I assume that somebody saw to it that all the proper forensic tests were carried out before the corpses were contaminated by havin' them blankets put over them,' Woodend said.

'This is Spain,' Paco Ruiz told him.

'Assume nothing.'

Aye, assume nothin', Woodend thought.

That just about summed it up. If he'd been conducting this investigation in Whitebridge, he'd never have allowed half a dozen of his bobbies to go tramping around all over the place, which was just what Captain López *had* let his Guardia Civil officers do.

'I suppose we'd better take a look at the stiffs, then,' Woodend said to Paco Ruiz. 'Can you ask the constable to remove the covering?'

Paco conveyed the request, and the constable who had been standing on duty over the bodies bent down and stripped the blankets away with a lack of care which made Woodend wince.

The body to the left of the door had been stabbed in the back, and there was evidence of bruising round his neck.

'What do you think?' Woodend asked.

'This man was used to persuade the other guard to come outside,' Paco Ruiz said. 'Once he had fulfilled that function, he was no longer of any use, so the killer dispatched him with a single thrust of his knife. That's not an easy thing to do. And I know, because I've done it myself. So whatever else the murderer is, he's certainly an expert at his trade.'

'He probably had plenty of practice durin' that Civil War of yours,' Woodend said.

The second victim had been stabbed in the chest. 'From the angle of the wound, I would say that the knife was thrown rather than thrust,' Paco said. 'Once again, that is not an easy trick to pull off.'

'No, it can't be,' Woodend agreed. 'Ask the constable who it was that found these poor buggers.'

A short exchange followed, then Paco said, 'The maid found them, as she reported for work.'

'She doesn't live in?'

'None of the servants do – apart from the bodyguard. Durán seemed to like his privacy, and if the rumours I have heard about his sexual activities are true, I can understand why.'

'Where's the maid now?'

'She's in the parlour.'

'Then we'd better go an' talk to her, hadn't we?'

The maid was called Conchita. She was in her early twenties, and looked very shaken up.

Paco gave her his warmest smile. 'What did you do when you found the bodies outside the kitchen door?'

'I went to tell Don Antonio. But he was ... he was...'

'He was dead as well.'

'Yes.'

'So then you phoned the Guardia Civil?'

'That's right.'

'Did you touch anything before they arrived here?'

'No,' Conchita said, far too quickly.

'You're sure?'

'No, I ... I mean yes, I'm sure.'

'We're investigating a murder,' Paco said gently. 'We're not interested in any lesser crimes.'

Conchita looked down at the floor. 'Don Antonio kept some cash hidden at the bottom of his tobacco jar,' she confessed. 'He didn't think I knew, but I did. When I saw that he was dead, I took it.'

'And where is it now?'

Conchita reached into the pocket in her uniform.

'I didn't ask to see it,' Paco said. 'I only wanted to know where it was. Is it in your pocket?'

Tears came to Conchita's eyes. 'I didn't *mean* to steal it, *señor*. It was just that—'

'You *didn't* steal it,' Paco interrupted her. 'Durán owed you back-wages, and by some happy coincidence, the amount he owed you was exactly equal to the amount in the tobacco jar. Isn't that right?'

'Yes,' Conchita said, unconvincingly.

'Then we'll say no more about it. Tell me, Conchita, what was the *Alcalde* like to work for?'

'Should I answer you honestly?'

'If you didn't, there would be no point in answering at all.'

'He was a pig. He treated me like a piece of dirt. And so did Luis, his chauffeur.'

'Did many people come to the villa? Did Don Antonio entertain a great deal?'

'He was the *Alcalde*,' Conchita said, as if puzzled as to why he'd bothered to ask the question.

'What's that got to do with it?' Paco wondered.

'Why should he pay out his own money to entertain others, when, in the hope of gaining some advantage, they were more than willing to entertain him?'

'But he did *have* visitors?'

'Not many.'

'Who has been to see him recently?'

'You came,' Conchita said evasively.

'Anybody else?'

'Perhaps.'

'Ah, I see,' Paco said. 'It was someone important! Someone you are afraid of. If you tell me who it was, I promise I will never say that I got the information from you.'

Conchita bit her lip. 'Captain López was here,' she said. 'Once yesterday, and once the day before.'

'And what did he and the Mayor talk about?'

'I don't know. But the first time, the Captain looked very angry when he was leaving.'

'And the second time?'

'The second time, it was the Mayor who looked angry.'

'I have just remembered something that happened when I was here the other day,' Paco said.

'You have?'

'Yes. I heard the *Alcalde* talking to you. He said that there were some fairly valuable things in this house that he wanted to give you as presents. I can't recall exactly what they were, but no doubt you can. Whatever they were, I would take them with you when you go home.'

'But what about the police?'

'They won't mind – especially if they don't see you doing it.'

Durán was slumped down on his desk. It wasn't easy for Woodend and Paco Ruiz to lift the fat man up into a sitting position – and when they had, they almost wished they hadn't.

'The cause of death is fairly obviously a stab wound to the heart,' Woodend said. 'An' there must have been some force behind it to cut through all them layers of flab.'

'And once he had killed Durán, the murderer began his real work,' Paco Ruiz added sombrely.

The *real* work had involved mutilating the

head. The killer had cut off both Durán's ears, then sliced through his tongue. All three organs had been placed neatly on the blotting pad at the edge of the *Alcalde*'s desk. Having completed that grisly task, he had then sliced Durán nose from top to bottom, hacking through the bone as he went. Finally – and it did seem to both Woodend and Ruiz that this *was* the last thing he did – he had gouged out the Mayor's eyes.

'Once more, I have to say that this was the work of a true craftsman,' Paco Ruiz said.

'So we've learned two things about him,' Woodend replied, 'the first bein' that he's exceptionally gifted with a knife.'

'And what's the second?' Paco asked.

'That whoever he is, he didn't seem to *like* your *Alcalde* much.'

Twenty-Seven

Woodend and Ruiz were already seated at the table in the interrogation room when the Guardia Civil constable led the American in. Mitchell looked rough – even worse than he had the day before. His eyes were yellow, and his cheeks so hollow that they seemed almost to be touching each other.

'Sit down, Mr Mitchell,' Woodend said.

Mitchell lowered himself gingerly into the chair opposite him; the constable took up a position next to the door.

'Is this another of those informal questioning sessions, or am I under arrest this time?' Mitchell asked.

'You're under arrest this time,' Woodend said.

Mitchell laughed, though the laugh rapidly turned into a cough.

'How ironic,' he said when he'd finally recovered.

'What is?'

'To be charged with a killing I fully intended to carry out, but didn't actually do because someone else got there first.'

'So you're no longer denyin' you came here to murder Durán?'

'I came here to *execute* Durán. But I alone had that intention. The others didn't know what I was planning. They thought we were just here to talk to him – to persuade him to confess his guilt.'

'Bollocks!' Woodend said.

'That's only your opinion. And even if you're right, it doesn't really matter – because that's what I shall tell the state prosecutor, and that's what I shall tell the judge.'

'Shall I tell you what *I* think?' Woodend asked.

'Why not? A man who's been placed under arrest has no other real demands on his time.'

'I think that you've worked out that even if one of your mates *didn't* kill the Mayor, somebody's goin' to have to go to gaol for even *plannin'* to do it. And I think you've decided that that somebody might as well be you, since you're already a dying man.'

Mitchell gave a weak smile. 'It's *that* obvious, is it?'

'It's *that* obvious,' Woodend agreed. 'My father had cancer. He looked just like you do now, towards the end. How long have you got left?'

'A month. Maybe two – if I'm unlucky.'

Woodend nodded. 'Well, since you're willing to take the blame for everythin' that's happened on your own shoulders, is there any harm in fillin' me in on any gaps in your story?'

'I suppose not.'

'You and the rest of them met when you were all in the International Brigade, didn't you?'

'Yes, we did.'

Dupont – or at least the man who was calling himself Dupont now – had been the first to reach Spain. He had been a member of the Commune de Paris Battalion, and arrived in Aragon in late 1936. Schneider had joined the German

Thaelmann Battalion, and got there a few weeks later. Sutcliffe, Roberts and Medwin had arrived in early 1937, with the British Battalion. Mitchell himself, having joined the Abraham Lincoln Brigade in New York, was not far behind them.

'Some of our group – some of the men who ended up on the beach – met at the Battle of the Jarama, when we were defending Madrid,' Mitchell said. 'We didn't get to know the rest until much later, when we were in retreat and making a last stand at the Battle of the Ebro, near Valencia.'

'What were you even *doin'* on that beach in March?' Woodend asked. 'I thought the League of Nations had evacuated the International Brigade long before then.'

'Why, so it had,' Mitchell agreed. 'The Brigade held its farewell parade in Barcelona in the middle of November. Unfortunately, due to circumstances beyond our control, we couldn't be there.'

It was a desperate final struggle on the River Ebro. The Nationalists had more artillery and more soldiers – as well as German planes and Italian troops to back them up – and though the Republicans fought heroically, the result was a foregone conclusion from the very start.

The British Battalion, which now included Dupont, Schneider and Mitchell, suffered seventy-five percent casualties, and towards the end of September, they were pulled out of the fighting. But not all of them crossed the river back into what was left of Republican Spain. Not all of them could.

'We were cut off from our battalion during the fighting,' Mitchell said. 'There were a hundred thousand enemy troops between us and safety.'

'So what did you do?' Woodend asked.

'What *could* we do? We took to the mountains. It was the only place we knew we would be safe.'

Snow was already starting to fall when they reached the foothills of the sierra, yet they had no choice but to push on. They survived the winter because there were still a few brave peasants around who were prepared to share with them what small amounts of food they had. And because Pete Medwin – funny little Pete Medwin – categorically refused to allow them to die.

When the snows melted, they headed for Valencia, travelling by night and hiding by day. It was a miracle they ever made it, but they did.

They found themselves in a city all but already defeated, but a city which still felt that it owed them a debt.

'Your escape is impossible from Valencia,' said the official of the crumbling government who received a deputation of the brigadistas *in his*

office. 'But if you attempt to leave from further down the coast – from a small port rather than a large one – there is a chance that you will make it.'

'Tell us what we have to do,' Medwin said, because by now Medwin spoke for them all.

'You must go to Benicelda. I am afraid I can spare you no transport to take you there, but—'

'We got this far under our own steam. We can make it a little further down the coast.'

'It has been arranged for a ship to pick you up. The local fishermen will ferry you out to it.' The official paused. 'There is one more thing. One more request I have to make of you who have already done so much for us.'

'Name it,' Medwin said.

The official pointed to four small crates which were in the corner of the room. 'Take them with you.'

'May I ask what is in them?'

'All that we can spare. Some gold bullion. Some foreign currency. Works of art which can be sold once you have reached England.'

'And what am I to do with the cash we raise?'

'There are four thousand Basque children in exile in an army camp in England. See that they get the money.'

'An' that's what Durán stole,' Woodend said.

'And that's what Durán stole,' Mitchell agreed. 'I think I hate him more for that than for anything else he did. We were soldiers,

242

and even if the ambush was cowardly, we had always known the risks we were running. But to steal money out of the mouths of children who were probably orphans by then – or would be orphans as soon as Franco got his hands on their parents – was unforgivable.'

'How many of you survived the ambush?' Woodend asked.

'Twelve. But even we didn't get away totally unscathed. Dupont had been hit in the shoulder, Roberts had taken a couple of bullets in the leg. They slowed us down, the two of them, but we didn't mind. We only did for them what they'd have done for us, if our positions had been reversed.'

'How did you escape in the end?'

'Over the Pyrenees. Once we were in France, we were fine. The French looked after us. They appreciated that in fighting against fascism, we'd been fighting for them. A few months later, of course, when Hitler invaded, they were involved in the same struggle themselves. But we were long gone by then.'

'How did you find each other again, after all these years?'

'We didn't have to.'

Medwin ordered a halt when they reached the orchard, and they took shelter from the sun under the trees. Some of the apples had already fallen to the ground, and were being attacked by a small army of wasps. Birds flew overhead, and tiny insects buzzed busily in the grass.

Medwin studied his men. Dupont's shoulder had given him a great deal of trouble during the trek, but now there was only a slight stiffness to show that he had ever been hit. Roberts still walked with a limp, but the gangrene they had feared would set in had never materialized. The rest of them were exhausted and undernourished, but now that they had reached safety at last, they would soon begin to recover their strength.

From his jacket pocket, Medwin took a folded piece of newspaper. 'I've had this with me since we were in Valencia, but I was waiting for an appropriate time to read it to you,' he said. 'That time has now come. This is a speech made by La Pasionaria.'

'La Pasionaria was one of the leaders of the Communists,' Mitchell explained.

'I know who she was,' Woodend told him.

'It is the speech she made at the Brigade's final parade,' Medwin continued. 'A parade which we missed because we had a few other things to keep us busy at the time.'

It wasn't much of a joke, but it was still the funniest thing they had heard for a long time, and the men laughed appreciatively.

'As I read the words, I want you to imagine that we were there,' Medwin said, growing more

244

serious. *'I want you to picture her saying the words to you.'* He cleared his throat. *' "You can go proudly. You are history. You are legend. You are the heroic example of democracy's solidarity and universality ... We shall not forget you, and when the olive tree of peace puts forth its leaves again, mingled with the laurels of the Spanish Republic's victory – come back!" '*

There was a lump in Medwin's throat, and tears in the eyes of all the men he was reading to.

'We can go proudly,' Medwin said. *'We are history. We are legend. And just as Spain will not forget us, we must never forget Spain. Or each other. People drift apart. That must not happen to us. We must keep in touch, and if one of us ever needs the others, the others must answer the call.'*

'We *did* keep in touch,' Mitchell said. 'And we read the papers – learned of the terrible things that were happening in the country where our comrades had spilled their blood. We didn't like what we read, but we didn't think there was anything we could do about it. Then it was announced that that butcher Durán was to have new honours heaped on him, and suddenly it all seemed too much to take.'

'So you came back.'

'Those of us who still could. Two of our comrades are dead, the others are not strong enough to travel. But we six, who still had the strength, *did* come back – as we had been invited to by La Pasionaria – to see justice done.'

'Who killed Durán?' Woodend asked.

'I don't know.'

'It has to have been one of you.'

'He must have had other enemies.'

'Enemies who could have killed him at any time, but who waited until you were here before they did it?'

'It's possible.'

'I'll find the murderer, you know,' Woodend said. 'I always do.'

'But why should you want to? If anyone ever deserved to die, it was that bastard Durán.'

'An' what about the others – the two young men who were killed. Did they deserve to die, too?'

'One of them perhaps did.'

'Why's that?'

'Someone pushed Pete Medwin off that balcony, and since it is unlikely it was Durán himself, it was probably one of them.'

'An' what if it wasn't? What if it was somebody else who was working for Durán?'

'Then their deaths were unfortunate.'

'Unfortunate?'

'Wrong!' Mitchell corrected himself. 'Then their deaths were *wrong*.'

'But they're still dead, aren't they? There's no way you can turn back the clock, an' make it right again.'

'I know.'

'That's the trouble with vigilante justice,' Woodend said. 'Once you've decided you've got the right to play God, you don't just cross the line – you stop seein' that there's any line there at all.'

Twenty-Eight

The constable who arrived at the interrogation room with Schneider was not the same one who had escorted Mitchell.

In fact he was *very* different, Woodend thought.

This man's eyes had a keener intelligence. He didn't look like a constable – a foot-soldier, a drudge – at all. Which meant that he probably wasn't. So what he was likely to be instead, Woodend decided, was the lieutenant that López had mentioned earlier –the one who had learned his English at the University of Salamanca.

Woodend fixed his gaze on the corner of the room. 'I'm afraid I'm goin' to have to ask you to leave, officer,' he said, in a flat, tone-less voice.

'*Qué?*' the Spanish policeman said.

Woodend swung round to face him. 'How did you know I was talkin' to you?' he asked.

The other man looked confused – as well he might.

So already López was going back on his word. Already he was trying to elbow his way into an investigation which he had promised Woodend he could conduct with complete independence. Well, the Chief Inspector supposed, that was only to be expected.

'If you want to keep on pretendin' to be a complete bloody ignoramus, then I'm perfectly happy to go along with it,' Woodend said. He turned to Paco Ruiz. 'Tell the "constable" that he has to leave now.'

Paco conveyed the message.

The constable-lieutenant shook his head agitatedly. '*No es possible.*'

'He says—'

'Even with my Spanish, I could understand that much,' Woodend said. 'So tell him this! Tell him to *make* it possible. Tell him that if he doesn't go now, I'm walkin' out of here and not comin' back. Ask him how Captain López is likely to feel when he realizes that my pulling out of the case is all his fault.'

Paco duly went through the charade, though it was plain from the expression on the officer's face that no translation was really necessary.

'Well?' Woodend asked.

The constable-lieutenant hesitated for a

moment, then made his way reluctantly to the door. The moment he had left the room, the portly German brought his hand together and began to clap.

'What's that in aid of?' Woodend asked.

'Your performance,' Schneider said.

'My performance?'

'What else would you call it, Chief Inspector? The man was clearly not what he was pretending to be, but it would have done no harm to have him remain. By sending him out against his wishes, you have demonstrated to me that, despite the fact you are a foreigner, you are also a man with authority. This is intended to make me much more willing to answer your questions.'

'Are you suggestin' that we rehearsed that little confrontation?'

'Of course not. It would have been far less convincing if he had only been playing a part. His reactions were perfectly genuine. You were the only real actor in the piece.'

'It wasn't like that at all,' Woodend protested. 'I just thought that the questionin' might go easier—'

He stopped suddenly, as he realized that though Schneider was accusing him of playing a game, the German was playing one himself. He probably didn't believe a word of what he'd said, but by pretending to believe it, he'd put his interrogator on the defensive – had, in effect, taken charge.

'You thought the questioning would go easier if ... ?' Schneider asked innocently.

'Sit down,' Woodend said gruffly.

The German studied the chair the Chief Inspector had indicated. 'Very narrow,' he said. 'I would be uncomfortable on that. Which is, of course, your intention.'

'It's no wider or narrower than any other chair in this station,' Woodend told him. 'You can accuse me of plannin' a lot of things, but you can't blame me for your own fat arse. So will you sit down, please, Herr Schneider.'

The German sat. 'It is not so bad after all,' he conceded.

'You must have learned your basic English in the Brigade,' Woodend said. 'But it's much better than basic now, so I expect you took advanced courses once you were back in Germany. Am I right?'

'I studied the language at the University of Bonn,' Schneider said. 'Or perhaps it was the University of Berlin. Then again, perhaps I married an English woman.' He laughed. 'If you are trying to make me say things which will help you to uncover my background, Chief Inspector, you will have to be much more subtle than that.'

'Even if you don't let anythin' slip, how long do you think it will be before your government is able to provide us with documents which establish your true identity?' Woodend asked.

Schneider shrugged his heavy shoulders. 'I should think it will not take more than a day or two. We Germans keep very good records. But that is still no reason why I should do your work for you.'

'You don't seem very concerned about us finding out who you really are.'

'Why should I be?'

'Mitchell was.'

'Mitchell has had problems in his country as a result of what he did in Spain. His government doesn't like it at all. In fact, American members of the Brigade were not allowed to fight against the Reich in the Second World War. Did you know that? They were not to be trusted, you see. My government does not view things in quite the same light. I am not a man who fought *for* the communists, but one who fought *against* the fascists – and in Germany that makes me a hero.'

'You're not worried that because you're travellin' under false papers you might actually go to prison here in Spain?'

'Perhaps. But after my years in the concentration camp that Adolf Hitler—' Schneider broke off and smiled – but it was a worried smile. 'Very clever, Chief Inspector,' he said.

The German raised his hands, so that, though the palms were pointing towards each other, they were at least two feet apart. His fingers began to undulate, as though he

251

was playing something.

A piano accordion! Woodend thought. In his mind, he was playing a piano accordion.

'*Now* you're concerned, aren't you?' he asked. 'You might have survived the concentration camp, but you were a lot younger then.'

Schneider's fingers came to a rest. He looked considerably calmer than he had a few moments earlier.

'As I said, I am a hero,' he told Woodend. 'My government will not let me remain in a Spanish prison for long.'

'Unless we can prove that you were implicated in the murder of Antonio Durán and his two bodyguards.'

'But I was not. And I have an alibi to prove it.'

'What kind of alibi?'

'I was with my comrades.'

'All night?'

'No, I was not with *all* of them *all* night. But at the time Durán was probably killed, I was certainly with one of them.'

'An' which one of them might that be?'

'I was with Dupont.'

'Ah, I see,' Woodend said thoughtfully. 'You were with *Dupont*.' He searched around in his mind for some sharp mental instrument he could use to break through Schneider's veneer of confidence. 'Are you lovers?' he asked. 'Is that why you spent the night together?'

Schneider laughed. 'Are you hoping to *shame* me into confessing to the murder? Do you think I would rather be taken for a killer than be thought a homosexual?'

'I don't know. Which one are you?'

'Neither! I have seven children. And Dupont claims to have three mistresses. Of course, he is French, so he may be exaggerating a little, to make himself seem more virile than he really is.'

'So if it wasn't for sex, why *did* you spend the night together?'

'For security, of course. After Medwin was killed, we decided that there was safety in numbers.'

'So why didn't *all of you* stay together?'

'Perhaps we would have done once – when we were young. But we are getting old, and we are getting soft. Two of us could sleep quite comfortably in one of those modest hotel rooms. More would have been difficult.'

'Then who got left out?'

'I am sorry?'

'Only two could sleep in one room, and there were five of you. So who got left out?'

'Mitchell.'

'Why him?'

'It was his choice, not ours. He told us that he would prefer to be alone.'

'Why do you think that was?'

'I didn't think at all. If you want to know the answer, you must ask him yourself.'

Dupont seemed as much at ease as his German comrade had.

'So you spent the night of the murder with Schneider, did you?' Woodend asked.

'*Oui.*'

'An' is he still as good a lover as he used to be?'

Dupont smirked. 'You English are so funny.'

'Are we? In what way?'

'You are so afraid of being thought a homosexual zat if you brush against each other accidentally, you are full of apology. Ze exception, of course, is if you are playing *le rugby*. Zen you maul each other as much as you wish. Me, I am French. I do not lust after uzzer men, but if I did, I would not be ashame of it. And my friend, Schneider, he have seven children – or so he claim.'

'You don't believe him?'

'Per'aps he have two or three. He only say seven to make him look like a stallion.'

'This isn't a joke!' Woodend said, finally losing his temper.

'It is not?'

'Four men have been killed!'

'*One* man have been killed – one man and three vermin.'

'You didn't even know the two guards who

were murdered. What right do you have to call them vermin?'

'I judge a man by the company he keep. If I were not me, I would be proud to be one of my comrades instead. Any man who work for that butcher Durán deserve what he get. Beside, somebody kill Medwin. You don't think that was one of Durán's bodyguards?'

'You can't go takin' the law into your hands,' Woodend said.

'Why not?' Dupont asked. 'It seem to work out pretty well for that bastard Franco.'

Woodend and Ruiz sat at a table in the bar closest to the Guardia Civil barracks. Woodend had asked for a beer, the Spaniard had chosen *sol y sombra* – a near-lethal mixture of brandy and anis.

'They've worked out their story together, and they think that they're untouchable,' Woodend complained.

'Perhaps they are. Perhaps, after all, they are not guilty.'

'They came here to kill Durán. They thought they had reason enough for that before they ever set foot in Spain. Then one of their number is murdered, and they suspect – naturally enough – that Durán is behind it. They wouldn't be human if they just sat back and took that.'

'They wouldn't be human if they just sat back and took it,' Paco repeated. 'Do you know what your problem is, Charlie?'

'No, but I'm sure you're about to tell me.'

'At least part of you is on their side. And does that part of you truly want to see them punished for murdering the *Alcalde*?'

'I don't know,' Woodend admitted.

'Have you ever let a guilty man go free before?'

Woodend thought of the investigation involving the Dark Lady of Westbury. 'Once,' he said.

Paco smiled. 'The second time is always easier.'

Woodend shook his head. 'I don't think it'll *ever* get easier. Besides, as much as I may dislike the guilty man being arrested, I've got an even stronger aversion to an innocent man taking the rap. And if we don't find the killer, that's what Captain López is goin' to make sure happens.'

'Ah yes, Captain López,' Paco Ruiz said enigmatically.

'An' what, exactly, do you mean by that?'

'I am not sure. But neither am I sure that López's involvement in the case is as straightforward as it might seem.'

'If you have somethin' you think that you should tell me...'

'I have nothing at all. Believe me, I would already have told you if I had.'

Woodend took another sip of his beer. That morning, it tasted like gnat's piss, though he was prepared to admit that the fault might not be with the beer but with himself.

'It would be nice if we could somehow tie López in with the killin's though, wouldn't it?' he said.

'It would be delightful,' Paco Ruiz agreed.

Twenty-Nine

The two Guardia Civil constables had been assigned the task of searching the hotel rooms which had been occupied by the *brigadistas*. They had begun their task full of enthusiasm – and in the clear expectation that they would uncover some vital piece of evidence which would both solve the case and put them firmly in Captain López's good books. So far, they had had no luck at all.

They had searched Mitchell's room first. They had admired his American clothes – such quality was simply not available in any of the shops they had access to – but since all the labels had been removed, there was nothing to be learned from them. They discovered several bottles of pills, but they seemed more like drugs prescribed by a doctor than anything he might have bought illegally for his own decadent pleasure.

Roberts's room had been next. Here they had found several packs of playing cards, a notebook full of complicated mathematical calculations, and several pages from old foreign newspapers with pictures of horses on them. Roberts's clothes, like the ones belonging to his friend Mitchell, had had all their labels carefully removed.

It was as they were about to enter the third room – Dupont's – that they realized they were not alone and, looking round, they saw that Captain López was standing in the corridor.

The two men snapped to attention and saluted. 'At your orders, my Captain,' the senior one said.

'You have not found anything?' López asked, without much expectation in his voice.

'No, my Captain. I am sorry, my Captain.'

López nodded. 'I cannot expect you to find something when there is nothing to be found,' he said, with uncharacteristic sympathy and understanding. 'This is the Frenchman's room, no?'

'Yes, my Captain.'

'I will search this one personally.'

The *guardias* exchanged an instinctive – and puzzled – look. It was not at all like López to get his hands dirty by doing actual police work. That kind of thing, he had

258

always said, was what he had constables for.

'You will search it, my Captain?' one of the constables asked, to make sure that he had heard right.

'I will search it,' López repeated.

'You do not wish us to assist you?'

'I do not. I wish you to search the German's room.'

The constables saluted again, turned as smartly as the narrow corridor would permit, and marched off towards Schneider's room.

López opened Dupont's door. He was not entirely sure that he would find something incriminating in the Frenchman's room, but that hardly mattered since he had brought something incriminating with him.

'So you and Roberts spent the night of Durán's murder in the same bedroom, Mr Sutcliffe?' Woodend asked the man with the shock of grey hair.

'Yes.'

'And neither of you left the room?'

'No.'

'Not even for half an hour?'

'Half an hour would not have been enough time. It would have taken much longer than that to walk to Durán's villa, do what had to be done, and return to the hotel.'

Woodend raised a surprised eyebrow. 'Now how would you know how long it would take to get to Durán's villa?' he asked.

'I am the eyes on earth of the Lord, and it is His divine spirit which leads—'

'You're a fake, Mr Sutcliffe,' Woodend interrupted.

Sutcliffe looked as if he'd just been slapped. 'I'm a *what*?'

'You're a fake. I'm not sayin' you're not sincere about your religion – I wouldn't know about that, one way or the other. But for all your hellfire an' damnation rhetoric, you're a practical man when we really get down to it.'

'I am a servant of the Lord who—'

'A practical man,' Woodend repeated. 'You'd never have survived the Civil War if you hadn't been. An' your comrades would not have allowed you to come back with them if they hadn't been sure you could play your part in the operation. So I'll ask you again – how do you happen to know how long it would take to get to Durán's villa?'

'It was my job to know,' Sutcliffe said sullenly.

'An' what does that mean, exactly?'

'In the old days, I worked with Whistling D—'

'Go on,' Woodend encouraged.

'In the old days, I worked with Dupont. We were the scouts. We went ahead and surveyed any area before the rest of the battalion moved into it. We saved a great many lives that way.'

'So you're sayin' that you scouted out Durán's villa?'

'Yes.'

'When was this?'

'The day I arrived. Before the others got here.'

'An' *why* did you do it? Because you'd already made up your mind that his villa was the place where Durán was goin' to meet his end?'

'No.'

'Oh come on, Mr Sutcliffe! That must have been your reasonin'. It would have been a wasted journey otherwise.'

'No journey a scout makes is ever wasted,' Sutcliffe said. 'He does not know what information he will eventually need, so he collects all the data he can.'

'He's a bit like a bobby in that way, then,' Woodend said.

'Yes, I suppose he is,' Sutcliffe agreed, as if he were surprised to discover that he might have something in common with a policeman.

'The scout an' the bobby have a wider view than most people. We don't just see the picture itself, we see what goes into makin' the picture the way it is.'

'That's true, we do.'

'Why was Mitchell the only one who slept alone on the night of the murder?' Woodend

261

asked, suddenly switching tack.

All signs of what had been a growing empathy drained from Sutcliffe's face.

'You would not understand,' he said, his tone now a mixture of pity and contempt. 'You, who value the material things of life above all else, could never even begin to comprehend the true nobility of Mitchell's soul.'

'He set himself up as the sacrificial lamb, didn't he?' Woodend said.

'I don't know what you mean,' Sutcliffe countered.

But it was plain that he did.

'He'd come to the conclusion that with all the security surroundin' Durán, it was goin' to be impossible to get to him, so he saw no choice but to go about matters another way entirely.' Woodend paused for a second. 'It's not too difficult to trace the lines his mind must have run along, you know. He'll have argued that Durán had hoped that by killin' Medwin he'd scare you all into leavin', but since that hadn't worked, the *Alcalde* would have no choice but to kill again. An' this time, Mr Sutcliffe – *this time* – Mitchell decided he was goin' to make it easy for him.'

'Why would he have done that?'

'Because there was always a chance that Durán would make a mistake an' get caught. An' that would mean that even if he couldn't be punished for what he did to your comrades on the beach – or for what he did to Medwin – he could at least be prosecuted for killin' someone else – a man who was dyin' of cancer anyway.'

'You're guessing,' Sutcliffe accused.

'I know I am,' Woodend agreed. 'But I'm right, aren't I?'

'Yes, you're right,' Sutcliffe said heavily. 'He told me his plan in confidence. I tried to talk him out of it. I told him to put his faith in God. But he wouldn't listen to me.'

'Of course, he wouldn't have to make the sacrifice at all if somebody got to Durán before Durán got to him,' Woodend said. 'And somebody did! Did you kill Antonio Durán, Mr Sutcliffe?'

'No, I did not.'

'To your knowledge, did any other member of your group kill Antonio Durán?'

'No, they did not.'

The denials were flowing far too easily, Woodend thought. Perhaps that was because he was not asking the right question.

'Did *God* kill Antonio Durán, using one of you as His chosen instrument?' he demanded.

'I have said all I intend to say,' Sutcliffe told him. 'You may flay my skin or cast me into the lion's den, but I will say no more.'

Captain López and his two uniformed constables stood in the spacious grounds of Don

263

Antonio Durán's luxury villa. In front of them was the crystal blue sea. Behind them towered the majestic brown mountains of the *sierra*. But they had not come to admire the view.

'We found nothing of any importance in any of the *brigadistas*' rooms,' the Captain said. 'That is regrettable. But perhaps we will have more luck with our search of the *Alcalde*'s garden.'

The two constables glanced furtively at each other, and reached an unspoken agreement that the senior of the two should ask the question that they both wanted answered.

'We are not quite sure what it is we are looking for, my Captain.' the constable said.

'You are looking for anything which will tie the foreign *hijos de puta* in with the murder of Don Antonio.'

'For example?'

López sighed heavily. 'I would have been better served by a team of trained donkeys,' he said. 'Or monkeys! Monkeys have brains. You, it seems do not.'

'If you could give us a hint of what you want, my Captain...'

'Find me a footprint or a scrap of clothing, for God's sake. Something – *anything* – that belongs to one of the *brigadistas*. *Now* do you understand what I want?'

'Yes, my Captain,' the constable said. 'I am

sorry to have been so stupid, my Captain.'

'I will put in a requisition for a troupe of monkeys in the morning,' López said. He looked around him. 'Start your search with the rose bed. And go carefully. I do not want you to damage any of the flowers.'

The constables walked over to the rose bed and – wishing they'd thought to bring gloves with them – began to gingerly part the prickly stems and peer between them.

'Have you found anything yet?' López called out impatiently.

'Not yet, my Captain.'

'Then keep looking. I have a strong instinct about that particular spot.'

He had no sooner spoken than the senior constable *did* notice something – an object gleaming in the sunlight, at the very centre of the rose bed.

'My Captain!' he called. 'My Captain! Come quickly.'

Thirty

'Do you know what makes you different to your comrades, Mr Roberts?' Woodend asked.

The thin-faced man grinned. 'There are many things which make me different,' he said. 'I'm a freer spirit than they are. I'm prepared to take chances they're not. If any of the others had run the risks I ran in the war, they'd be dead. But I have a charmed life.'

'You're not just saying that, are you?' Woodend asked, with genuine curiosity. 'You really do believe it.'

'A gambler has to believe it if he is to continue to gamble,' Roberts replied. 'But what's the thing that *you* think sets me apart from the others?'

'They're all travelling under false names,' Woodend said. 'An' I can see why they would be. A man plannin' a murder wants to be as anonymous as possible. But you're *not* using an alias.'

'Aren't I? What makes you so sure of that?'

'*Sutcliffe* makes me sure of it. He was prepared to swear he hadn't known the others

266

under the names they're usin' now, but he wasn't willin' to do the same for you.'

'So you're right, and I really am called Roberts,' the other man admitted. 'What of it?'

'Why didn't you bother to take the same precautions as the rest of your mates did?'

'I thought that would make the whole thing far too easy,' Roberts said. 'Where's the thrill in staking all you have in a game of poker against a man you *know* you can beat? What's the point of taking a bend in the road at speed – and on the wrong side of the road – if you're certain there is nothing coming in the other direction? Life without the element of chance – without the possibility of failure – is no life at all.'

'Did you kill Durán?'

'It's a waste of time your asking that particular question.'

'Why?'

'Because if I had, I wouldn't be likely to admit it, would I?'

'Murderers have surprised themselves by confessin' before now,' Woodend said.

'Ah, I see what you're after!' Roberts said. 'You want to *hear* me deny it. Or rather, you want to study me as I say it, to see if I'm lying. But that wouldn't work with me. I have a poker face.'

'Try it anyway,' Woodend suggested.

All expression drained from Roberts' face,

and he looked Woodend straight in the eye. 'I did not kill Durán,' he said. 'Correction – I did kill him. I'm the murderer. No, I'm not. It was somebody else.'

'You're right, I can't tell when you're lyin' or when you're not,' Woodend admitted. 'Tell me one more time.'

'I did not kill Durán,' Roberts said.

Woodend sighed. 'You spent the night Durán died in the same room as Sutcliffe, didn't you?'

'That's right.'

'An' did either of you leave the room at any point?'

'I didn't.'

'What about Sutcliffe?'

'You surely don't think Sutcliffe killed Durán!'

'It's a possibility.'

'You're on completely the wrong track. Sutcliffe's very good at talking about violence – he can quote every gruesome death in the Old Testament at you chapter and verse – but that's not the same as saying that he killed Durán.'

'Are you tryin' to tell me he went through the whole Civil War without spillin' blood?'

'No, he will have killed some of the enemy. It was hard not to, if you weren't to be killed yourself. But he'll have done it with a rifle. From a distance. He doesn't have the stomach for close-quarter fighting.'

'What about you? Do you have the stomach for it?'

'I could do anything I set my mind to.'

'*Could* do? Not could *have done*?'

Almost miraculously, Roberts started to look uncomfortable. 'I bayoneted a man once,' he said.

'In the guts?'

'That's what they always tell you to aim for.'

'An' how did you feel when it was over?'

Roberts skin was slowly acquiring a slightly green tinge. 'I didn't feel *anything*,' he said. 'It was a job I had to do, and I did it. Then I moved on to something else.'

'I bayoneted a man once, myself,' Woodend said.

'So why did you need to ask me what it felt like?'

'To see if our experiences matched.'

'And did they?'

'Not exactly. I kept on fighting, because there wasn't much choice about that. An' when the battle was over, I told myself that I could put it all behind me – that I could forget the look of agony on his face, an' the squelchin' sound as the blade sank in. The man I killed couldn't scream, you know. He wanted to, but he didn't have the air left in his lungs for it.'

'What's any of this got to do with me?' Roberts demanded angrily.

'I was quite calm until we camped for the night,' Woodend said. 'Then I started gettin' these terrible pains in my stomach. An' before I knew what was happenin', I was spewin' my ring up. Of course, you'll never have experienced anythin' like that, will you?'

'No,' Roberts gasped. 'Nothing like that. As I said, it was all in a day's work.'

'It's interesting that you don't seem to think *Sutcliffe* was involved in any fighting at close quarters,' Woodend said. 'After all, he was a scout behind enemy lines. I would have thought he'd have found himself in any number of situations when a rifle would have been too noisy to use, an' he'd have to resort to a knife instead.'

'He ... he would have told me if anything like that had happened to him,' Roberts said.

'Oh, close friends, were you? Confidants?'

'Yes.'

'Funny, that. I can't really see the man of God an' the professional sinner bein' close mates. But let's go back a bit, shall we? *Did* Sutcliffe leave the room that night?'

'I don't think so.'

'But you're not sure?'

'I was asleep.'

'Asleep?'

'That's what I said.'

'You fell asleep on the very night when you were afraid that Durán would send one of

270

his men down to the hotel to deal with you in the same way as he'd dealt with Medwin?'

'I wasn't *afraid.*'

'Of course not. You're Roberts the Gambler. You don't know the meaning of fear. So let me put it another way. You felt some *concern* that your lives might be in danger?'

'That's more like it,' Roberts agreed.

'An' in order to increase your chances of survivin' the night, you decided to sleep two to a room?'

'Yes.'

'But you didn't take it in turns to stand guard? You just *fell asleep.* You put yourselves in a position where anybody could have walked into your room and slit your throats!'

Roberts bit his lower lip. 'The door was locked,' he said.

'Locks can be picked,' Woodend pointed out. 'You knew that. If you'd thought a locked door was all the protection you needed, you'd never have doubled up.'

'All right,' Roberts agreed reluctantly. 'The plan was for us to take it in turns to stand guard. Sutcliffe took the first watch, but fell asleep himself, and the first thing either of us knew, it was morning.'

'You mean the first thing *you* knew, it was mornin'?'

'Like I said, Sutcliffe fell asleep as well.'

'Are you a heavy sleeper, Mr Roberts?'

'Not normally, no.'

271

'But you were that night?'

Roberts grinned awkwardly. 'Must have been the sea air.'

'Or else you were drugged.'

The very idea seemed to offend Roberts. 'Drugged!' he repeated. 'What do you take me for? An amateur?'

'Anyone can be drugged.'

'I'm a professional gambler,' Roberts said angrily. 'Gambling's not just dealing the cards and placing a bet, you know. It's a whole approach to life. There are always some toe-rags on the gaming circuit who'll try to slip you a Mickey Finn to take the edge off your play. You learn how to avoid it. If I'd been drugged, I'd have known about it. You can believe me on that.'

Captain López burst into the room without knocking. 'You must come up to the *Alcalde*'s villa immediately,' he told Woodend.

'An' why should I want to do that?'

'I have found vital evidence, and I do not want to touch it until you, too, have seen it where it lies.'

'What "vital evidence" are we talkin' about here?' Woodend wondered.

'The murder weapon,' López told him. 'My men and I have found the murder weapon.'

Thirty-One

'Look there,' López said, pointing into the centre of the *Alcalde*'s rose garden. 'What do you see?'

Woodend peered through the bushes. 'I see some kind of dagger,' Woodend said. 'Is it lyin' exactly where it was found? Or have you moved it?'

'Neither I, nor my men, have laid a finger on it,' López said. 'We leave that task to the "expert" from England, who did not find it himself, but will no doubt claim all the glory.'

Ignoring the comment, Woodend took a step forward and examined the ground around the knife.

'I don't see any footprints,' he said. 'An' none of the bushes look as if they've been trampled. Now why do you think that is, Captain?'

'Perhaps the killer *threw* the knife into the bushes,' López suggested.

'Perhaps he did,' Woodend replied, though he sounded far from convinced by the theory.

The Chief Inspector took a large white handkerchief out of his pocket. He knelt down at the edge of the rose garden, stretched his trunk out slowly over it, then carefully picked up the corner of the knife handle with the handkerchief, which he held between his thumb and forefinger. Having established a firm grip, he stood up again, and held the dagger out for López's inspection.

It was an evil-looking weapon. The point was as fine as a pin; the two edges looked as if they could slice through a brick with ease.

'What do you make of it?' Woodend asked.

'As you have reminded me on more than one occasion, I am not a detective,' López replied.

'I'd still like to hear what you think.'

'Fresh cord has been wound around the handle.'

'Why do you think that is?'

'Perhaps the old cord had been worn away. Or perhaps the handle had no cord on it originally, but had become so smooth with use that it was necessary to add this cord to improve the grip. Whichever is true, the evidence would suggest that it is quite an old knife – perhaps as much as thirty years old.'

'Interestin' you should say "thirty", rather than "twenty" or "forty",' Woodend commented. 'Anythin' else you'd like to add?'

'I do not think so.'

'Interestin' again. What about the hairs an'

274

the bloodstains?'

'There *are* no hairs or bloodstains.'

'Exactly,' Woodend agreed. 'An' if this was the dagger which was used in the murders, there should have been, shouldn't there?'

'Maybe the killer wiped the knife clean before he threw it away,' López suggested.

'So let me see if I've got this straight in my mind. The murderer comes running out of the villa with his weapon in his hand?'

'Yes.'

'He wants to get rid of the knife, but he's in such a hurry that instead of botherin' to hide it properly, he just throws it into the bushes?'

'Yes.'

'But he *does* find time to wipe it clean? Clean it *so well* that there's not a trace of his grisly work left on it?'

'He would not have cared about the blood and the hairs. But he would have been worried about leaving his fingerprints, so he would have wiped them away. And in doing so would have removed all traces of blood and hair as well.'

'But what did he wipe it *on*?'

'Does that matter?'

'Yes, as a matter of fact, it does. You've searched the house, an' there's no sign he cleaned the knife on anythin' in there. So what did he use? Did he wipe it on his clothes?'

'Of course not. That would be absurd.'

'Then what?'

'He had a handkerchief, as you have. Or a rag. He would have used that.'

'Then where is it?'

'Perhaps he took it with him.'

'So he ditches the knife because he thinks it might incriminate him, but he keeps the bloodstained rag?'

'It's possible.'

'An' where does he keep it? Does he carry it in his hand, where anybody he runs into will see it? Or does he stick it in his pocket, thus stainin' his clothes with the blood?'

'I think you are making difficulties where none exist,' López said. 'Why do you not turn the knife over?'

'Why should I?'

'To see what is on the other side.'

Woodend turned the knife over, and saw the words which were engraved on the hilt – *Marat et Cie, Paris*.

'A French knife,' López said.

'You don't seem at all surprised,' Woodend said accusingly.

'Do I not?'

'Bloody right, you don't. Do you know what I think? I think this is all too bloody convenient. I think you decided that Dupont was guilty – or, at least, that he was the one who was goin' to take the blame – then you arranged for the evidence to point in his direction.'

'Are you saying that I planted the knife?'

'Yes.'

'And you have reached this conclusion because I was not surprised when the knife turned out to be French?'

'Partly. You see, it could have come from anywhere. It could have been German. It could have been American. But you *knew* it was French!'

'I did *not* know. I merely suspected that was a strong possibility.'

'Because you've seen it before!'

'Because while you've been having friendly little talks with all the suspects, I have been doing some real police work.'

'You! Real police work!'

'That is what I said.'

'I'd pay a lot of money to see some evidence of that!'

'Then come with me into the *Alcalde*'s study, and I will show you all the evidence you need,' López said with quiet confidence.

López spread the photographs out on the dead *Alcalde*'s desk.

'How long have you had these?' Woodend demanded.

'Since yesterday.'

'An' why didn't you show them to me before?'

'Until I had examined them carefully, I

could not be sure that they were important.'

'But you're sure now?'

'Yes, I am.'

'Then prove it to me.'

'These are photographs taken in the *briga-distas'* camp while they were waiting for the boat to pick them up,' López said. 'From their poor quality, I would guess that either the photographer did not know his job or else he didn't want the others to be aware of the fact that he was taking their pictures. I am inclined to the second explanation.'

'So am I,' said Woodend, with new-found respect slowly edging into his voice.

'Despite the poor quality of the photographs, they still reveal much,' López said. He pointed to one of the pictures. 'Look at the two men in the foreground here. One is Medwin, the other Sutcliffe.'

Woodend peered at the picture. 'Agreed,' he said.

'But the most interesting thing is revealed in this series of pictures over here,' López continued. He reached into his jacket pocket, produced a magnifying glass, and handed it to Woodend. 'Look at the man in the corner of the picture.'

Woodend did as he'd been instructed. 'It's Dupont,' he said.

'His hand is by his side, isn't it?'

'Yes.'

'And what is he holding in it?'

278

'I'm not sure.'

'It is clearer in the second picture, when he has raised his arm.'

'It's a knife!' Woodend said. 'But we can't see it clearly enough to say that it's the knife we found in the rose garden.'

'That I *planted* in the rose garden, at least, according to you,' López said.

Woodend looked shamefaced. 'Aye, well, I might have been a bit hasty there,' he admitted. 'An' if I was, I apologize.'

'Look at the third picture,' López said. 'What is Dupont doing now?'

'He's throwin' the knife at a tree!'

'And why would he want to do that?'

'For practice!'

'Which would suggest that he is an expert in that field?'

'Yes.'

'And whoever killed the *Alcalde*'s bodyguard was also an expert with a throwing knife?'

'True. But that still doesn't mean that Dupont did it.'

'You are right,' López agreed. 'That is why I had Dupont's photograph flown up to Paris and delivered to the Ministry of the Interior.'

'An' I suppose they had a file on him.'

'Most certainly. Not that he has done anything criminal, you understand. It is simply that the security forces in France like to keep a check on men of a known left-wing back-ground. And he has certainly had an inter-esting career.'

'You're enjoyin' this, aren't you?' Woodend said.

'And why would I not?' López asked. 'Why shouldn't the Spanish political thug enjoy himself, when it turns that it is he, not the English Chief Inspector, who is the real detective?'

'I've apologized once,' Woodend said, 'but if it'll make you any happier, I'll do it again. I'm sorry I jumped to conclusions. Now bloody get on with what you've got to tell me!'

'Dupont's real name is Claude Sant. He has worked as a technical advisor to the film industry, and has helped to train the French Foreign Legion. His speciality is the use of the knife. And he has a nickname. It is one he earned during his time in Spain. Can you guess what that nickname is?'

Woodend thought back to his conversation with Sutcliffe, earlier in the day. He had been a scout, Sutcliffe had said. He had worked as a team with Dupont. Except that he hadn't called him Dupont at first.

'In the old days, I worked with Whistling D—' he had begun, before he had realized he was saying too much and stopped himself.

'Well?' López asked.

'If I had to guess, I'd say his nickname had

280

been "Whistling Death",' Woodend said.

'Whistling Death,' López repeated. 'You are standing alone on guard duty, on a dark, dark night. You hear a whistling sound in the air, and before you have time to wonder what it is, you feel a pain in your chest as the dagger buries itself there. A whistling sound must have been the last thing the *Alcalde*'s bodyguard heard, don't you think?'

Thirty-Two

The sun was setting over the sea as Woodend lifted his glass and took a sip of the local beer which he was really coming to quite enjoy.

It was the end of the case, he thought. And here they were, he and Paco Ruiz – sitting at their *usual* table, in front of their *usual* bar, ready to dot the final *i*'s and cross the final *t*'s, just as if he was back home in Whitebridge, closing things up with Rutter and Paniatowski.

It was amazing how quickly he had got to know Paco, and how well they had learned to work together. It was almost a pity that the investigation was over, and he would have to go back to trying hard to be a tourist again.

'The first time I met López, I thought he was a political thug who was more concerned with gettin' *a* result than with gettin' the *right* result,' he said. 'An' maybe that *was* the case then. Maybe it even will be again. But you can't deny that he's pulled off a nifty piece of detective footwork on this case.'

'So you believe he has the right man, do you?' Paco asked, knocking Woodend completely off balance.

'Well, I must admit that before the knife turned up, I'd have put my money on Sutcliffe,' the Chief Inspector said, a little shakily. 'The way I had it figured, he had two motives for killin' Durán. The first was the one he came here with – the desire for revenge. An' the second one – which perhaps became even *more* important – was that he wanted to get Durán before Durán could get Mitchell. So all in all, he was lookin' a very promisin' prime suspect. But you can't argue with the hard evidence, now can you?'

'Can't you?' Paco asked. 'Your first thought, when you saw the knife in the rose garden, was that it had been planted there. Why should the killer have abandoned it so close to the crime? you wondered. And where was the rag that he used to wipe it clean? They were good questions, Charlie.

Why are you not still asking yourself them now?'

'Because there are often loose ends in an investigation. Because, in the heat of the moment, murderers sometimes do stupid, irrational things. You have to learn to balance that against the main body of the evidence.'

'Balance it?' Paco asked. 'Or merely use the evidence you *do* like to discredit the evidence you *don't*?'

'Look, what are the three standard tools a bobby should apply to every investigation?' Woodend asked exasperatedly.

'You know what they are as well as I do,' Paco said, a little morosely.

'Maybe I do,' Woodend agreed. 'But just to make sure we're talking the same language, why don't you tell me what *you* think they are?'

'Motive, means and opportunity.'

'Exactly. An' we've certainly got a motive. Durán slaughtered over thirty of Dupont's comrades – or perhaps I should say *Sant's* comrades – on that beach. We've got the means, too. Sant was an expert with the throwin' knife – such an expert that he even instructed the French Foreign Legion – an' so was the man who killed Durán and his bodyguards.'

'Opportunity?' Paco asked sceptically. 'Schneider said Sant spent the night with him.'

'An' he probably thinks that he did.'

'But he is wrong?'

'Yes, he's wrong. We're almost certain that Roberts was drugged on the night of the murders, even though the cocky bugger refuses to admit it himself. When Sutcliffe was my main suspect, I thought he was the one who'd done it.'

'But you no longer think that?'

'No. I think that Sant drugged Sutcliffe, Roberts *an'* Schneider. An' that once he'd accomplished that, he went up to the villa an' did what he'd been plannin' to do all along, which was to kill Durán.'

'I thought you were the same sort of policeman that I once was,' Paco said, sadly. 'I thought you were one who had faith in his own instincts – in the feeling in his gut.'

'An' what does *your* gut tell you?'

'That López has to have been involved in framing Sant in some way.'

Woodend shook his head. 'You've got it wrong this time, Paco.'

'López had two disagreements with Durán shortly before the *Alcalde* was murdered,' Paco argued.

'An' didn't you say, from what the maid told you, he appeared to have come out on top in the second one?'

'Yes, but—'

'So if one of them had a motive to murder the other, it was Durán who had a motive to

284

murder López.'

'Perhaps they had a third argument,' Paco said. 'One that we know nothing about. One that put Durán back in control again.'

'An' perhaps there's a spring up in the mountains that gushes nothin' but Lion Best Bitter,' Woodend countered. 'It'd certainly be wonderful if there was. But things don't happen just because we'd like them to, Paco. If López had killed Durán, I can't see he'd have used a knife. An' I can't see him workin' alone, which it's plain is just what our killer did. Besides, look at the way the killer treated Durán after he'd killed him. He gouged his bloody eyes out! He slit his nose! That suggests a hatred that's been festerin' for a long, long time.'

'Perhaps that is simply what López wanted you to think.'

'López may be a complete bastard,' Woodend said. 'I suspect that he is. But that doesn't make him a murderer.'

'I'm very disappointed in you,' Paco said.

'An' I'm very disappointed that you feel the *need* to be disappointed,' Woodend countered, angry at the way things were developing, yet seeing no way to defuse the situation. 'Life's full of disappointments. I'd have thought that after all you've been through, you'd have known that. I'd have thought that your experiences would have helped you to grow up a little!'

They were teetering on the edge of their first argument – an argument that neither of them wanted. Perhaps they would have found a way to resolve it amicably, or perhaps it would have developed to the point at which they almost came to blows. They were never to find out, because at that moment a breathless clerk from the hotel appeared at their table.

'I have been looking everywhere for you, Señor Woodend,' the young man gasped.

'Why? What's happened?' Woodend said.

And already he could feel his entrails turning to water.

'Señora Woodend...' the clerk said.

'What about her?'

'She ... she is ill. She has been taken to the hospital.'

Woodend was finding it difficult to take in air – difficult to speak.

'Which hospital?' he said, forcing the words out.

'There is only one hospital in Benicelda,' Paco Ruiz told him. 'I will drive you there.'

Thirty-Three

The workshop was in the back room of a house in the old part of town. It differed from most establishments of its nature, in that all the tools of the trade – the numerous bottles of coloured inks, stacks of paper of various qualities and various ages, the expensive camera – were on open display.

And why shouldn't they be? Pablo Vasquez asked himself.

The police weren't going to raid *him*, because he was under the protection of the most important – and probably the most corrupt – policeman in the whole of Benicelda.

Not that it was always a soft option, being protected by López. The Captain wasn't an easy man to handle. He was vain. He was short-tempered. He was greedy. But then, Vasquez supposed, that was almost the definition of any captain in the Guardia Civil. And if there was one thing which could be worse than dealing with him, it would be *not* dealing with him.

Vasquez heard a knock on the door – three

short raps, a pause, two long raps. He stood up, crossed the room, and drew back the bolts. Though he had just been thinking about Captain López, it was still something of a surprise to find the man himself standing there.

López looked quickly over both shoulders, up and down the street, before stepping over the threshold.

Once he was inside, Vasquez quickly bolted the door behind him. 'I was not expecting you, my Captain,' he said.

'Weren't you?' López replied. He frowned. 'Does that mean you have not completed the work I set you to do?'

'No.'

'No!'

'I mean, it is finished but...'

'But what?'

'They are saying in the town that you have arrested the Frenchman for the murder of the *Alcalde*.'

'And so I have.'

'Then ... then I do not see why you would need my help any more.'

'Your *help*?' López asked, with a sudden dangerous edge creeping into his voice.

'My ... my assistance,' Vasquez said, then, seeing that López's frown was continuing to deepen, he asked desperately, 'What do you *want* me to call it, my Captain?'

'You need *call it* nothing at all. I give you

orders, and you obey them. We are not partners in any sense of the word. We are not even *associates*! Is that clearly understood?'

'Y … yes, my Captain.'

'Then show me the work you have done for me,' López said.

Vasquez led him over to the bench.

As the Captain examined the documents, his temper seemed to improve. 'You asked me why I still needed these papers now that I had arrested the Frenchman,' he said.

'Y … yes, I did. But if you don't want to tell me...'

'I will tell you. Listen and learn. There are only two kinds of people in this world, Vasquez. There are those like you, who grub along from day to day, hoping that things will not go wrong – and are always caught on the hop when they do. And there are people like me – who can see beyond their own noses and plan ahead. I will never end up in gaol – something which is almost certainly your fate – because I am always ready for the unexpected. That is why, though your tiny brain sees no need for me to have documents any more, I have still come to collect them.'

'I … I have made a good job of them,' Vasquez said.

'You have made an *excellent* job of them,' López said. 'But then a mule will make an excellent job of carrying my baggage and my cat will make an excellent job of catching mice. I *expect* excellence. The moment you cease to be excellent, your usefulness to me is over, and your life as a convict will begin.'

Vasquez looked down at the floor. 'I am well aware of that, my Captain,' he said.

López nodded. 'Good, then we truly do understand each other.' He reached into his jacket pocket, and produced a wad of banknotes. 'I've brought you your money.'

Vasquez licked his lips at the sight of the cash. He felt a powerful urge to reach over and snatch it from López's hand, but he knew that would be a very big mistake.

'I want no payment,' he forced himself to say. 'That you allow me to continue with my work is reward enough for me.'

López nodded again. 'Perhaps you are gaining a little wisdom after all,' he said. 'Perhaps you, too, are finally learning to look ahead.'

Vasquez, who had devoted many hours of painstaking labour to the documents, watched as López picked them up and thrust them roughly into his pocket. He winced at the Captain's lack of care with his precious work, but he knew that it didn't really matter. In fact, the professional in him recognized, the rougher López was with the documents, the better they would be.

Thirty-Four

Joan was lying on a bed in the intensive care unit, with tubes running from her into pieces of machinery whose function Woodend couldn't even begin to guess at. She was pale and drawn, but at least she was conscious.

'Are they lookin' after you, lass?' Woodend asked.

Joan gave him a half-smile. 'It's a hospital,' she said. 'What else do you expect them to do?'

Woodend's grin owed more to relief than amusement. Joan might be weak, but at least she was still *his* Joan.

'What happened?' he said.

'Since there wasn't much chance of seein' you, I thought I might as well go for a walk. I was just outside the hotel when it hit me.'

'When what hit you?'

'This pain in my chest. Like indigestion, only a hundred times worse than any indigestion I've ever known. I tried to reach the nearest bench, but my legs just wouldn't let me. I fell over, Charlie! In the street! It was all very humiliatin'.'

291

'Bollocks!' Woodend said.

'Watch your language!' Joan warned him.

'It's a hospital, not a church,' Woodend told her. 'Anyway, what I meant was, you'd no cause to feel humiliated. You couldn't help bein' taken ill. What do they think it was?'

'A heart attack. They're almost certain it was. They think it was quite a mild one, but they say I'll still need plenty of rest, which means you'll have to go in a minute.'

'Aye, I suppose I will,' Woodend agreed.

'Anyway, you're probably itchin' to get right back to work on that case of yours.'

Woodend felt as if he had been struck in the stomach with a sledgehammer, wielded by a very large – and very angry – navvy.

'The case doesn't matter a toss to me,' he protested.

'Your cases *always* matter to you, Charlie. That's just the way you are,' Joan said, her tone suggesting that it was his dishonesty at that particular moment – rather than the obsession which drove most of his life – that she really disapproved of.

'Anyway, the investigation's all over, bar the shoutin',' Woodend said awkwardly.

'Then you should be off celebratin' with your new mate, Paco.'

That's just what I was doin' while they were sticking all them tubes in you, love, Woodend thought guiltily – except that it

292

hadn't turned out to be much of a celebration at all.

'I want to stay here,' he said.

'They won't let you stay here. There's sick people to deal with, an' they don't want you gettin' in the way.'

'Then I'll go an' sit in the waitin' room.'

'There'd be no point in that. They won't let you see me again until the mornin', so you might as well go back to the hotel, have a few pints an' then get your head down.'

'If you're sure,' Woodend said hesitantly.

'I'm sure.'

'Well, I'll be off then.'

He had almost reached the door when Joan said, 'Charlie?'

He turned round. 'What is it, love?'

'I was just thinkin'.'

'What about?'

'All your life you've drunk like a fish, smoked like a chimney an' lived off greasy food. An' *I'm* the one who gets the heart attack. Odd, isn't it?'

'Odd?' Woodend repeated. 'It's not *odd*! It's bloody unfair – that's what it is.'

Paco Ruiz entered the foyer of the hotel where the *brigadistas* had been staying – where all of them, with the exception of Sant, were *still* staying. He was very clear about his reasons for being there. He was looking for evidence – *any* evidence – which would prove that he had been right, and Woodend had been wrong.

He recognized the man behind the desk. His name was Manolo, and several months earlier, when he had landed himself in trouble, it had been Paco who had pulled him out.

The desk man positively beamed with pleasure when he saw who was entering the lobby.

'Señor Ruiz,' he said. 'What a surprise.' A look of concern crossed his face. 'You don't want a room, do you? You haven't fallen out with that lovely *señora* of yours?'

Paco grinned. 'No, I haven't. I'm here to ask a favour.'

'Name it.'

'I wondered if it would be possible to see the Frenchman's room.'

'For you, most things are possible,' the clerk said, but he made no move towards the pigeon holes which held the keys.

'I'll need some way of getting in,' Paco suggested.

The clerk looked puzzled for a moment, then smiled. 'Oh, I see what you mean,' he said. 'But on this occasion, a key will not be necessary.'

'It won't?'

'No. The door is open. The maid is in there at this very moment, parcelling up the Frenchman's things.'

'So the police have finished with the room already, have they?' Paco asked, surprised.

The other man shrugged. 'The first time they came, when they were searching for evidence, they were upstairs for a long time. The second time – after the Frenchman had been charged with the murder – they had no sooner gone up than they were coming down again.'

'So the second time they didn't really search at all?'

'That's right. They said they had all they needed, and as soon as I'd sent the Frenchman's possessions to the Guardia Civil barracks, I could have the room cleaned and let it out again. I didn't argue with them. We've probably already lost three days rent, since I don't imagine the Frenchman will pay for his stay here. So it's time the room started earning its keep again.'

Paco thanked the clerk, and made his way upstairs. He had not expected to hear crying as he approached Sant's room, but that was just what he did hear.

He looked into the room. A young maid – little more than a child – was on her hands and knees, peering under the bed and sobbing.

'What's the matter?' Paco asked.

The maid jumped up so quickly that she banged her head on the bed, but the pain did not seem to bother her half as much as the fact that someone had seen what she was doing.

'Are you from the police?' she asked, panicked.

'No,' Paco said gently. 'I am a friend of Manolo's. He sent me upstairs to see if you were all right.'

'Then he knows,' the maid moaned. 'And soon, everybody will know. My mother! My father! My friends! They will all know.'

'Know what?'

'They will say I stole it. But I swear to you, I did not.'

'Why don't you calm down, take a deep breath and start at the beginning,' Paco suggested.

The maid nodded, then gulped in air as if she had been on the point of suffocating before he arrived.

'I clean this room every day,' she said. 'I do a good job – a thorough job – just as they taught me to.'

'I'm sure you do.'

'The last time I cleaned it was just before the policemen came.'

'Which time? The first? Or the second?'

'The first. I cleaned all the cupboards – even in the corners. And then I turned over the mattress, and saw that something was hidden there. It must have been valuable, don't you think, or the *señor* would not have bothered to hide it like that?'

'Valuable to him, at least,' Paco agreed. 'What did you do when you'd turned the mattress?'

'I put it back where I found it. And now it is gone! The *señor* cannot have taken it away, because he has not been back. And the room has been kept locked, except when the police were here. So *where* has it gone? They will blame me. I know they will blame me.'

'No one will blame you,' Paco said soothingly. 'I promise you that.'

'Truly?'

'Truly. Now tell me exactly what this valuable thing you found under the mattress was.'

And the maid did.

Thirty-Five

Woodend had almost reached the main exit of the hospital when he felt a tap on his shoulder. He stopped and turned around, to find himself facing a tired-looking young man in a white coat.

'You are Señor Woodend,' the man asked.

'That's right.'

'I am Doctor Sanchez.'

'Are you one of the doctors who looked after my wife?'

'No, I ... I have been very busy with another patient. That is why I am here now. This patient of mine is dying, but he wants very much to talk to you. Will you come?'

'I'd be glad to, if it'll help, but I don't *really* see what good I can do for him,' Woodend said. 'Are you sure it's me he wants to see?'

The doctor nodded. 'He was very insistent about it.'

'But I'm not a doctor, or a priest. I'm a policeman.'

'I know. He kept saying, "Get me the English cop. I need to talk to the English cop." '

It was the slight American twang the doctor put into the last few words which gave it away.

'This patient of yours isn't called Mitchell, by any chance, is he?' Woodend asked.

'That is the man,' the doctor agreed.

They had put Mitchell in an isolation room at the end of a long corridor. The air was full of the cleansing scent of antiseptic, but even that didn't quite manage to mask the stink of impending death.

Mitchell himself was lying on the room's single bed, though his wasted body seemed to make hardly any impression in the mattress. His face had turned the colour of sulphur, and despite all the drugs that had been pumped into him, it was clear that he was still suffering agonies.

His eyes flickered, acknowledging Woodend's presence. 'Whatever else you might tell me, don't – for God's sake – try to persuade me that this is just a temporary relapse,' he said.

'I won't,' Woodend promised him. 'You're dyin', Mr Mitchell, and we both know it.'

Mitchell forced a grin to his pain-wracked face. 'They promised me another month at least. Think I can sue?'

Woodend returned the grin. 'No harm in tryin'. What was it you wanted to see me about?'

'I don't suppose there's any point in my confessing to having killed Durán and his bodyguards, is there?'

'None. I've got a boss back in England who'll believe almost anythin' if it suits him, but even *he* wouldn't swallow the idea that you'd had the strength to carry out the murders.'

Mitchell's eyes flickered 'In that case, I want you to find *another* way to get Sant released,' he said.

'I'm not one to turn down a dyin' man's request,' Woodend said. 'I'd do almost anythin' you asked of me – but I can't do that.'

'Why not? He's innocent.'

'That's not the way the evidence points,

I'm afraid.'

'What evidence?'

'Sant is an expert with a throwin' knife an'—'

'He *was* an expert with a throwing knife. And I should know that better than most – I saw him use it often enough in the old days. But he couldn't do it now.'

'Sorry, but that's not true,' Woodend said. 'Up until recently, he was instructin' the French Foreign Legion.'

'He taught the Legionnaires the *techniques* of his skill. But he couldn't demonstrate those techniques himself – not after that night on the beach.'

'What do you mean?'

'I told you he took a bullet in the shoulder, didn't I?'

'Yes, you did.'

'If we'd been able to get him medical attention right away, it might have mended properly. But we couldn't. We were on the run from Durán, and the whole of Franco's army. It was months before we got him to a doctor, and by then it was too late. Sant can't throw a knife like he used to, because he can't raise his right arm above shoulder level.'

'I see,' Woodend said, noncommittally.

'You don't believe me.'

'I think it's the easiest thing in the world to fake an injury. If I'd been plannin' to do what he did, I'd have faked it an' all.'

A look of total despair crossed Mitchell's face, only to be replaced, a moment later, by the faintest shadow of fresh hope.

'The night Durán was killed, we were all in the hotel,' he said. 'Do you know about our sleeping arrangements?'

'Aye. Sutcliffe shared a room with Roberts, Sant shared a room with Schneider, an' you were alone.'

'And do you know why things were arranged in that way?'

'Sutcliffe thinks you wanted to be alone because that would give Durán a chance to kill you – an' that just might lead to his own downfall.'

'Yes, yes, that's what I wanted,' Mitchell said impatiently. 'But that's not important now.'

'Then what *is*?'

'The way *the others* divided up.'

'The two Englishmen shared one room, an' the Frenchman an' the German shared the other. An' that's about it, isn't it?'

'The two Englishmen shared one room,' Mitchell said, speaking in a croak, 'and the two *former lovers* shared the other!'

'Funny you should come up with that,' Woodend said, 'because, as it happens, I did ask them if they had a thing for each other.'

'Then you could see for yourself that they were very special to each other!'

301

'No. I couldn't see anythin' of the sort. The only reason I asked the question was to throw them off balance. I didn't believe it myself, an' I wasn't the least surprised when they denied it.'

'If they denied it, they were lying.'

Woodend shook his head. 'I'm afraid that simply won't wash,' he said.

But he was starting to think that maybe it *would*. They made an odd couple – there was no doubt about that – but he'd seen odder couples in his time.

And there was more! Schneider had denied they were homosexuals, but had cast aspersions on Sant's heterosexual virility. And Sant had done the same thing with regard to Schneider's.

There was a symmetry about it which he should have noticed before – but hadn't. It was almost as if they'd rehearsed it – almost as if they'd discussed, beforehand, what would be the best kind of smokescreen to throw up.

'You're convinced now, aren't you?' Mitchell said.

'Not entirely. If it was true, why didn't they come clean about it when I asked them?'

'Because most people in the societies they come from consider it *unclean*. Schneider *is* married, and *does* have children. Sant says he has mistresses, and I believe him. They've both changed over the years – but whatever

302

happens, first love is the hardest of all loves to destroy.'

'Can I get confirmation from the others on this?' Woodend asked.

'No. They don't know. If I hadn't caught them together one night – out on the *sierra*, during the Ebro Campaign – I wouldn't have known about it myself.'

'An' you never told anybody else about it?'

'Not a soul. It was a beautiful thing they had together, you see, but most people wouldn't have understood. Do *you* understand?'

'Well, I'm certainly not goin' to condemn it,' Woodend said, and the moment the words were out of his mouth he realized that he believed everything Mitchell had told him.

'I'd have taken their secret with me to the grave,' the American said. 'But I can't – not if I'm to save Sant.'

'You're sure they still felt the same way about each other that they used to?' Woodend asked.

'I'm convinced of it,' Mitchell replied. 'I've been watching them over the last few days. They were *aching* to touch one another, but they didn't dare while the others were there. Then they were given a heaven-sent opportunity. They had the chance, on grounds of security, to spend the night together. Do you understand what that meant to them?'

'I've a pretty good idea, but I'd still rather hear it from you.'

'Even their hatred of Durán would not have got them out of their room that night,' Mitchell said. 'They had this one chance to relive their old passion. They wouldn't have sacrificed that for anything.'

As Woodend stepped out of the main hospital door, he saw Paco Ruiz's little car parked on the other side of the road. It shouldn't have surprised him, he thought. Nothing Paco did should *ever* surprise him.

He walked across the road and came to a halt beside the Seat.

'How is Joan?' Paco Ruiz asked, through the open window.

'She's goin' to have to be careful, but it looks like she'll be all right,' Woodend said.

Paco nodded his head, slowly and seriously. 'Good!' he said. 'Excellent!' Then he took a deep breath. 'Sant didn't do it,' he continued, the words gushing from his mouth like water from a burst dam.

'I know he didn't do it,' Woodend replied.

Thirty-Six

It was dark by the time they reached the Guardia Civil barracks, and as the double doors closed behind Paco's small car, sealing it into the courtyard, Woodend couldn't help wondering if he'd done the right thing.

The lieutenant who spoke English – and had pretended to be a private – approached them as they climbed out of the Seat.

'Captain López will see you,' he said, addressing the remark to Woodend, 'but you –' turning to Paco – 'must remain here.'

'Open the gates again, will you, lad,' Woodend said.

'I beg your pardon?'

'If your Captain doesn't want to see both of us, then he gets to see neither of us.'

The lieutenant flushed. 'I think you forget where you are.'

'An' I think you forget who I *am*,' Woodend countered. 'You might push your own countrymen around – you shouldn't, but you might – but don't try the same thing with me, laddie. Because Her Britannic Majesty *requests an' requires* that her subjects be allowed to pass without hinder. She doesn't like it when her subjects are bossed about by foreigners, you see – especially when the subject in question happens to be a senior police officer.'

The lieutenant hesitated for a moment, then said, 'Wait here,' and disappeared into the building.

'That was a very pretty little speech you just made,' Paco Ruiz said.

'Thank you.'

'Was it rehearsed?'

'It was spoken straight from the heart of a true Englishman born and bred, you cheeky Dago bastard,' Woodend said.

'In other words, it *was* rehearsed.'

Woodend chuckled. 'It was more like an improvisation on a theme,' he said. 'I thought it might be useful to have a few well-chosen words to hand, so I was composin' them on the way over here.'

The lieutenant returned. 'My Captain will see you both,' he said, looking at Woodend with loathing.

Captain López was sitting at his desk. His feet – clad in highly polished jackboots – were resting on an open drawer of his filing cabinet, and he made no move to get up when Woodend and Ruiz were shown into the room. Woodend was unimpressed. His boss back in England played tricks like that

306

and – if anything – did them slightly better.

'So what do we have here?' Captain López asked. 'Who has come to see me in the dead of night? Why, it is none other than the Laurel and Hardy of criminal investigation.'

'Now that *is* what you call a carefully rehearsed line,' Woodend said, in an aside to Ruiz.

'What are you saying?' López demanded.

'Only that you're not even *half* as relaxed as you're tryin' to look an' sound. Because if you were, you'd never have agreed to see us.'

'Why should I not be relaxed?' López asked, almost lazily. 'I have my murderer under lock and key.'

'You certainly have *somebody* under lock an' key,' Woodend admitted. 'Unfortunately, it's the *wrong* somebody. You couldn't wait for me to find the real murderer, could you, Captain? However hard you tried, you couldn't resist tamperin' with the evidence.'

'I don't know what you're talking about,' López said. 'Sant is an expert knife thrower—'

'*Was* an expert knife thrower,' Woodend interrupted. 'By the time he comes to trial, he'll have sworn statements from half a dozen French Foreign Legion doctors. An' they'll all be prepared to stake their professional reputations on their opinion that he couldn't have raised the knife *high enough* to throw it.'

López frowned. 'I see,' he said. 'If that is true, then I clearly have the wrong man.'

'An' the wrong *knife*,' Woodend said.

'How can it be the wrong knife?'

'Because it's *Sant's* knife.'

'I don't understand. If Sant is not the killer, then the knife cannot belong to him.'

'But it *does*,' Woodend insisted. 'He's had it for nearly thirty years, an' though he hasn't been able to throw it since the ambush on the beach, he always carries it around with him as a good luck charm.'

'Then the real killer stole the knife, and used it for the murder,' López suggested.

'Wrong again,' Woodend told him. 'The knife could only have been used in the murder if it had been dropped into the rose garden *at the time* of the murder. After all, it's not likely that the killer would have risked comin' back to the scene of the crime the next day, now is it?'

'The knife *was* dropped in the rose garden at the time of the murder,' López said.

'No, it wasn't. It was still in Sant's room the next mornin'. The maid saw it when she was cleanin'. But later, after you'd been to the room yourself, it was gone. An' later still, it appeared in the rose garden. It's like I first thought – it was planted there. An' you're the one who planted it.'

'What do you want?' López asked.

'Want?' Woodend repeated innocently.

308

'If your only aim had been to get Sant released, you would never have brought up the problem with the knife. But you *did* bring it up – and that can only have been to gain leverage over me. So I ask you again, Señor Woodend, what is it that you want?'

'Well, what Señor Ruiz here would like is for you to prove, to his satisfaction, that you didn't kill the *Alcalde* yourself,' Woodend said.

'What!' López exploded.

'You heard me.'

'You believe that *I* killed the *Alcalde*?'

No, Woodend thought. No, I don't. I was never really convinced by Paco's argument, an' now I've seen the look on your face I'm sure I'm right – because *nobody's* that good an actor.

'I did *not* kill Durán,' López continued. 'I may have arrested the wrong man, but I am still convinced that one of the *brigadistas* is the murderer.'

'Which one?'

'Whichever one of them it was who betrayed the others.'

'What are you talkin' about?' Woodend demanded.

'You must know the story as well as I do, by now. Two hours before the *brigadistas* arrived, Durán's militia moved the fishermen out of their shacks and began to dig pits for their machine guns in the sand. And why did they do that? Because they knew for a fact that the *brigadistas* were coming. Because somebody had betrayed them.'

'But the traitor could have been anybody,' Woodend said. 'One of the fishermen might have sold them out. Or one of the villagers who was providin' them with food. That seems a lot more likely an explanation to me than that one of the *brigadistas* did it.'

'That is what I would have thought, too, until I found a very interesting document among Durán's personal papers.'

'A document!' Woodend sneered. 'How convenient for you that a document should turn up – just at the right moment to implicate one of the *brigadistas* in even more dirty dealin's. An' exactly what is this *document* of yours? A scrap of paper in a handwritin' which *could* be Durán's – if you looked at it in the right light? A scribbled note in which he confesses that he had an English spy workin' for him?'

'No, nothing like that,' López said, with a confidence which *almost* convinced Woodend that he really did have something of value.

'I don't suppose we could see this document of yours, could we?' the Chief Inspector asked sceptically.

'But, of course,' López replied. 'As long as you promise that in return for my showing it to you, you will abandon this crazy idea of yours that I was the one who planted the knife in the rose garden.'

'You don't really expect me to buy a pig in a poke like that, do you?' Woodend asked.

'I don't understand the expression.'

'You don't really expect me to agree to pay your price before I see if what you have is worth it?'

'Perhaps not. But once you *have* seen it, I will have lost all bargaining power.'

It seemed as if they had reached an impasse. Woodend chewed the problem over in his mind for a second.

'If what you've got is real proof that there was a spy in the *brigadistas'* camp, I'll forget all about how the knife found its way into the rose garden,' he said. 'You have my word on that.'

López nodded.

'Very well,' he said. He swung his feet off the filing cabinet, reached into the drawer, produced a yellowed piece of stiff paper, and held it across the desk for Woodend to take. 'Here is all the proof you need.'

Woodend looked at the document. It was a printed form, with some of the spaces on it filled in with typewriting. 'Tell me what this means,' he said, passing it to Paco Ruiz.

As Ruiz examined the document, the frown on his forehead grew deeper and deeper. 'It is a bank transfer form,' he said finally.

'Is it genuine?' Woodend asked.

'I am not an expert on forgery, but it looks real enough to me.'

Then it probably was, Woodend thought. 'Go on,' he said.

'It is dated late 1939. It talks about a lot of other attached documents, because, at the time, it was very difficult to transfer money out of the country without a great many formalities being gone through.'

'So the money left the country,' Woodend said impatiently. 'An' where was it sent to?'

'To London. To a company called Gee-Gee Trading Ltd.'

'Was it a lot of money?'

'A very large amount. Almost a fortune.'

And there was no doubt how the money had been raised, was there? Woodend thought. It had come from the sale of what had been in those boxes that Durán had killed upwards of forty men to get his hands on. It was blood money!

He was beginning to see things clearly for the first time. Medwin hadn't been killed by Durán's men at all. He had been killed by the same person who had killed Durán himself. And the key to both those murders lay in a deal which had been struck up early in 1939.

Bits of previous conversations, which he had stored away in his mind, now began to fit together. He was almost sure that he knew who the murderer was. He just needed one more thing to confirm it.

'I want the photographs,' he told López.

'Which photographs?'

'Which photographs do you bloody well think? The ones of the *brigadista* camp! The ones the murderer took!'

Thirty-Seven

Roberts was sitting alone at the table in the square which Woodend and Ruiz had been using since the investigation began. He did not look surprised when the other two men sat down beside him. In fact, he might almost have been expecting it.

'Can I help you gentlemen?' he asked.

'We think so,' Woodend replied. 'You see, we're looking for what my friend Paco here calls "the butcher beyond".'

'Very cryptic,' Roberts said. 'And what does that mean, exactly?'

'It means that we're not lookin' for the man who killed your comrades – that was Durán, an' he's dead himself now – but we *are* lookin' for the man who made it possible for the killings to take place, an' he's—'

'The butcher beyond,' Roberts said. 'I see. Very clever. But what I still don't understand is why you'd want to talk to me about it.'

'The first time I interviewed you, you referred to Mitchell as "Ham-'n'-Eggs",' Woodend said. 'Back then, I thought it was a slip of the tongue – a very helpful slip of the tongue from our point of view. But it was no such thing, was it?'

Roberts smiled. 'Wasn't it?'

'No, an' if I'd known you better then, I'd have realized it immediately. You never raise the stakes at the poker table without havin' at least some idea of how your opponent's goin' to react to it. You never bet on a horse unless you think you know somethin' that's goin' to give you the edge. A man like you doesn't say anythin' – doesn't *do* anythin' – before he's thought out all the consequences first.'

'I'm flattered you have such a high opinion of me,' Roberts said. 'But what, pray tell, was the point in revealing Mitchell's nickname to you?'

'It was the most indirect way you could come up with to let me know that you'd all been mates for a long time. An' there was a bonus in doin' it that way, because, since it involved a cravin' for some pretty ordinary food, you were also tellin' me that you'd been together through some pretty hard times. It was a signpost, if you like, pointin' me towards the fact that you'd all been *brigadistas*.'

'And why would I have wanted to do that?'

'Because *brigadistas* are still not welcome in Spain. Once the authorities had found out what you were, you'd have been out of here on the next plane out. That would have meant that nobody would have got the chance to talk to Durán.'

'What you meant to say was "Nobody would have got the chance to *kill* Durán".'

'No, I didn't. You didn't mind whether he lived or died. But if your mates were determined to kill him, you were very concerned that he shouldn't *say* anythin' before he died.'

'We think that one of the *brigadistas* who isn't here – one who was too ill or too old to come back with you – is a very rich man,' Paco said.

'Interesting,' Roberts replied. 'And what led you to that conclusion?'

'It's the only supposition which fits the facts,' Woodend told him. 'The traitor was faced with two choices, you see. He could come back to Spain and try to bury the truth. Or he could disappear before the truth came out.'

'Disappearing would have been the easier option,' Paco Ruiz said.

'It would indeed,' Woodend agreed. 'The traitor didn't have to stay in England. There's lots of places in Europe for a feller to hide, if he knows his way around. And if he didn't fancy Europe, he could go the States – or even South America. An' what would be the chances his old comrades could track him down? Virtually nil!'

'Unless one of his old comrades was rich,' Paco said.

'A rich man, you see, could hire the best private investigators that money could buy – a whole team of them, if needs be. They'd keep lookin' and lookin', and eventually they *would* find the traitor. An' once they'd done that, of course, he was a dead man.'

'So burying the truth was not just one option,' Paco said. 'It was the *only* option.'

'From what you've said, I take it you think that I was the traitor,' Roberts said.

'We *know* you were the traitor,' Woodend said. 'The photographs prove that.'

'What photographs?'

'I can pick out everybody else on them,' Woodend said, ignoring Roberts's claim to ignorance. 'Medwin, Sutcliffe, Mitchell, Dupont, Schneider – they're all there. There's a lot of other lads, too.'

'And we have a second set of pictures – taken of the dead on the beach,' Paco said. 'Several of the faces from the first set are missing from this one, because some of the *brigadistas* survived.'

'But there's only one face that's missin'

from the *first* set,' Woodend said. 'An' whose do you think that might be, Mr Roberts?'

'Mine?'

'Yours,' Woodend agreed. 'An' the reason your face is missin' is because you were the one takin' the photographs.'

'Why would I take photographs?' Roberts asked.

'Because Durán insisted on it. He should have handed the treasure over to the advancin' Nationalist army, but he had no intention of doin' that. So anybody who knew what was in the boxes had to die. He calculated he'd kill most of them in the ambush, but it was possible that a few of the *brigadistas* might escape. If that did happen, he'd have to hunt them down – an' he'd need photographs for that.'

'Anybody could have taken the pictures,' Roberts said. 'It could have been one of the villagers who brought us food.'

'None of them would have stayed long enough to photograph everybody in the camp,' Woodend said. 'It had to be an inside job.'

Roberts smiled again. 'True,' he said. ' "You've got me bang to rights." Isn't that the phrase?'

'This isn't a game!' Woodend said angrily.

'Of course it is,' Roberts replied. 'Life is a game. Or if it isn't, I've unwittingly been playing by the wrong set of rules.'

'So you admit you betrayed your comrades?'

'Why not? You seem to have put together a pretty good case, and when I know the deck's stacked against me, the only thing to do is fold.'

'Since you knew all about the ambush, why were you on the beach yourself?' Woodend wondered. 'Surely it would have been easy enough to slip away in the darkness?'

'The others might have smelled a rat if I'd suddenly disappeared. Anyway, that would have been cheating.'

'Cheatin'!'

'It would have been like slipping a card from the bottom of the pack. If you're a true gambler, there's no pleasure in winning unless you've taken a risk. And what a risk that was! If I died, I'd get nothing. If I survived, I'd be a rich man. It was the ultimate challenge. I've never felt so alive in my life.'

Woodend shook his head. 'I simply don't understand you,' he said.

'Of course you don't,' Roberts agreed easily. 'I'm a front-line gambler, and you're a mere civilian.'

'Why did you help the others to escape? Wasn't your deal with Durán that they should all be killed?'

'My deal with Durán was that I should make it *possible* for him to kill them. It's scarcely my fault that he bungled it.'

'You could have got a message through to him somehow. You could have set your comrades up again.'

'I was wounded by then. If Durán had seen me in that state, he might well have decided to renege on our deal, and finish me off as well. Besides...'

'What?'

'Chance had decreed that the others should survive, so who was I to say that they shouldn't?'

'We've seen the record of the money transfer Durán made to London,' Woodend said.

'Oh yes?'

'It was paid into an account owned by Gee-Gee Trading Ltd.'

Roberts laughed. 'Someone's been playing silly buggers with you, you know,' he said.

'A lot of people seem to have been doin' that recently,' Woodend admitted. 'But how, especially, have I been taken in this time?'

'With the name! Gee-Gee Trading! It's as good as a confession! Why would I have been that obvious?'

'Perhaps because it gave the whole thing that edge of danger that you seem to live for.'

Roberts nodded. 'You're quite right, of course. I probably *would* have called myself Gee-Gee Trading if I'd come up with the idea. But I didn't.'

'Then who did?'

'Does it matter now? After all, I'm perfectly willing to admit that Durán did send me money.'

'An' a lot of money it was,' Woodend said. 'Where is it now?'

'Gone. Long gone. Placed on horses which didn't run as well as they should have done. Lost at poker games in which I underestimated my opponents. To tell you the truth, I was glad when I'd spent it all.'

'Because it was blood money?'

'Because it made my life too *easy*. Because there were no challenges any more. It didn't matter whether I won or lost when I knew I still had plenty of money in the bank. But once I was one step away from poverty again, then I could really begin to enjoy what I was doing.'

Woodend shook his head again. 'Can we talk about the night you killed Durán?' he asked.

'Certainly. It's very courteous of you to ask for my permission, if I may say so.'

'You gave us the impression that, even though you wouldn't admit it to yourself, Sutcliffe had doped you. That was very clever, because, in fact, it was the other way around. You had doped Sutcliffe.'

'Exactly.'

'Why did you think that was necessary? He was all for revenge. Couldn't you have risked telling him what you were doing?'

'Spoken like a true amateur,' Roberts said. 'There are some risks it is necessary to take. There are some risks you take because you enjoy taking them. Telling Sutcliffe even a half-truth didn't fall into either of those categories. It was so much easier to drug him.'

'An' once he was out for the count, you ran up to the Mayor's villa as fast as you could.'

'I *cycled* up. I'd already arranged for one of the local lads to provide me with a bicycle.'

'When I talked about the man I'd bayoneted, you went quite green,' Woodend said.

'Yes, I did, didn't I?' Roberts agreed. 'It's a very useful trick. I've used it countless times at the poker table.'

'An' you've never had the slightest scruple about killin' people at close quarters?'

'None at all. Do you know why I left the first unit I served with in Spain?'

'Is that relevant?' Woodend asked.

'Very. Strictly speaking, of course, I didn't really leave it. *It* left *me*. All my comrades were killed, but with my gambler's luck—'

'Get to the point!' Woodend said.

'In that first unit, I used to do the same kind of work as Sant did later on. In fact – and in all modesty – I think I'm better with a knife *now* than Sant was even in his heyday.'

'Yet you never told Medwin and the others how good you were. Why?'

321

'Children show off their skills and accomplishments. Gamblers keep them hidden until they need them. It gives them the edge.'

'Why did you mutilate Durán once you'd killed him?' Woodend asked.

Roberts began to look a little uncomfortable – and this time, Woodend thought, he was *not* faking it.

'I did it to make it look as if whoever killed him really hated him,' Roberts said.

'Which you didn't?'

'Of course not. We were business partners, and I was merely dissolving our agreement.'

'You could have mutilated him less, an' still made your point.'

'True. So perhaps I also did it, in some small part, for my comrades who died on that beach.'

'Why did you kill Medwin?'

'How do you know that I did?'

'He was here on a mission to kill Durán. He knew there was a danger of Durán finding out, an' strikin' first. He'd never have run the risk of takin' somebody who might have been one of Durán's henchmen up to his room. It had to be somebody he trusted – or somebody he desperately wanted to *regain* his trust in.'

'I don't know how he first became suspicious of me,' Roberts said. 'Perhaps it was something I inadvertently let slip. Or perhaps he knew me better than I thought I did.

But you're right. He *did* want to regain his trust in me. He desperately wanted me to prove to him that I wasn't the traitor. But, of course, I couldn't – so poor old Pete simply had to die.' Roberts paused. 'Could I ask you a question now?'

'What is it?'

'I'd rather like to know if either of you is armed.'

'Would that make any difference, one way or the other?' Woodend asked.

'Just as I thought. You're not. British policemen don't carry weapons around, and Spanish ex-policemen aren't allowed to. But you see, I don't fall into either of those categories, and I've got a gun in my jacket pocket which is pointing straight at you.'

'You're bluffin',' Woodend said.

'It's an essential tool of my trade to be able to do so,' Roberts agreed. 'But part of the skill of bluffing well is that *sometimes* you don't bluff at all. And maybe this is one of those times.'

'What do you want?' Woodend asked.

Roberts raised a quizzical eyebrow. 'Aren't you supposed to say, "You'll never get away with this"?' he asked.

'I'd only be wastin' my breath. You *know* you'll never get away with it. So what do you want?'

'I want the two of you to get up from the table, ever so slowly and ever so carefully.'

'An' then?'

'And then, I would like the three of us to walk together to the edge of the square.'

'To the top of the cliff, you mean,' Woodend said.

'That's right,' Roberts agreed. 'To the top of the cliff.'

The bulge in the gambler's pocket might well be a gun, Woodend thought when they had all stood up and he could take a closer look at it. On the other hand, it didn't have to be a weapon at all. But as Roberts had said, bluffing was what he was good at.

They reached the wall at the edge of the cliff. It was no more than three feet high, and beyond it lay a sickening drop.

'You can see Pete Medwin's balcony from here,' Roberts said conversationally.

'I know,' Woodend agreed.

'Do you think he knew he was going to die as he fell from it, and plunged down to the beach?'

'He was certainly screamin' as if he did.'

'Yet there must have been one small part of him, don't you think, which believed that he could beat the odds and survive the fall? There's always a small part of *everybody* that believes that.'

'Maybe,' Woodend said.

Roberts glanced quickly over the wall. 'It's not quite as long a drop from here as it is from the balcony. What odds would it take to make you bet that somebody could survive the fall from here?'

'I wouldn't make the bet at all.'

'Oh, come on,' Roberts said, disappointedly. 'Anybody will bet on anything if the odds are long enough. The bigger the gamble, the bigger the rewards. What if I gave you odds of a thousand to one? That way you'd only be minus a pound if you lost, but you'd have earned yourself a thousand if you won. Certainly worth the risk, don't you think?'

'I don't want to play this game,' Woodend said.

'But I *do*,' Roberts told him. 'And I'm the one holding the gun. So what odds *would* be acceptable to you? A hundred thousand to one? A million to one?'

'A million to one,' Woodend said reluctantly.

'I'd have gone up higher to get you to bet, you know,' Roberts told him. 'Looking at that drop, I might have even given you ten million to one.'

'It doesn't matter.'

'But it *does*. Have you got a pound on you?'

'I don't know.'

'Then find out – or my finger just might tighten a little too hard on this trigger.'

Woodend reached into his pocket. 'I've got a five peseta note,' he said, when he'd withdrawn it again. 'I don't know exactly what it's worth, but it's much less than a pound.'

'It'll do,' Roberts said. He held out his left hand. 'I want you to hand it to me very carefully.'

'This is sick,' Woodend said.

But he did as he'd been instructed.

Roberts pocketed the note. 'A million to one,' he said reflectively. 'That could make you five million pesetas. And I always honour my debts – when it's at all possible.' He brought his right hand smoothly out of his pocket. It was empty. 'I was bluffing about the gun,' he said, as if the admission surprised even him. 'Remember now, if I live, I owe you five million pesetas.'

He vaulted over the wall. There was no scream as he fell, just a sickening thud when he hit the rocks below.

Epilogue

It was ten days since Roberts had plunged to his death, and the holiday was finally over. It would have been much more comfortable for the Woodends to have travelled back to the airport in the bus the hotel provided, but Paco Ruiz seemed eager to drive them there in his little car, and they felt it would have been rude to refuse. Now the Chief Inspector, his wife, and the Spanish private investigator stood together in front of the departure lounge.

'I hope that you enjoyed your short stay in my country, Joan,' Paco Ruiz said.

'Oh, I did, Paco,' Joan Woodend agreed. 'I will admit that the first few days were a bit rough – what with the foreign food, an' sittin' around on my own while my Charlie was out playin' his usual game of "Catch the Killer". An' then, of course – though I hardly like to mention it – there *was* my heart attack. But after that, it was grand.'

Ruiz looked doubtful.

'You'll not get higher praise than that out of a Northern woman,' Woodend told him, grinning.

'I think I'll just go an' look for an English paper,' Joan said.

'I'll get it for you,' Woodend told her.

'No, you won't,' Joan countered. 'I might have one foot in the grave, but I can still use the other one to hop over to the newspaper kiosk. Besides, I know you of old, Charlie Woodend. You'll need at least five minutes alone with Paco, so you can talk about how clever you've both been.'

There was no point in arguing. Woodend watched as his wife walked towards the kiosk, and fretted as he wondered whether her step was quite as firm as it used to be.

'Do you think that you'll ever come back to Spain, Charlie?' Paco Ruiz asked.

'Aye, we might well,' Woodend said. 'In fact, I've been eyein' up some of those little villas on the edge of town, an' thinkin' this might be a nice place to retire to – providin', of course, that the next mayor's a little better than Durán.'

'I think I can guarantee that,' Paco said.

'You can?'

'Yes. Madrid selects all the new mayors, so we would be foolish to expect a saint. But what he *will* be is one of the younger men from the Movement – a man brought up after the Civil War; a politician who wormed his way into power, rather than a thug who butchered his way into it. And unlike the veterans who run the country now, he will understand that a time will come when it will take more than simple loyalty to Franco to hold on to his privileges – that he had better do a good job, or else he will be out.'

Woodend nodded. 'My, but he was a nasty piece of work, that Durán, wasn't he?'

'He was an *hijo de puta*,' Paco agreed. 'He almost turned me to a life of crime.'

'He almost did *what*?'

'A man cannot right all the wrongs in the world, but at least he can try to improve his own little corner of it. For the last few years, that has been my ambition. I have been like the tall, handsome stranger of the Western films, who rides into town and sorts out all its problems.' Paco grinned. 'Not that I am handsome, tall, American or own a horse. But you get the idea?'

'I get the idea,' Woodend agreed.

'More times than I care to remember, Durán has blocked me in what I tried to achieve. What did it matter that I could prove something was wrong, when he said it was not – and his word was law? Such a situation can be very frustrating for a man like me.'

'I still don't quite see where your comment about him almost turnin' you to a life of crime comes into this,' Woodend admitted.

'Oh that,' Paco said offhandedly. 'As I told you, the frustrations had been building up, and three or four days before I met you I had finally decided that, since nothing else seemed to work, I would have to kill Durán myself. I will always be grateful to Roberts for saving me the trouble.'

Pablo Vasquez felt uneasy – as he always did whenever Captain López paid him a visit.

'A drink, Captain?' he asked.

'Do you have a good brandy?'

'The best. Lepanto. I have been saving it for you.'

Another man would say he was honoured. López merely grunted his assent. Vasquez went over to the cupboard and poured a generous ration of the precious brandy into a glass.

'You're not drinking yourself?' López asked.

'I have some delicate work to do today, my Captain. I will need a steady hand.'

'I may soon have some more work for you myself,' López said.

He sounds as if he thinks he's doing me a favour, Vasquez thought. He treats me as if I were no more than a cobbler or a shirt-maker.

And suddenly, he felt a tiny flame of rebellion flaring up inside him.

He was always complimenting López – why didn't López, for once, return the compliment? Would it hurt if, occasionally, the Captain said something nice to him?

'I see myself as an artist, and you as my patron,' Vasquez said. 'You do think of me as an artist, do you not, my Captain?'

The words came out almost as a challenge. López said nothing, and for a moment Vasquez worried that he had gone too far.

Then the Captain chuckled. 'You are indeed an artist,' he said, thinking of the stunningly convincing title deeds and stock certificates that Vasquez had produced for him in the past. 'A great one, in your own grubby way. For while most other artists have to wait until they are dead before their work becomes valuable, yours is like money the moment the ink is dry.'

Vasquez let out a silent sigh of relief, and immediately fell back into his familiar role of stroking the Captain's ego. 'This last scheme of yours was brilliant,' he said. 'Perhaps the most brilliant of all your schemes.'

'It was not bad,' López said. 'I particularly liked my idea of using the word Gee-Gee on the document. That could almost be called a master stroke.'

'Yes, indeed,' Vasquez said enthusiastically.

López smiled at him, in the way a snake might have smiled if it had had teeth. 'I was not aware that you knew the word,' he said.

He's paying me back, Vasquez thought in a panic. I challenged him, and now he's paying me back by making me squirm.

'I ... I don't know what it means,' he said.

'But you said it was brilliant, and your assurance is good enough for me.'

'It is what the English gambler called horses,' López said. 'Now do you understand?'

Vasquez nodded enthusiastically. 'Yes. It was very clever. But not as clever as you knowing who the killer was.'

López frowned again.

What have I done wrong *now*? Vasquez wondered.

'Do you know what "irony" means?' the Captain asked.

Of course I know the meaning, Vasquez thought. What am I, an ignorant peasant?

'No, my Captain, it is not a word that I have ever come across,' he said aloud.

The 'admission' brought a return of López's good humour.

'I did not know who had killed our beloved *Alcalde*, nor had I any particular interest in finding out,' he said. 'Yet I understood well enough that for my career to prosper, *someone* had to be arrested. Under normal circumstances, I could have arrested anyone I chose to, because the policeman's skill comes not in making the arrest but in extracting the confession. But these were *not* normal circumstances. The English detective was involved, and so there would need to be at least *some* evidence. And who was likely to find that evidence, and get the credit for

332

solving the case? Why, the English detective! Unless, of course, I did not have to *find* the evidence but merely *create* it. Which is exactly what I decided to do. My original intention was to frame the Frenchman for the murders, but because, as I told you, I am a far-sighted man, I arranged to have a back-up plan in case that didn't work. That's where you came in.'

'I know, my Captain.'

But López, enchanted by the sound of his own voice, was not listening. 'I told you to forge a document which would suggest that Durán had sent money to Roberts as a payment for Roberts's betrayal of his own comrades. You can imagine how much I laughed inwardly when that English policeman took my bait and concluded that Roberts was the murderer. What a fool I'd made of him, I thought to myself.'

'But...'

'But this is where the irony comes in, my dim friend. Because the story I invented turned out to be the *truth*! Durán *had* sent Roberts money, and Roberts *did* kill Durán. Without ever intending to, I framed the man who was actually guilty! So perhaps I am not such a bad detective after all.'